Praise for *Betrayal of a Hustler*

"If you ain't ready grown folks, B.L.U.N.T. just might burn you with her hot and steamy tale from the hood! Power, revenge, love and deception are all served up in B.L.U.N.T.'s debut novel, *Betrayal of a Hustler,* giving the reader a smorgasbord of entertainment, leaving them hungry for more!"

-Lakesa Cox, best-selling author of
After the Storm and *Water in my Eyes*

"B.L.U.N.T.'s ghetto tale will leave street fiends craving for their next fix! I really look forward to this talented author's next release. I'm sure *Betrayal of a Hustler,* is just the beginning of what she has in store. B.L.U.N.T. is definitely a force to be reckoned with in the genre of street fiction!"

-Jewel Cherise, author of
Death's Destiny, My Body for His Soul
– In Stores Now!

BETRAYAL OF A HUSTLER

B.L.U.N.T.

D&D Publishing

For information: D&D Publishing, Post Office Box 15473, Richmond, Virginia 23227. www.4blunt.com

Printing by: Designs With Distinction, Printing Specialist Richmond, Virginia, in conjunction with Marketing Strategies, www.designswithdistinction.com

DEDICATION

This book is dedicated to Marquise DeLafayette Barnes: "The Prodigal Son" - You are always in my head and will forever remain in my heart. May you rest in eternal peace.

To my beloved Grandmother, Dorothy Garnett, Mama - We all miss you so very much. Our family will continue to remain strong and united. We will never forget the love, strength, and values you have instilled in all of us. I know you have your hands all over me. You were, and always will be, one of a kind.

To my son- Daniel William Johnson a.k.a Dolla- a chip off the old block. Let's do this son!! You're next to shine. I love you!!

To my daughter- Jenia Deonna Johnson Smith- Tell me that's not a name fit for a queen. I thank GOD for Mommy's Star!

To my honey, Damon D. Smith - you are my rock.

To my mother- M.J.B., my mentor. I am very proud

of all of your accomplishments. You are the epitome of a strong black woman. Hey Ma, see what finding that diary led to?

To my father- T.J., I see so much of you, in me...Love always.

To my sister- Doreen Plaskett, You have held me down from day one. I truly appreciate all you've done and all you continue to do for me. Your support and faith in me, means everything.

To my sister- Janice Brewer, I know we used to tell you that you were adopted and that we found you in a gargabe can. But you know you are my true blood – we've shared a room for many years. Remember, you were Felix Unger and I was Oscar Madison. Love You Much! Thank you for pushing the book!

To my brother- Timothy Johnson, I am so very proud of all of your accomplishments. You are the founder and CEO of your own company, and you're a wonderful father. Hey, Elijah & Ephraim.

To my sister- Ashley Johnson, I was used to being the baby of the family. But when I saw you, all I could do was love you. As I still do, and always will.

To my niece, my sister - Lakima Garnett, I am so very proud of you. I admire your scholastic achievements. Obtaining your Masters degree at 29 years of age. You Go Girl! Our dreams can become reality. Love Ya!

To my nephew - Ray Garnett, You served your country bravely in Iraq. We are so very blessed and happy to have you back home with us. Much love. To my nephew- Michael Plaskett a.k.a Pork, My soldier and bodyguard. To my nephew- Devin Plaskett a.k.a. Baby Shaq and most definitely my baby. You are so special and multi-talented.

ACKNOWLEDGMENTS

First and foremost, I must give all praise to GOD- For through HIM, all things are possible. I know that it is YOU who steers my course of direction, and every step that I take. I am truly blessed.

My best friends who I consider to be a part of my family: Cheryl Wallace, Timothy Scott, and Kathleen Benjamin.

Thanks to all of my people at my 9 to 5 who showed me support from day one and gave me the courage to do the damn thing!: Phillipe Washington, Hustle Inc.'s about to blow! Thanks for the cover! Paul Robinson, Carolyn Jones, Michell (Shelly)Camp, Jamai Lewis, Latrice Scales, Emmanuel Bethune, Mark A. Dove-Thanks John Stringer. Chrischanda Hickson, Chinae Massenburg- Thanks for the prayers!, Roz Cousins-You know you are crazy as hell-Be easy - T.C., Shannah Jones, Allyson Gourley, Mary Smith, Janette Bailey-Ibrahim, James Baldwin. Last, but certainly not least, Jewel Cherise- See you on the bestseller list chick!

Carl Weber - Thanks for all of the advice. Thank you for simply taking the time to talk to me. I now consider you, a friend.

Lakesa Cox - Thank you for all of your help and guidance throughout this whole process. You've truly been a blessing.

Shannon Holmes- Thanks for keeping it real wit' a chick!

LaJill Hunt- Thanks for the words of encouragement.

Darien Simon- Brooklyn, Brooklyn...You my ni***a!

Danja Mowf - Extra special thanks for turning the promos and the cover into a masterpiece, in my eyes. You are a very talented brother. I am in awe of your creative ability.

Matthew Williams - You are also a very talented and creative individual. You took my website, 4blunt.com, and turned my words into a technical collage of vision, and for that, I thank you.

My publicist and friend- Sharon McCreary, My sister in print, my visionary- No worries.

My editor and friend- Laura Robinson, Thank you for believing in me enough to lend a helping hand. You did a great job!

Readers-P.S.: Holla at a chick: hollaatblunt@yahoo.com or Ru4blunt@aol.com. Let me know your thoughts. Please check out my website @ www.4blunt.com to purchase additional copies. Find out who B.L.U.N.T. really is...and all of the other projects I have coming your way!

PROLOGUE

"You said you would spend more time with me Donell!"...
How much of this would she take? How much could she take?
Lisa was just about through with this man. "Donell, please,
please don't leave. I love you baby. I'm sorry, whatever I did,
I'm sorry!" Lisa yelled. Donell looked at Lisa. She had a look
of complete fear in her eyes.

"I told you to stop stressin' me when I gotta' take care of
shit." Donell screamed.

"I just worry about you Daddy. You just came home. I
don't want you to fuck around and end up back in the
penitentiary!" Lisa squealed, barely catching her breath as the
tears flow down her honey bronze skin onto her thick lips.

Donell wanted to stay and be with his woman. They had
been through mad shit together. Lisa even waited for him
through his six year bid he had to do for a robbery he pleaded
innocent to, but copped a raw deal at trial. Yes, he wanted to
stay and make mad, passionate love to this fine chocolate
thick ass woman that was all his, but his stickman was waiting
on him. He had a deal to complete.

Donell realized he was taking way too much time. He had
to go. Shit could be jumping off right now! Donell looked at
Lisa and slowly planted his tongue on her lips, outlining the
edges of her succulent lips, working his way to the center of
her hot awaiting mouth. He plunged his wet tongue into hers.
Lisa melted. He then took his fingers and moistened them
gently in her mouth never removing his tongue from hers.
Donell took his fingers and slid them down to Lisa's thighs.

9

Knowing his woman rarely wore panties, Donell was pleased to discover all he had to do was lift the tight black miniskirt to finger her moist alcove of pleasure. As Donell began fingering the tip of her clit, he stuck his tongue in Lisa's ear, placing his tongue everywhere possible.

He then whispered, "Daddy'll be right back, you keep my pussy hot and wet for me."

Lisa had no choice but to give him his way, as she moaned in ecstasy, a wave of uncontrollable liquid spilled from her being ...He kissed her forehead and walked out of the door.

THE JUMP OFF

"Where the fuck is this nigga at?" shouted Chino. "I swear, if he is the reason for any of this shit going down improperly, he'll wish he would have stayed in the fucking pen."

Just as Chino was about to spit in disgust, Donell pulled up beside him, nearly running over his feet in the oversized midnight blue Lincoln Navigator Lisa bought him as a coming home present.

"What the fuck took you so long man?" Chino asked. "You trying' to get us killed? I'm tellin' you Dee nothing, you feel me, nothing can go wrong. This shit is too important. "

"Look nigga, I'm here right, which we both know I shouldn't be, so shut the fuck up!" Donell stated.

"Yeah nigga I know your dick is saluting every piece of pussy you see. As soon as this shit goes down, you can go back to your woman and handle your business, but right now, I need you to help me handle mine. "

Chino was still lecturing Donell when a black Honda Accord slowly drove by. The guy in the front passenger seat gave Chino the signal for them to follow. Chino quickly jumped in the Navigator and followed suit. The Accord headed onto the Major Deegan Expressway and went in the direction of the Farmer's Market.

"Damn, why did they have to pick a spot that smells like dead fish?" Chino scowled. "That shit is going to fuck up my hair and get in my clothes, Shit!"

Donell interjected, "Stop bitchin', you've been bitchin'

11

ever since I got here nigga', shut the fuck up. This shit is way deeper than your fucking clothes and your hair. Take a motherfuckin' shower when we get out of here, let's just make sure that we get out of here."

Donell studied his best friend of twenty years. The two of them had known each other since first grade, and to Donell, Chino had not changed since the first grade. Chino had always been concerned about his appearance. Even at the age of six he would tell his mother what he would and would not wear. This habit drove Donell absolutely nuts at times, but other than that, Chino was his number one dawg. He would do anything for this man, which was why he was risking his freedom right now.

"You know I don't fuck with these cats, if it wasn't you I wouldn't even be here, shit even for you I shouldn't be here, man, I just got out!" Donell exclaimed.

Donell looked at Chino, but Chino didn't look back. He knew the last thing Donell needed was to get caught up in some illegal shit right now. He was still facing five years if he violated parole, but Chino also knew Donell was the only one he trusted. There was no one else he could go to with a deal such as this. Fifty kilos of uncut cocaine to be purchased and distributed by Chino and his "junior army." They were referred to as the "junior army" because their ages ranged from nine to fifteen years of age. Donell totally disagreed with the way Chino operated his business, but there was a certain logic to his plan. The kids were too young to be tried as adults in the state of New York for cocaine possession.

Neither man had children of their own, so Chino never took the time to fully comprehend how deeply he was destroying these young boys mental, emotional and physical

12

well being. Any human being with a conscience knew that it was morally disgraceful to lead their youth down paths of destruction.

The car pulled up near the 145th street Bridge and stopped. Donell also stopped. He then waited for the signal that it was cool to proceed. Just at that moment, the two men spilled out of the Accord. One of the men rushed to the drivers' side, the other to the passenger side, both with guns drawn.

Chino, not sure of how he should react, asked the guy on his side of the vehicle, "Wha's up man?" He eyed them suspiciously. "Wha's up with the artillery and shit? Shark knows how I get down. Wha's the problem?"

"No one said there were going to be two of you. Shark said we were dropping off to Chino, other than that, ain't no problem," slurred a big burly dude who went by the name of Gauge. They called him Gauge because he was shot with a twelve-gauge shotgun in the chest and amazingly survived.

"We just gotta' make sure y'all are straight. This some major shit goin' down right now - so I hope you all ain't takin' this shit lightly!"

"Na man, nobody takin' nothin' lightly. We straight. Tthe money is on me." Chino stated, motioning to his body.

"On you?" Gauge looked at him curiously.

"Yeah man." Chino ripped his shirt open and displayed what looked like hundreds upon hundreds of one hundred dollar bills taped to his body. "I wasn't taking no chances, you never know, you know."

Gauge's partner, Blue, clumsily dropped the gun that he was holding on Donell, as he bent down to pick up his piece, Donell opened his door with force, knocking Blue to his feet,

13

leaving him scrambling for the gun.

Chino automatically knowing his stickman, yelled unexpectedly, "What the fuck is going on?" when all along he was reaching for his 9 millimeter. Once in hand, he shot Gauge in the temple. Donell was already out of the truck positioning himself to quickly execute Blue.

"Don't do it man!" squealed Blue, as Donell pulled the trigger on the glock, furnished with a state of the art silencer. Blue, realizing he was about to be cancelled from this contract we call life, urinated and defecated on himself before breathing his last breath.

Chino made his way to the Accord. He reached in his jacket pocket and retrieved a pair of driving gloves. Chino searched the trunk until he found what he had been looking for, the cocaine. Donell was busy placing the bodies back in the car, which they planned to push off of the bridge. There was minimal blood due to the weapons chosen and the format in which they had been used. Chino secured the cocaine in the Lincoln and went to assist Donell. The two moved swiftly and silently. This was not the first time they had done something of this nature, but it was damn sure the first time they ever tried to cop this much work from someone as notorious and reputable as Shark. Donell let Chino know up front that if it came down to it, he would deny that he knew anything about it.

"Did you figure out what the fuck you were going to tell Shark?" questioned Donell.

Chino smiled, "Yeah, I'm going to tell his big, bald ass that they never made it. I'll call him now and act like I'm here at the meeting point and ain't nobody here to meet me."

Donell didn't quite agree with that approach. "What if

14

they already called Shark once they met us. Before they even brought us here?"

"There's only one way to find out." Chino pulled out his cell ... "Yo man, yo where your boys at?"...."Well, I'm here at the meeting point where I'm supposed to be and ain't nobody here with my fucking candy."

Shark apparently was not aware that his men had in fact made contact with Chino. He told Chino to hold on while he called them on his other phone to see where they could be. Chino looked at Donell smiling. He couldn't believe it was going to be that easy. The car phone started to ring. Donell was a little startled by the noise the ring caused, but caught himself. The sound was amplified because of their location. Shark came back on the line with Chino. "Look, I don't know what the fuck a gwon', but if these niggas don't answer soon me a' put an NPB out on them motherfuckas. NPB stands for Niggas Perpetratin' Bullshit. I knew them niggas was gettin' itchy to fuck me over. Straight up!"

Chino could not believe how sweet this was turning out.

"Well look man I still got this cash for you baby, and I need my candy, so as soon as you find out what the deal is, hit me back."

Shark was thinking of at least twenty things all at once as to what could have happened when Chino hung up.

"Yo man, let's hurry up and breakout." Chino said. "Yo, he think his boys did him dirty, he doesn't even suspect me."

Donell looked at Chino, "Don't let that shit fool you man. That man didn't get where he is today by lettin' niggas get over on him. You better make sure you know what the fuck

15

you're doing." Donell continued, "I thought you had it all figured out, and now I'm finding out you're just figuring shit out as you go along. I told you that's not the smart way to do business. You've been a lucky motherfucker so far. I will definitely give you that."

"Come on man, not now." Chino scowled. "Let's clear this shit out and be out!"

Donell and Chino took care of the Accord, and its passengers, by disposing of it and them into the Harlem River.

WELCOME BACK

"I don't know where the hell they are ... but I told Donell, I don't have time for this dumb shit!" Lisa found herself venting to her best friend Camaria.

"I already told you what the deal would be." Camaria said. Camaria and Lisa had a relationship similar to Donell and Chino's. They too had been best friends since the beginning of time. Camaria and Chino used to date, but she could not handle Chino's lifestyle. She continuously warned Lisa about what she could and should expect from Donell ... not much. Of course she would have the finest clothes, jewels, and cars, but for how long, and at what cost. Camaria was worried now more than ever, especially now that Donell was back home. She almost had Lisa ready to leave Donell and the life that came with him, but he made parole.

"I can still leave Donell. I'm not going to be going through this. I can't. I just can't do it any more." Lisa felt exhausted and Donell hadn't even been home a month.

"Girl, look, you are too damn pretty to be wasting your time and your life on Donell. Damn, he already wasted six years of his life and yours. Besides, you've really only been with him for two years for real. I wouldn't even count all that time he was locked up." Camaria hoping there was still possibly a chance to get her away from Donell wouldn't just stop there. "Besides Lisa, he has been away for a long time. How do you know he even still likes women?"

Lisa looked at Camaria like she was crazy.

"I know you did not even go there!" Lisa was furious.

17

"Now hold on," Camaria said. "You mean you haven't thought about it?"

Lisa placed her hands on her hips, tilted her head and asked Camaria, "Thought about what?"

She wanted Camaria to come straight out of her mouth with it. Well, Camaria gave her just what she wanted.

"Shit, for all you know he could have been fucking one of those other inmates!"

"Camaria! " Lisa just stared at her.

"I'm dead fucking serious Lisa. The man has been gone for six years, not six months and you know they have those men in there that look damn near better than we do, shit some of them do look better than we do." Camaria would not back off.

"Donell is stronger than that Camaria." Lisa stated, trying to defend her man.

Camaria gave up, "Yeah, whatever!"

Lisa heard the key in the door. She went toward the foyer to greet Donell. Donell entered with Chino.

Lisa instantly knew what Donell went to take care of.

"Hey baby, I was worried about you." Lisa totally ignored Chino.

"What's up Lisa? How's it going?" Chino asked.

Lisa decided she'd better acknowledge him, "I'm doing pretty good, and you?"

"I'm chillin." Chino said slyly.

"Baby, fix us some drinks. Not no fruity shit either, just give us some Remy on the rocks."

Donell led the way to the den. Chino followed, looking

18

back at Lisa. He watched her go to the bar and start pouring. He always watched Lisa. Secretly, he loved her. Chino took care of Lisa for the six years Donell was away. He made sure she never had to work. Every week Chino would deposit a thousand dollars into her account. He wondered if and when she would tell Donell what had happened between them.

"Yo man, what the fuck are you up to?" Donell asked.
Chino caught himself still looking in the direction in which Lisa went. "Nothing man, I'm just tripping off the shit we just pulled off."

He began to take his shirt off to remove the money from his torso when Lisa came in with their drinks. Lisa handed Donell his drink first, then gave Chino his drink. Lisa saw all the money Chino had taped to him but declined on saying anything about it. She knew what the deal was.

"Baby, Camaria's here. She's in the kitchen."
Donell's face tightened. "What the fuck is she here for? She can't stand my ass. Wait a minute, I been home almost a whole month and I ain't seen that bitch. What the fuck she come over tonight for?"

"I asked her to come over baby. It was getting late and I was getting worried." Lisa whined.

"And what the fuck was she supposed to do? Change into her "Super Bitch" costume and come save me?" asked Donell. Chino laughed, spitting out some of his drink.

"Donell don't be like that. Camaria has been there for me and you know that!" Lisa said.

Donell reached for the remote to the stereo, and made a comment, "Well she may have been there for you, but what

19

the fuck has she done for ME lately?"

Chino cut in, "Yo man you just sounded like Janet Jackson when you said that shit man. Remember that shit? "What have you done for me lately? OOH OOOH YEAH!"

Donell had to laugh, "Aw fuck her man. You know what? I ain't even mad at her anymore. Life's too short, y'all come on in here and let's chill."

Lisa could not believe her ears, "You serious baby?"

Donell smiled, "Yeah, I'm serious. Fuck all that minor bullshit from now on."

Lisa immediately called for Camaria to join them. After a few moments of Camaria not responding, Lisa decided it would be best to just go and get her. She may not be able to hear her calling. As she approached the kitchen, Lisa overheard Camaria on her cellular phone. "Fuck that, I'm not telling her, if he's not, that's on him, but I cannot and will not … " Camaria felt a presence behind her. She swiftly turned around. She noticed the inquisitive look on Lisa's face.

"Let me call you back!"

"What was all that about?" Lisa asked.

"Oh nothing girl, that was Karen. She's carrying on about me telling Sugar that Warren is cheating on her." Camaria was good, damn good and quick.

Lisa said, "Karen needs to mind her damn business. She's always in the middle of somebody's damn relationship. That's why she doesn't have a damn man."

"You're probably right," Camaria agreed, hoping to divert the conversation.

"Oh trust. I'm right. You need to stop fucking with her," Lisa added.

Lisa got back to the matter at hand of why she came looking for Camaria in the first place. "Girl, you won't believe what Donell just said. He said that whatever you guys were at each other about, it's all forgotten. He wants us to all chill together, no more hostility. He said and I quote, "Fuck all that minor bullshit from now on!"".

"Really?" Camaria was a little surprised. She didn't expect Donell to step up and be mature about their relationship, or rather their lack of one.

"Yes, really. I told you my baby has changed." Lisa gloated.

Camaria snapped her back to reality, "No, what you told me is that, you wasn't going through this bullshit anymore and ... "

Lisa snapped, "Shut up Mari!"

Lisa and Camaria joined Donell and Chino. Chino had already finished removing the money from his torso and was lounging on a burgundy paisley embroidered chaise.

"Camaria, you sho' done got fine in your old days."

Camaria's neck snapped. "Old! Motherfucker who are YOU calling old? I'll have you know I ain't a day over twenty-six and yes, I'm still fine as a bitch! You better ask some motherfuckin' body!"

Chino loved to rattle Camaria. She made it so easy. Chino loved him some women. He usually had at least three or four at one time. Normally everyone would have at least one girl who would be classified as their "main" girl, but not Chino he had three or four main girls. They all knew and understood they could leave at any time, but Chino was not changing his habits for anyone. Donell always believed Chino just hadn't found that right one yet. Chino knew he would never find that right one because she was already taken, by Donell.

"Yo man. We didn't even sample the goods."

Chino retrieved the packages and started to assess exactly what they had.

"Damn man. This shit is unbelievable. I need to start packaging this shit right now. It won't be long before Shark starts feeling funky about how shit went down," Chino said.

"Well you're not gonna cut that shit up in here!" Lisa snapped.

Donell looked at Lisa, he didn't expect for her to object, he thought Camaria would open her big mouth if anyone.

"What's the matter baby?" Donell asked.

"What the hell do you mean, what's the matter? What the fuck do you want Donell? You want me to just call the motherfuckin' cops and have them pick your ass up now to save me the heartache? What part of, I'm not going to be dealing with this shit anymore, don't you understand? You apparently don't give a fuck about me or our future. This shit means more to you than I do!" Lisa stormed out.

Camaria followed her. She called to her, "Lisa ... "

Lisa was fuming. That was it! That was all she needed to see to know things were not going to change a bit. Now she just had to find a place to stay for a while because she meant business. She was leaving Donell. Even if it was just to jar him into reality, she was leaving.

"Yo man, don't let a woman decide what you can do in your own home, even if it is your main woman."

Donell snapped, "Look nigga, don't tell me how to handle

my motherfuckin' household. I got this shit. "

Donell started to go after Lisa, but decided not to. Lisa knew who Donell was when he went away and no matter how much time he has done or how much time he was facing, he was, and always would be from the streets. "Just go ahead and divide this shit up, leave my cut and break out and bag your shit up elsewhere!"

Chino saw that look that told him to just do as Donell said. He'd talk to him when he calmed down. He had more than a few of his women in which he could trust that would allow him to package his goods. "A'ight man, I'm out!" Chino separated the work, left Donell forty thousand of the eighty he had taped to himself, and left.

Donell went to find Lisa. He found her and Camaria in their bedroom. Lisa was packing.

"Lisa, come on baby, he's gone. I told him to break out with all of that shit!"

"Donell you know you shouldn't be getting mixed up in no dumb shit. You just came home!" Camaria boldly stated.

"Look, I just told Lisa that I wanted to out all the bad blood between us, but I don't want you all up in my shit Camaria. What I do is my goddamn business. I'm a grown man and I'll make my own decisions when it comes to what I will and will not get myself into. I know what I'm facing. I'm not stupid. I'm the one who did the fucking six years!"

Lisa jumped in, "You are not the only one who did six years, my life was like a prison the entire time you've been away."

"I'm sorry baby. I didn't mean to make it seem like it was nothing for you. I know I hurt you and I know it was not easy at all being alone for all this time." Donell went to hold Lisa, but she pulled away.

"I'ma' go ahead an' split, you know, let you take care of your business." Camaria hesitated. "I don't know why I am saying this, Lisa, but I really don't think you should leave."
Lisa was very surprised. "I don't care what either of you think! I have to get the hell out of this house. Donell if you really wanted a life with me, you would have never done what you did tonight. I tried to tell myself that maybe this would be the last time, but who the hell would I be fooling?" Lisa continued to pack.

Camaria wasn't sure of what she should do. She offered to take Lisa wherever she was going, but Lisa didn't want to involve Camaria, especially since Donell was willing to bury their differences. Lisa asked Camaria to leave and she would catch up with her later. Camaria left, unsure of just what the outcome of this evening would be.

"Lisa, look ... " Donell attempted to stop her. He grabbed her arms.

"Get the fuck off me Donell!" Lisa yelled. "You don't give a shit about me so you might as well just let me leave. I really thought things were going to change, but I guess I'm the stupid one for believing that you could leave the streets alone!"

"Oh, so now the life I lead is so unbearable? I didn't hear any of that bullshit while you were out shopping, buying all this shit for yourself. Gucci, Fendi, Dolce & Gabbana, is it comin' back to you now?" Donell added, "Lisa, you know what? Fuck it –go. You're full of shit!"

"I'll be full of shit, and my bags are going to be full of shit too, my shit motherfucker, I'm out!" Lisa grabbed the two oversized Louis Vuitton duffle bags she had packed and headed downstairs. "Don't get it twisted. I paid my damn dues in this goddamn relationship." Lisa made it to the door. Donell was on her heels, cursing her, calling her weak, telling her to go. He would have her replaced within the hour.

Lisa was on fire. How dare he say those things, after six years of her visiting him on every visiting day, making sure he had everything he needed. Whenever there was beef, she was always right there by his side, and this was the thanks she got. Cool!

"Replace me motherfucker? You wish you could replace me. I wouldn't care what skank ho you decide to hook up with and trust, you can fuck her until the cows come home. I'm straight. I don't need you, your house or your clothes. I got mad niggas that want this. And you know it ... ask your boy!" Lisa slipped.

"Ask my boy? Ask my boy, who?" Donell's face twisted as if he just swallowed his least favorite food. "I know you not trying to say one of my boys is trying to fuck you?"
Donell went to lunge at Lisa, but she moved out of the doorway and ran to the car. Donell lost his balance and tripped, almost falling to the ground.

Lisa didn't want any trouble between Donell and Chino, they had been friends for years and actually Chino didn't make the first move, so Lisa played it off, "You have plenty of "boys" it could be, but don't worry because I'm weak so they won't want me. Right Donell?" Lisa taunted as she got into her champagne colored Lexus and sped off.

SOMETHING JUST AIN'T RIGHT

"There is no way in the world that a car with two huge blood clad muthafuckas just disappeared into thin air." Shark howled. "I know one thing. Somebody betta come up with some damn answers, some cocaine, or my muthafuckin' paper, sien!"

Shark was screaming to Lil' James. Lil' James' was Shark's right hand. At four feet nine inches it was amazing the hurting this man could put on a full size human being, actually it was totally unbelievable. Shark could not help but take Lil' James under his wing after he saved his life in Memphis on a deal gone bad.

"Shark I don't know man, them niggas was shady anyway. You know they wanted a higher position and they knew I was next in line if anyone, so they probably took the shit to start off on their own." Lil' James tried to calm Shark. Shark had one hell of a temper and Lil' James was just not in the mood. But Lil' James also knew that this was very serious. No one was crazy enough to fuck with Shark, not anyone from New York anyway.

"You really think them niggas did me dirty?" Shark asked.

"You think Chino set this shit up?" Lil' James shot back.

Shark reflected on how loyal Chino had always been. He's known Chino since he was a snotty-nosed kid coming up on 112th and Lexington in Johnson Projects. Chino's father used to work for Shark until he was gunned down in a robbery. Ever since Chino's dad passed, Shark has taken care of

26

Chino's entire family. It couldn't be Chino ... na. It couldn't be ...

"Let the circuit know what the fuck went down tonight," Shark said. "If there is a burst of coke on the street, I wanna be the first to know 'bout it!"

Lil' James did as he was told.

Shark's English was nowhere near perfect, he was a native of Jamaica and he never finished grade school. Shark left school in the middle of fifth grade. He had to. The all too familiar story of his father leaving his mother with seven kids, being the reason. Shark, the oldest, knew what he had to do.

Shark called his best friend, his woman, Shelly. Shelly was a down ass bitch, down for whatever her man needed. She did four years in the pen for a rap Shark should have taken, but he promised her that if she took this bid, she would be straight for the rest of her life. Shelly being no fool, had Shark set up a one million dollar trust fund in their daughters' name. This trust fund can't be touched until the child was eighteen years of age. Shantel, their daughter, would be eighteen in six more months.

"Hey Daddy, what's up? " Shelly asked.

"You won't fuckin' believe this raas clad shit baby... "

Shelly knew instantly it must be serious, "What Daddy, what happened?"

Shark rambled into the receiver, "Blue and Gauge set me up! Dem muthafuckas stole my goddamn cocaine and split. They broke the fuck out with my blood clad shit!"

Shelly was calm, she knew she had to be because Shark

was about to blow up and when Shark blew up a couple of people would be feeling his wrath. "Shark, baby, calm down and tell me what happened."

Shark told Shelly exactly how everything went down. Shelly knew Blue was shady, but she didn't think Gauge was weak enough to be persuaded to do some dumb shit like that. Shelly really wasn't sure of what to think either. She loved Chino, in more ways than one. So to make it easier on her mind, she instantly blamed Blue and Gauge.

"Daddy I told you about Blue. It was only a matter of time. He even tried to scoop me!"

Shelly was never going to tell Shark that Blue tried to pull her from Shark. There was no need. Blue could have never given Shelly the lifestyle she was used to.

"Are you telling me that mufucka tried to take you from me?" Shark yelled.

"Tried is all he could do, that nigga must have been smoking some good shit to think I would even consider leaving you Daddy. I knew he was trippin'. I paid him no mind. "

That was all Shark needed to hear. He was convinced it was Blue's idea and that he must have gotten to Gauge, maybe even killed him.

"Shelly, get your ass over here. We've got some shit to take care of. Blue is a dead mufucka, that's my blood clad word."

"Coming Daddy, I'm on my way."

Shark went over and over in his head what he assumed went down that night. That just made him more upset. He wanted to know the truth now, fuck guessing. Shark felt he treated all of his workers fairly and with the respect he himself expected. He was also aware of a jealous man's envy and he had encountered that one too many times. Blue had been acting strange for the past few weeks, like he was getting ready to make a move. Shark recalled, he kept mentioning being tired of the city. He thought about how Blue questioned his decisions lately, as if Shark was losing his touch. Shark then thought about the fact that Blue tried to cop Shelly. Was he crazy? He must have known he would have never been able to pull that off. Blue always asked Shark what he saw in her, telling him he could do a lot better. Now Shark realized he was just frontin'. 'What the hell? He thought he was just gon' be me, wit' my shit and my 'oman?' Shark thought about Gauge. Gauge was still earning his place. Blue must have told him some good shit if he told him anything at all. Shark felt he could trust Gauge. He was due to move up in the organization after this job, so he had to have a bonafide reason to do something like this. Shark figured a half a million dollars would be considered reason enough.

Lil' James returned to the living room. He had gone to the den to make some calls. Nobody knew anything. No one had seen anything. It was as if Blue and Gauge had dropped off the face of the earth.

"Either niggas truly don't know nothin' or ain't nobody talkin', cause I done called everybody. Ain't nobody seen Blue or Gauge. I asked about Chino, they saw him, but he ain't up to nothin' new."

"I smell a fuckin' fish!" Shark was furious. The thought of someone taking him for a joke made his blood boil. "Oh somebody know somethin'. I'm not tryin' to hear nobody knows nothin!"

THAT'S WHAT FRIENDS ARE FOR

Chino was bagging up at his own place. He figured things would be too hot to trust anyone right now, even his main girls. Anyone would sing for the right price, or, to save their own life.

His phone rang, he answered, "Talk to me."

"Chino." Lisa hesitated. "Uh, it's me, Lisa."

Chino was very surprised. Lisa was the last person he expected to be on the other end of his line.

"What's the matter Baby Girl?" "Baby Girl" was a nickname Chino gave Lisa while Donell was locked up, while he was loving her.

"I left him." Lisa stated.

"What! Lisa what the hell happened? Where are you?" Chino asked.

"I can't do it anymore. Both of you need to stop living the way you're living." Lisa's voice was strained. "I just feel like shit is about to explode Chino!"

"Donell told me he could replace me in an hour. He told me to go, after all the shit I've been through with him and for him, he didn't give a fuck. He treated me like a bitch on the street!" Lisa broke down.

Chino could not control his feelings for Lisa. He didn't even know how they became so strong. He had control with any other woman, no matter how fine or how good the pussy was.

"Baby Girl, calm down. Tell me where you are and I'll come get you."

31

Lisa thought about it, "No! That's not a good idea. I almost slipped and told Donell about us."

Chino didn't know how to react to that statement. He knew there may come a day when it came out, but right now would be the wrong time.

"A'ight, then at least tell me where you are so I can get you straight. You need some money?"

Lisa left the house in such a hurry she didn't realize she left her wallet on the dresser.

"Shit, I left my wallet." Lisa blurted out.

"Tell me where you are Lis!" Chino demanded to know.

"I'm at the Marriott on 59th."

Chino was there in less than thirty minutes. He asked for Lisa Spencer and was told he had to be announced. He was then told she was in room number 417 and to go right up. As Chino got off of the elevator and headed toward the room, he couldn't help but reflect on what he was about to get himself into. He knew he should not be involved in what was going on between Donell and Lisa. He had so many other things to worry about right now, namely Shark, but the unexplainable feelings he had for this woman, his best friend's woman of eight years, blocked out all of his apprehensions. He loved her in a way he loved no other. Lisa had never ever cheated on Donell, until Chino. Chino knew how loyal Lisa was, and probably still is, to a man who didn't deserve her love and devotion. He admired the fact that even though they grew up to live and love the life of the streets, Lisa took her education very seriously. She already had a bachelor's degree in computer technology and was working on her master's. She was fine and she was smart, one of the sexiest women he had ever met. He could not for the life of him understand why she stayed with Donell, she could have anyone she wanted, namely, him. The whole bid. She did the whole bid with him.

He was in front of Lisa's room. Chino knocked once. Lisa immediately opened the door. She was wearing a beige fitted halter lounge dress from Victoria S.. Her caramel skin glistened through the sheerness of the garment.

"Damn, why you put that shit on Lisa? "

He looked intently at Lisa. He could not resist her. Chino moved slowly toward her placing his hands gently on her shoulders, he fingered her neck, his tongue traced his fingers, he placed hot breaths over her earlobe, his hands flowing over her soft silky skin, her scent, so sensuous. Chino turned Lisa around so that her back was facing him. He placed hot, wet, kisses from the nape of her neck down to the small of her back. Lisa groaned in ecstasy. He also knew all of her spots. Chino slid down and slowly slid his tongue over Lisa's calves, leading his way up to her thighs. He was engulfed under the sheath of beige, his tongue touched the tip of Lisa's clit, she moaned uncontrollably. Chino placed soft wet kisses on the outer lips of her passageway to pleasure then gently licked the rose-colored flesh of her inner lips. He loved the way she tasted. She always, always tasted so sweet. He began to suck her pussy like a newborn baby sucking their first bottle. He never wanted to stop. Lisa was mesmerized with the feeling of lust Chino was bestowing upon her.

He panted, "You know what you do to me, Baby Girl, why you doin' this (Lick)-(Suck) to me?"

Chino raised himself up and slid the dress off of Lisa. He stood back just to marvel at her coca-cola bottle shape. She had the perfect shape. Pert titties. Not a sag anywhere. Lisa was silent. She was always silent when they were together in this way. She felt guilty for betraying Donell, but at the same time, Chino made her feel like only the two of them existed when he made love to her. Chino began to undress, but thought Lisa may change her mind, so he just took his pants off and pulled his pulsating scepter out of his boxers. Lisa watched as Chino licked the tip of his fingers and started rubbing his dick, slowly, looking directly into Lisa's eyes.

"Come on Baby Girl, come here."

Chino reached for Lisa. Lisa knew what Chino wanted. She came to him. Chino turned her on. He was fine as a bitch. He had olive colored skin and the softest brown eyes, with brown wavy "good hair" to match. His physique was tight. He stood at six foot four inches. The nigga was fine. Lisa took him in her hand, caressing his hot, throbbing shaft. She removed his boxers. Lisa took him into her hot, waiting mouth. She licked around the head of his penis slowly and continually, teasing him with the heat of her mouth and the swiftness of her tongue. Lisa guided him fully into her mouth sucking his dick as if she had been created specifically for providing this pleasure. She licked herself into a frenzy, accumulated the generated saliva and showered it all over Chino's dick. Chino wanted to shove his dick down her throat. She was giving it to him–just like he liked—just the way he taught her. He was ready to explode in her hot mouth, but he pulled out, he had to feel the tightness of her love cavity.

Chino led her to the bed. As they lay together, Chino looked deeply into Lisa's eyes. They both felt the same but words would make it too real. So instead, he simultaneously thrust his tongue and his dick into her hot holes. They made love feverishly. Their lovemaking was so very passionate, probably because it was so forbidden.

"Uhm ... Baby Girl, your pussy is sooo good. Tell me I can always have you. Tell me. I ... aah ... aah ... shit!", Chino exclaimed as he pulled out and shot his thick creamy cum all over Lisa's shapely being.

Chino got up and went into the bathroom to get a hot soapy rag to wipe Lisa's body down. Lisa had been through a lot. Her body just gave in. Chino wiped her body down as she lay, asleep. He just watched her for a while, he knew if and when Donell found out, that they would no longer be best friends, shit they probably wouldn't even be friends. Chino could not believe he had taken things this far with Lisa, but he could not deny that she made him feel more alive than any other woman, and he's had plenty.

Chino left five thousand dollars on the dresser and a note, which read:

Baby Girl,
Whatever you do, don't tell Donell about us. Not right now. There is some major shit that is about to go down and I need him with me, not against me. Feel me? Take the loot and get a crib. Hit me up and let me know where you are at all times. I know you know how I feel about you so I don't have to tell you. Fuck it. I love you Lisa.   *Chino*

HAVE YOU SEEN HER?

Donell called Camaria. He was sure that even though Lisa told Camaria to leave, that she had to be at Camaria's. She didn't trust anyone else.

"Good Morning!" Camaria cheerfully answered.

"Mari ... "

"Donell?" Camaria was not shocked it was Donell, but this was still a rare moment.

"Let me speak to Lis!"

Camaria said curiously, "Donell, Lisa never came over here. I thought you guys had worked it out when I didn't hear from her."

Donell didn't know what to think. "She never even called you?," he asked.

"No, and now I'm worried. She was upset as shit last night. Donell, what happened?"

Donell gave Camaria a briefing of what was said between the two of them. Camaria could not believe what she was hearing. "Donell, I know you didn't say that shit you just told me you said? You told Lisa that you could replace her in an hour and you called her what? A bitch, nigga is you crazy? Do you know what that girl has been through for your dumb ass?"

Camaria screamed on him, "She doesn't deserve that shit Donell!"

"Look Mari, not now. I know I fucked up. I was just mad as shit cause' we were all chillin and here she comes with this holier than thou shit. She knows what I'm about. It's never been a problem before. What the fuck is the problem now?"

Camaria still could not believe her ears.

"Donell, did your mother drop yo ass head first when you were a baby? Did you not just get finished doing a SIX year stint? Ain't your ass still on parole? Doesn't Lisa want to spend the rest of her life with your dumb ass and have your damn kids? For the life of me I still don't know why she wants to, but that's beside the point. Where is your head at?"

"I just really need to find her Camaria. She doesn't even have her wallet. She left in such a fucking hurry, she forgot her damn wallet!" Donell was furious. "Camaria, tell me! Did Lisa fuck around on me while I was locked up? Does she have some other nigga somewhere else?"

Camaria knew that would be the next question, but to her knowledge there was no one else.

"No Donell, Lisa unfortunately feels that you are the only one for her, imagine that!"

Donell was relieved. He knew if there was someone else, Camaria would love to tell him, just to fuck with him. Alright, so there was no other man. Donell didn't know what he would do if he felt another man was with his Lisa. His Lisa! Donell did what he always does when he felt stressed. He called Chino.

"Talk to me." Chino answered.

"Yo man, Lisa is gone, man. Something happened to her, man. Camaria hasn't seen her, she left her wallet, her mom hasn't heard from her."

Chino interrupted, "Whoa, man hold up. Lisa's what? What happened?" As if he didn't know. But of course he could not reveal the truth.

"She just flipped and broke out last night man." Donell

37

was beginning to come to the realization of what was happening. Lisa left him. "This shit is your fault man, if I would have never went with you, none of this shit would be happening."

"Look man, I know you love Lisa to no end man, she knows you do too, maybe, and don't get me wrong when I say this, but maybe she was just waiting for an excuse to leave." Chino went there.

"What the fuck are you talking about Chino? Huh man, what the fuck are you tryin' to say?"

"I'm not saying anything man. It just seems strange that's all. What did you do to her?" Chino was playing the role to the hilt.

"We had some beef after you left. I fucked up and told her I could replace her in an hour. I told her she could go and I called her some names."

Donell thought to himself now, how stupid he was. What was he thinking? Lisa had been nothing but good to him.

"Damn man, what made you say some shit like that to her Dee?"

Chino really didn't want to hurt Donell. He honestly never meant to fall in love with Lisa, but when Lisa would get weak and break down about Donell, he was there to console her. He was the one taking care of her needs while Donell was gone for all those years. They spent a lot of time with each other and one day it just happened. Neither of them meant for it to go down this way, but it was done, and with the feelings they shared, there was no turning back. Chino still did not know how this shit was going to play out, but he knew for sure it was not going to be smooth.

"You talked to Camaria?" Chino asked.

38

"Yeah, but she actin' like she don't know shit!" Donell answered.

"I don't believe that bullshit. Camaria is her fuckin' shadow." Chino said.

"Well I called Camaria and she said she knew nothing. She said she thought we had settled everything when she didn't hear from Lisa because she felt Lisa would come straight to her house, but she hasn't seen her either!" Donell started to sound worried. "Yo, if something happened to her man, I don't know what I would do."

"I'm sure she's ok man, Lisa is smarter than you guys give her credit for," Chino said.

"What the hell you mean by that? I know my woman! I never said she wasn't smart." Donell said defensively.

"She's very smart, very beautiful, and I fucked up man. I just don't believe this shit right now."

"It'll be cool man, this is a big ass city, but we'll find her." Chino reassured his best friend.

Donell felt better already. Chino knew everybody, if anyone could find Lisa, he would be the one. He thought to ask Chino if he had heard anything about the heist the night before, but he figured if something was wrong, Chino would have told him by now. So he ended the call by setting up a time and place for them to meet and begin their search for Lisa.

Chino knew Donell didn't know how to handle Lisa. He had been away too long, the woman he knew was long gone. Lisa was a totally different woman now. Chino had been handling her for a while now and he knew for sure that Lisa was too much for Donell sexually. 'He had to have noticed a difference in her skills,' Chino thought.

Chino tried to think of several ways he could tell Donell how things happened with Lisa and him, but none were good. There was:

"Look man, I know you're not going to believe this shit, but while you were away, me and Lis." Na ...

"Yo, Dee the craziest shit happened while you was locked up. Lisa and me ... we ..." Na .

"Yo man, Lisa needed somebody. She was going crazy. " Na ...

"Fuck that, man, I got wit' Lisa while you were gone, she needed somebody and I figured you wouldn't want just some regular nigga fuckin' with her so ..." Oh hell no, that ain't good!

Chino figured it was best left unsaid for now, until he could figure something out. Maybe he would never tell.

MEMORY LANE

Lil' James arrived back at the penthouse. He was getting nowhere with his search for Blue and Gauge. No one claimed to have seen either of them. Which meant one of two things, either they did in fact try to fuck over Shark and were long gone, or they were no longer alive to tell what went on. Lil' James had seen it all. He still had Chino pegged as the culprit. He had no proof, but the more that he thought about it, the more his gut told him it was Chino that set Shark up. He would have to prove it without a shadow of a doubt. He knew how Shark felt about Chino. Poppo, Chino's father, used to be Shark's right-hand man, until he got killed.

Poppo was a smooth ass hustler, he could rob you looking dead in your face and you wouldn't be the wiser. Lil' James felt the apple didn't fall too far from the tree. Now Poppo would have never, ever tried to do Shark dirty, but his son was a different story. 'These young kids don't care', thought Lil' James. Shark and he were considered old timers. Shark being forty-five, Lil' James his junior by five years. You had hustlers as young as sixteen and seventeen actually taking over territories that used to belong to some fo' sho' hustling ass niggas.

Poppo got shot to death in a bank robbery. Shark assured him it was cool. It would be a piece of cake. One of Shark's broads was a bank teller at First National Savings Bank on 110th and Amsterdam Avenue. All Poppo had to do was present her with the withdrawal slip from a healthy account. The slip had already been completed with matching

41

signatures. Everything was cool until the teller next to Charlyn, Shark's broad, recognized Poppo as one of the guys who robbed a jewelry store she happened to be in. He had actually held her down at gunpoint, but let her go when the heist was done.

She panicked and pressed the silent alarm. Charlyn was getting the head teller's approval on the withdrawal. It was over her cash limit. The police had arrived, but Poppo hadn't noticed. His back was to the door. He was waiting patiently for Charlyn to return with the thirty thousand dollars that had been requested. The police questioned the security guard who said he saw nothing suspicious, and had no idea who signaled the alarm. Just as the teller who signaled the alarm went to talk to the officers, Charlyn was on her way from the vault with the cash. Poppo was about to reach for some of the money when one of the officers came up behind him and asked if he could come with them. Poppo was already on ten years probation and only did the heist because Shark guaranteed it was safe and he needed the money for his family. Poppo panicked, he knew as soon as he talked to the officers, it was over. He tried to make a run for it. Without turning around, he pulled the .38 special out of his waist, threw his left hand in the air as if to surrender, and shot the officer in the stomach with his right hand. The officer's partner was caught totally off guard. He fumbled for his weapon. Poppo disarmed the wounded officer and attempted to run, firing at the police officer with both weapons. He slept on the security guard, who pulled out his dusty old .38 revolver, and nervously pointed and unloaded the weapon until it emptied, fatally shooting Poppo in the head, neck, and back. Chino was thirteen when his pops got killed. Shark had taken excellent care of his family ever since. He practically raised Chino as his own son.

Lil' James felt Chino was using Shark at times. Chino started making some not so intelligent decisions in the game. Shark had to cut him off for a while, but Shark did everything for Chino out of love, even if some of it was tough love. Chino had been there for Shark through some tough times too, even put his life on the line a few times. Maybe it wasn't Chino. Lil' James didn't really know what he was thinking.

"Hey Shelly, what are you doing here?" Lil' James asked.

"I live here motherfucka!" Shelly snapped.

Shelly didn't care for Lil' James. She felt he stayed up Shark's ass too much. Lil' James would still always show Shelly mad respect because he knew how Shark felt about her. For the life of him he didn't know why Shark felt the way he did. She wasn't the best looking thing in the world, but that's not all that matters, right?!

"I know you live here, sometimes," replied Lil' James.

"Don't fuck with me you little midget ass motherfucka. I'm not in the mood!" Shelly shot back.

"Why you always gotta' disrespect my height?"

"Do I fuck with you about how beautiful you COULD have been?" Lil' James couldn't resist that one. "Where's Shark at Shelly?"

Shelly just looked at him like he was the lowest form of human flesh.

"WHAT! You mean you came out of his ass and done lost him? We got some real shit jumpin' off right now, Lil' James, so naturally Shark is busy." Shelly continued, "What the fuck you been doing? They just took my man's shit! What the fuck you got to say about that? Where the fuck have YOU been?"

"Out trying to find out who the hell is behind this shit!" Lil' James said. "I done checked out every possibility. Everybody claim they ain't see shit."

"What the hell was there to see? Didn't the transaction go down in the wee hours of the night at a secluded spot? Who was supposed to see anything?" Shelly asked.

"See, that's what I mean Shark got your ass playing Inspector Gadget, and you don't even know what the fuck you're doing!"

"It ain't hard to tell that Blue done fucked Shark over and either killed Gauge or convinced him to roll wit' him." Shelly said.

"And it's that simple, huh genius?" Lil' James replied snidely.

Lil' James decided he wouldn't even entertain her with any more information. For all he knew Chino was fucking her ugly ass too.

"All I'm saying is that from what Shark told me, it seems like that's what went down. Chino called Shark to ask where they were. So that means they never made it to the meeting."

"I see I gave you more credit than I should have. I thought you were smarter than to believe whatever the hell someone, no matter who, tells you when shit like this here goes down. Everybody is guilty until we find out what really happened and that includes your pretty boy surrogate son," snapped Lil' James.

"Sounds like you jealous of Chino. Sounds to me like you want it to be Chino so bad you can taste it in that nasty ass mouth of yours."

44

"Well I'll be goddamn! I know you ain't say nothin' about nobody having a nasty ass mouth! What Shelly, you fuckin' him?"

"FUCK YOU! How bout' that!" was Shelly's reply.

"Alright you two. Cut the shit. I been sittin' in the den listenin' to both of you. Both of you have nasty ass mouths," yelled Shark.

"I tried to keep it clean Shark, but she be fuckin' wit a nigga."

"That's right, bitch up motherfucka, see, I told you Daddy, you got a bitch out there doing a man's job!" Shelly boldly stated.

"Shelly, do me a favor baby, I want you to go out and see what you can find out. Bring Daddy back some bona fide info." Shark went over to Shelly and put his hand under her chin and brought her lips to his and placed a soft kiss. Shark was a massive, but gentle human being. He stood six feet three inches tall, and he weighed three hundred twenty pounds, all muscle. He was still a handsome brother at the age of forty-five. A pecan complexion, bald head, eyes like an eagle, always watching. Shelly totally loved Shark.

Shark took Shelly off the streets when she was just coming into her teens. He was out conducting business as usual and he saw a girl arguing with two dudes. He pulled over just to watch for entertainment. From what he could hear, she tried to lift one of the guys' wallet and the other one busted her. So here he watched as this female held her own, spitting some serious gift of gab to these niggas so they wouldn't break her neck, and from what he was hearing, she was doing a good job. Shelly swore up and down that she thought she knew the dude. She tried to convince him that they had gone out and he never called her back so she wanted to get his wallet so she could call him and invite him to dinner. Then he could retrieve his belongings. She told him once he would have realized who she was, he would see what he missed out on and they could have gone out again and picked up where they had left off. The guy Shelly lifted the wallet from was actually buying the bullshit story, but his stickman wasn't going for it - at all. He started getting buck with Shelly, like he was going to hit her.

Shark saw how Shelly stood her ground, even took her heels off and told both of the dudes, "Fuck it, let's go, I don't give a shit- you think I won't go for mine- I told you I thought I knew you." Shark thought she was hilarious. He also knew a down ass bitch when he saw one. He got out of his car and went over to the situation. One of the dudes knew Shark. Shelly had heard of Shark. Everybody had heard of Shark.

"Yo Ice!" Shark called. "You got your shit back mon, gwon' go."

"Yo Shark, man, na man, she tried to lift my shit. I can't go out like that man," Ice was heated. "This little bitch is trying to play me Shark. She think I'm some new nigga!," snapped Ice.

Shark added, "From what I heard, she almost had you playa. She's cool mon, gwon na', you got your shit, break out."

Shelly was putting her shoes back on.
"Thank you Mista Shark."

Shark laughed.
Shelly asked him, "What's so funny?"

46

"Nobody ever called me Mista Shark before."

"Well, like I was saying, Mista Shark, I sho' appreciate you straightenin' that for me."

Shark asked Shelly, "Where you live?"

"Here, there, I have a granma. She let me stay there sometimes." Shelly replied.

Shark asked, "How old are you?

"Fifteen, Mista Shark."

"Please stop callin' me Mista Shark, ... fifteen! What you doin' on your own so young?"

Shark looked at her closely. "You need some real money, not that lifting wallet bullshit."

"I'm not sucking no dick, and ain't nobody fuckin' me, Mista Shark."

"What kinda' man you take me fa'?"

Shark had decided that he would take Shelly under his wing. Make sure she was living right. Shelly was straight up. He liked that. With guts like hers, she would be very valuable to him and his organization. When Shelly turned eighteen, Shark finally gave in to his loins. He wanted Shelly physically when he met her, but when she told him her age, he knew she was off limits. That was eighteen years ago ... and a child later.

47

THE SO-CALLED SEARCH

Chino scooped Donell up at their meeting spot, under Yankee Stadium on 161st in the Bronx.

"Damn man I need to wash my shit. I don't like my shit all dirty an' shit." Chino was referring to his baby, his money green Cadillac Escalade.

"You think she's fucking around on me man?" Donell asked.

"Chill man. I'm sure she's ok. She's probably just trying to scare you. I'm telling you man. I don't think Lisa wants to be found right now."

"Fuck all that, I gotta' find her and I'm gonna find her!" Donell yelled.

"A'ight, man, just chill, you gon' buss' a motherfuckin' blood vessel. I got you man, we'll find her."

Chino proceeded to Harlem. They were going down 112th and Lexington, when Chino spotted Kareem. Kareem was one of Chino's oldest employees at sixteen years of age.

He told Donell he was going to ask him if he had seen Lisa and if not, to put the word out. Chino made it seem like he was asking Kareem if he had seen Lisa, but under his breath, he whispered, "I'll be back in five hours, make sure you have all of my money. No shorts. No bullshit!"

Loudly Chino asked, "You sure you haven't seen Lisa?"

Kareem looked directly at Donell, "Which Lisa you talkin' about? I know mad Lisas. I just fucked a broad named Lisa last night!" Kareem looked at Donell with disgust. He despised him. Donell had fucked over Kareem's oldest sister, Rachel. He was cheating on Lisa, with her. He got her pregnant and then denied that the baby was his. He then threatened her to have an abortion.

She had a horrible experience. The physician turned out to be unlicensed and uncertified to perform CPR let alone a delicate procedure such as an abortion. Needless to say, Rachel had a botched abortion. The doctor had left half of the fetus inside of her. Rachel had never been the same ever since, she can never have children. Although this happened eight years ago and Kareem was only eight years old when all of this happened, he never forgot the man who ruined his sister's life. He noticed, she hadn't smiled the same since.

"Na, I ain't seen her!" Kareem yelled.

"Yo man, tighten up. Let that shit go." Chino told Kareem. He knew what was going through his head. "You a man now nigga."

Chino got back in the truck. He received a page on his two-way. 'Call me-Baby Girl.'

"I need some cigarettes. You need something from the store?" Chino asked.

"I don't believe you man!" Donell exclaimed.

"What?" Chino asked.

"I don't believe you out here acting like a small time nigga—man with that hit we made, you was supposed to have a sho' nuff' connec' to get rid of the whole shit—not no street level bullshit that you trustin' some little fucking kids with!" Donell snapped.

Chino was definitely tired of people, especially Donell. He was underestimating Chino's abilities. Kareem was just the tip of the iceberg. Chino had a slew of adolescent employees that

49

would not hesitate to follow his every command. People slept on his "junior army". But they would soon see, actually, they wouldn't, and that was his whole plan.

"Like I said, you need anything from the store?" Chino stressed.

He wanted to catch Lisa. He would deal with Donell when he returned. Chino exited the vehicle, slamming the door to let Donell know that he didn't appreciate his attitude. They knew each other well enough to read each other's body language. For the first time ever, Donell felt he could not trust Chino. He felt Chino was keeping things from him.

Chino called Lisa, "Baby Girl—this is not a good time. I'm out with Donell looking for Lisa."

He played it off, just in case Donell wandered into the store.

"Chino, Mari said Shelly was asking Karen all kinds of questions about you and Dee. She asked if you guys were spending a lot of money, or buying up a whole bunch of shit."

"What did Karen tell her?" Chino asked.

"Nothing. What could she tell her? What the fuck is going on, Chino?" Lisa questioned.

"Nothin' that I can't handle Baby Girl. I got this. When can I see you?" Chino asked.

"Chino, I know you two were not stupid enough to fuck with Shark! You know how that motherfucker gets down Chino. You're playing with your life and Donell's!"

"Don't worry, Baby Girl, you know I ain't trying to check out no time soon, trust a nigga. I got this! Now when can I see you?"

"Come tonight. Call first!" Lisa hung up.

'She didn't ask how Donell was doing. That's good.'

Chino thought.

Donell came up behind Chino. "Look man, I'm trying to find my woman. You got about fo' or five of em'– let's be out!"

Chino double-checked, "You sure you don't want nothin' outta here man?"

"Na, I'm sure." Donell replied.

Chino and Donell headed out again to supposedly look for Lisa.

Donell looked at Chino long and hard, "Yo dawg, what's happening to you? You changin' up on me, man? This shit got you THAT caught up?"

Chino had had it. "Man look, I'm not caught up in a motherfuckin' thing. I'm running one of the largest operations in the N-Y. What? You jealous?"

"Come on, nigga pleeze!" Donell said.

"Then what the fuck is your problem man? You been trying to tell me what to do and how to do it since you stepped out the bing, but you been off the streets too long. You don't have a fucking clue as to what the fuck is happenin' out here man. You need to watch a nigga and learn, that's what the fuck you NEED to do! I always drop Kareem off a package. So why would I move any differently? I copped my regular amount of work from my regular connect. I'm doing everything as I normally would do - on the regular! How long you think this shit is gon' keep? It ain't. It's gon' lose its potency. We can't just sit on it! You think Shark is stupid enough not to be checking for a big deal to go down? Na, dawg, it's YOU whose thinking like a small time hustler, nigga!"

Donell thought about all the shit he went through, for, and

with this man sitting next to him. All of a sudden, it just wasn't worth it.

"Fuck you Chino! You think you got all the answers, don't you? Where the fuck is my woman? Huh, tell me that? My fucking woman is gone. Shark probably got niggas watching us right now!"

"Yeah what if niggas are watching us right now, you ready? Cause that's what the fuck I need, a partner whose always motherfuckin' ready!"

"You don't think about nobody but yourself man. That shit ain't gonna get you nowhere in the long run." Donell was ready to tell Chino his opinion of how he felt he'd been handling things while he was locked up. "Look man, what you really need is..."

Donell started sweating profusely, his words even started to slur. Chino didn't pay him any mind at first, but when he looked over to Donell, his eyes were rolling in his head and he started to shake uncontrollably.

"Yo Dee, what the fuck is up man? You a'ight? —Yo, I'm taking you to the hospital."

"No!" yelled Donell "I'm not going to no more fucking institutions."

Chino persisted, "You don't look good man. Let me get you to a doctor. "

Donell gained his composure. "No I'm not going to see no doctor plus I ain't got no goddamn insurance. I ain't sittin' in no emergency room with four hundred motherfuckas with one sorry as intern frontin' as a doctor."

Chino couldn't help but laugh. "Yo ass ain't that sick.I see you remember that shit huh! Look man. I gotta' take you somewhere, where someone can watch over you. Someone we trust." Chino didn't want to, but he called Camaria. She was the only person he could think of.

"Mari , I need a favor" Chino said.

"Now why the hell would I do a favor for yo' ass?" Camaria asked.

"Alright, well do it for Lisa then!"

"What do you know about Lisa, Chino?"

"Look, Donell is sick, real sick."

"Well take his ass to the hospital!" Camaria demanded.

"Camaria, I'm serious, he just passed out, sweating n' shaking n' shit. Then he came back around."

"Chino honestly, he sounds like he needs a hospital."

"I asked him if he wanted to go to the emergency room, but he refused to go. He said he doesn't have any insurance and all this other shit!"

Camaria blurted out, without really thinking, "Well don't bring his ass over here to die!"

"Camaria, I got some serious shit I have to take care of—and I'll come right back to get him. Come on Mari, for ole' time sake." Chino attempted to persuade her.

"Nigga please, don't even go there. It wasn't all that with you and me!"

Camaria agreed for Chino to bring Donell over. She figured if Lisa called, she would tell her what had happened and she'd have no choice but to surface. Lisa was being too secretive. Something was going on. Camaria could feel it! Donell was still sweating and shaking when Chino got him to Camaria's apartment.

"What'n the hell?" Camaria asked. "Oh hell no, you

should have taken his ass to a hospital."

Chino assured her, "I'll be right back. Give me three hours."

"Three hours! He ain't gon' last no three hours Chino. What the hell is wrong with him?"

"He probably got a virus or something, I mean damn-- the nigga just got out from doing six years. Maybe the fucking air don't agree with him. I don't fucking know, but what I do know is, I gotta' go!"

Chino took Donell into Camaria's guest room and laid him out on the bed. He covered him up with the comforter that was at the foot of the bed.

"Look man, I'll be right back. When I come back man, we goin' to the hospital. I don't give a fuck what you say!"

"Chino, you gotta' find Lisa man, find her."

"I know, don't worry about that right now, I'll find her." Camaria listened as Donell pleaded with Chino to find Lisa. She felt a little bit sorry for Donell. She didn't know why, but she did. Chino emerged from the guest room.

"What do you think is wrong with him?" Camaria couldn't help but ask again.

"I don't know. Did Lisa mention him being sick to you?" Chino asked.

"No, she didn't."

"From what I know, he's never been sick, not like this." Chino placed his hand on Camaria's waist and led her toward the door.

"Look, Mari, I don't think you should tell Lisa what's going on with Donell until we find out what's wrong with him. I don't want her to worry unnecessarily."

Camaria thought to herself, 'What the hell is he talking

54

about not worrying Lisa unnecessarily, she's the one who should be worried and watching over this motherfucker. Something was just not right, but she still couldn't really piece anything together, not yet.

"Chino where are you going that's so important, that you can't take Donell to get checked out?"

"Look, I tried ok! For the last time, he doesn't want to go and I can't make that man do something he doesn't want to do. I can't tell you where I'm going, because you're better off not knowing, I'll be right back!" Chino left.

BACK TO BUSINESS

Chino had lost a lot of time. He was running late for his meeting with his "junior army". Chino sent word for all of his troops to meet at the clubhouse, an apartment in the Roosevelt Housing Projects in Bed-Stuy out in Brooklyn.

Chino kept watching to make sure he wasn't being followed. He knew Shark was going to suspect him for a while. He wouldn't be where he was today, if he didn't. Chino also knew Shark was still at the top of his game. He didn't send back up with Blue and Gauge because he trusted Chino. Chino was able to pull this job off, only because Shark trusted him. He knew Shark's kindness was not to be taken for weakness. He also knew he'd better pull this shit off correctly or --- there would be no "OR"!

Chino arrived. Everyone was present, all of his soldiers. To all, he acted as their "father", to some, "mother" and "father".

"Y'all know what's going down!" Chino started.

"Has everyone checked their two-way for instructions?"

All the boys said they had.

"I've trained all of you to be on top of your game and ultimately knowledgeable in your street endeavors. Don't let me down." Chino continued, "Shit is real in the field. If anybody is having second thoughts about their participation, speak now, or forever hold your peace!"

There was silence.

"Good! I'm proud of you."

"Now check it. I don't want to hear no bullshit counterfeit stories about my motherfuckin' money! I don't want to hear no shit about the cops because I've taught you too well. And I damn sure better not hear no 'my mama found my package (whining) bullshit–cause you know what I expect!"

One of his soldiers, by the name of Knees interjected "You expect us to beat our mama's ass if we have to, but we better get you yo' money one way or another!"

"That's right!" replied Chino.

"And what about some pu putt ass nigga tryin' to rob any of my lil' niggas, young or old ?"

In melodic unison, they all replied, "Blast his ass, and make sure we bring you yo' motherfuckin' money!"

"Aah, music to my ears."

Chino gave everyone their package and additional instructions.

He hollered at a few of them. He was very special to the boys, and the boys were very special to him. He didn't feel what he was doing was wrong. It's how he came up. And to him, he came up just fine. He tried working nine to five jobs, but he just couldn't do it. What he made in a week, on the street, he made in less than an hour. How could you compare the two? As long as he operated intelligently, he didn't see how he could lose.

Knees was pretty much the leader of the troop. They called him Knees because he had lost his legs in a shooting. He was only ten years old when it happened, that was five years ago. You would think he would be bitter, but Knees was a special human being. It was almost as if he had been here before. He seemed much older and wiser than a fifteen year old. He had the patience of a masterful chess player, and he was as

57

cunning as a fox. Knees was always in a good mood. Chino
liked that. That is why Chino chose him to steer the other boys
in his path.

"Knees!" Chino called.

Knees smoothly maneuvered his electronic state-of-the-
art wheel mobile, (it was too fly to call it a wheelchair), in
Chino's direction. With a smile on his face, he spoke,"What's
shakin'?"

"You man, wha's goin' on? You straight?" Chino asked.

"No doubt!" Knees noticed Chino looked distant. "What
about you Boss? How you be?"

Knees loved talking in slang, almost everything he said
had some kind of twist or turn.

"I'm cool, just some major shit hoppin' off right now and
I'm tryin' to keep everything in perspective, you know what
I'm sayin'?"

"No doubt!" Knees responded. "Well you know if you
need me, just holla!"

"I'll do that Baby Boy, I'll do just that." Chino dubbed
Knees, "Baby Boy". Just like Lisa, he cared a lot for Knees.

They gave each other dap and broke up the mini-
conferences going on amongst the others.

"A'ight!," Chino announced, "Y'all know what time it is,
let's do this!"

While everyone was dispersing, Chino's cell phone rang.

"Talk to me ... "

"Yo, Chino ... "

"Yeah, this is Chino who's this?"

It was Lil' James, but Chino didn't recognize his voice.
Lil' James thought he would take advantage of that fact.

58

"You better know what you doin' nigga, cause I damn sure know what you did!" Lil' James thought he could fuck with Chino's mind.

"Word, you know what I did. Damn so yo' mama told you that I fucked her in the ass last night and I made that bitch suck the cum off my dick. Damn, that's fucked up!"

"You think this shit is a game, don't you?" Lil' James yelled, almost blowing his cover.

"Look man, I don't know who this is, but I will in a matter of hours, so whoever you are, YOU better know what the fuck YOU'RE doing – you dig motherfucka–cause you about to be late!" Chino hung up.

Chino looked at the display on his phone. It read 'unavailable'. Chino locked the call in anyway. He had a trick for that. One of his main women worked for one of the most advanced tele-communications firm in the U.S. She had the ability to trace any call made to that phone. He felt sorry for the person on the other end of that line, because they had just signed their own death certificate.

FRIEND OR FOE?

Donell really didn't look well. Camaria wondered what on earth could be wrong with him. She would hate to think the worst, but he had been locked up for a long time. She guessed it could be just about anything. Camaria wondered why Lisa hadn't called back. She would never stay gone this long, especially without someone, knowing her whereabouts. She decided she would two- way Lisa. 'Call me asap- Donell is here sick'.

"Mari," Donell strained as he spoke.

"I'm re..ally wo..rr..ied abou..t L..isa, th..is is not li..ke he..r at all..."

"I must say, I agree, she has not even called me back, and that is unheard of. All of a sudden, everything is top secret." Camaria replied.

"Wha..t do you me..an, top se..cret?"

"Well, Chino didn't want me to tell Lisa you were sick until we find out what's going on with her, but I thought if I told her you were sick, it would make her come check for you." Camaria said.

Donell was stumped. What would Chino do that for? Chino knew how badly he wanted to find Lisa.

"Did you te..ll her?" Donell asked weakly.

"I paged her, but she hasn't called back or paged back."

"Chi..no kn..ows som..eth.ing." Donell was convinced.

"Knows something, like what? You mean he knows where Lisa is?" Camaria asked. She believed anything to be possible. What she couldn't believe is that it took her so long to figure it

60

out.

"He wa..s ac..ti.ng like he w..as hel..p..ing me lo..ok for Lisa to.d..ay, he wa..sn't do..in' shit, but hyp.in' it up li..ke he wa..s loo..k.ing for her." Donell was losing his strength again.

"Calm down Donell. You shouldn't get yourself all worked up until we really do find out what's up!" Camaria tried to convince him to take it easy, but her own mind was going one hundred miles a minute. 'What IS going on?' She thought about it for a second, but dismissed the idea, there was no way ...

*   *   *   *

"Who is it?" Lisa asked.

"Me-- Baby Girl." Chino answered.

Lisa opened the door, exposing the very revealing negligee she chose to wear. A red number. Totally sheer stopping at the base of her butt cheeks, a red lace thong set hugged her beneath. For someone who didn't want Chino, she sure didn't know how to show it.

Lisa turned and walked toward the balcony.

She knew exactly where Chino's eyes would be, so she quickly shot a glance back to see him joyfully watching the bounce in her ass.

"What you looking at?" Lisa said slyly.

"You know what I'm looking at - that juicy fat ass of yours." Chino replied.

"Whatever," Lisa said jokingly.

Chino reached out for her. "Come here Baby Girl." Chino

61

came up behind Lisa and wrapped his arms around her waist. He lay soft kisses on the nape of her neck, slowly licking the frame of her earlobe, he then plunged his tongue in her ear, making her shudder.

"Chino ... stop ... we ... stop ... I ... "

"You know I can't stop when I'm alone with you. Please don't make me stop."

Chino began to rub Lisa's shoulders in a massaging motion to relieve some of the tension he knew she had with everything that had been going on.

"Umm, umm, yeah, that feels so good." Lisa moaned.

"Yeah, I know, just relax. Let Daddy take all your tension away. Calgon ain't got shit on me!"

Lisa laughed, "You crazy Chino, just damn crazy. With all the shit you mixed up in, you still got jokes."

"Can't ever stop jokin' and laughin', Baby Girl, no matter what the fuck is goin' on, or you will lose your damn mind."

"How's Donell?" Lisa asked.

Chino hesitated. He wasn't ready to tell her about Donell yet, he wasn't ready to share her again, not just yet.

"He's cool."

"That's it - He's cool?" Lisa quizzed.

"Yeah, Baby Girl, I mean, like I told you earlier he asked me to help him look for you, but since I knew you wasn't tryin' to be found, I just played it off."

"Where is he now?" Lisa asked.

"Home I guess. I don't keep tabs on the nigga!" Chino snapped.

"What the fuck are you getting nasty for?"

"I'm sorry Baby Girl, it's just that you know how I feel about you and now this nigga is back home and I just—I don't know, I guess I don't know how I thought it would be when he came home. All of this shit is catching me off guard."

"I feel you. I feel the same way. I know I love Donell. I know that for a fact, but I can't deny that I love you too." Lisa looked at Chino. She licked her lips, then she licked his.

That was all he needed. Chino grabbed her by the waist and pulled her close, the thickness of her body scent drowning him, making his dick swell. He caressed her breasts softly, with two fingers circling in a slow steady motion, making her nipples talk to him. Chino lavished her with his tongue. Her breasts, so supple, so soft, he couldn't get enough of Lisa.

"Bend over." Chino commanded.

Lisa, already in ecstasy, moaned. "What you want huh?"

"You know what I want."

"Uhm, no Chino, not now." Lisa pleaded.

"Yeah, now, come on ... don't I treat my pussy real good?"

"Yeah baby, you do."

"I do what?"

"You treat your pussy real good, baby."

"So let me get that ass."

Chino placed Lisa up on the ledge of the balcony, looking over the city lights he began devouring her relentlessly, showing no mercy, he slid his tongue to the edge of her asshole, teasing the passageway with his tongue, preparing his lamb. He couldn't let her go back to Donell. Donell knew nothing about this Lisa, Chino's Lisa.

"Come on, baby." Chino lifted Lisa off of the ground of the balcony placing her in a patio chair on her knees.

Chino continued lubricating his target, driving Lisa into a frenzy.

"Fuck me, fuck me in my ass Chino, please baby, ... "

"Oh yeah, I'm a fuck you in your ass, you know I'ma' ... " Chino entered. Ooh it was so tight ... Oh damn he loved this shit. He was gone, she had him gone ... "Ooh yeah, this is my ass baby, you can give that nigga the pussy cause you have to, but this here, is my ass! aah ... aah ... aaahhhh." Chino pulled out spilling hot liquid all over Lisa's chocolate fat juicy ass.

"Ooh damn Chino." Lisa was in heaven.

"You're mine, you hear me, you can't go back to him!"

"Chino, ... "

"No, fuck that, I mean that shit Lisa, promise me, promise you not goin' back with that nigga."

The mood was gone.

"That nigga is your best motherfuckin' friend Chino. He just did some shit that he could get locked up for a long time, for your ass and we here fucking like he's still locked up. Look, Chino I think I should just chill, I mean I don't know what I want for real. Donell isn't really ready to get his shit together and stay out the game and I don't have no time to be getting caught in no dumb shit behind his ass, or your ass either."

"Na see, Baby Girl, I'm getting out. I just pulled off the deal of a lifetime and as soon as the time is right, I'm outta here." Chino took Lisa back in his arms. "Look, I'm sorry, I know Donell took mad risks for me, but let's not forget, I've done mad shit for that motherfucka my damn self!" Chino looked deeply into Lisa's eyes, "What the hell am I supposed to do about you being with this man? I thought it wouldn't mean shit, but I can't deal with the shit. When he took too long that night when we did the hit I knew y'all was fuckin. I couldn't take that shit. I'm not playing Lisa, look, I'm out, give me four weeks and we're out. You can finish school wherever we are. We can have some kids an' shit. A little Chino and Lisa, wha's up wit' that?" Chino swayed Lisa back and forth in his arms.

He made it sound so easy, but Lisa didn't think it could be so easy. How would they just leave in four weeks? Everybody was in New York. Both of their families. Where would they go? Donell would kill them both if he knew. Why was she considering his offer? All Lisa knew, was that Chino physically made her feel like no other. Mentally, she admired his strength. Chino was not intimidated by anyone and even though he used his smarts in the streets, he was still very smart. Emotionally, Lisa was intrigued with the effect she had on him. Lisa knew Chino's ways, but she also knew he didn't love any of those women, but he did love her and he would leave it all, for her.

Lisa wanted Chino from the day she saw him. It was eight years ago, but she was introduced as Donell's main girl and that meant she was off limits. When they would double date, Lisa would pretend to dislike Chino so Donell would never think anything. When Donell got locked up, Chino was the only one, besides Camaria that she could depend on. Donell had been taking very good care of her. He was even paying her way through college. Chino took care of all that now.

They lay together, Chino contemplated everything he had on his plate. He had mad moves to make. He got up, took a shower and put his clothes on. Lisa had fallen into a light sleep.

"Lisa" Chino lightly whispered. He kissed her forehead, then brushed her face with the palm of his hand, "Baby Girl, I'm out."

Lisa looked up groggily.

"Remember what I said. Our secret must still remain our secret. Our lives depend on it. Shit is real right now, Baby Girl. If you go back, just go back like you broke out for a while, you know, like you went out of town real quick, to clear your head.

You feel me?"

"Yeah Chino."

He rubbed her ass gently, kissed her lips deeply, and left.

WELL CONNECTED

Chino had a lot on his mind. He had to find out who that was who called. Whoever it was, they either knew, or suspected that he had taken Shark off and it would only be a matter of time before that person would attempt to make a profit or move up a notch in Shark's organization.

He didn't recognize the voice at all. He had to get the phone to Tanya. It would take about a half a minute for her to do her thing and have a name. Tanya was a telecommunications engineer for the Xenon Corporation, one of the largest conglomerates of the country. Chino fucked with nothing but the best.

"This is Tanya Charles."

"Hey baby, I need you like yesterday. You tied up?" Chino asked.

"Never too busy for you."

"That's what I know. Look, I need to bring the phone by. I need to trace a call that came up unavailable."

"What happened to you last night? You were supposed to come give me my fix."

"Look baby, there's some major shit hoppin' off right now. I can't get into it. I'm on my way to you."

"Ok Chino. I'll be right here."

Chino parked in a garage on 52nd and 8th. One thing about the city, Manhattan that is, you could never find "on the street" parking during business hours. And if you wanted your shit, you'd make sure you parked in a garage, even if they were

67

charging twenty dollars for a measly half hour!

He made his way through the crowded streets, dodging all the employees that were obviously running late for work. One man nearly knocked him down. "Damn man, take my fuckin' shoulder with you next time!" Chino yelled. The man didn't even turn around to acknowledge him. You know, the typical New York state of mind.

Chino entered the Xenon Corporation. The building reeked of success with its marble walls, signature gold emblems and plush red carpet. The floral arrangements were larger than life. He entered the elevator bank that ranged from the twentieth to the fiftieth floor. He caught an elevator just as it was about to close and selected the 39th floor.

"I'm here to see ... "

"Tanya Charles!" the receptionist interrupted.

"Yes, Tanya Charles, can you tell her ... "

"Mr. Wells is here," she interjected again.

She was annoying the shit out of Chino. Just as he was about to let her know how much, Tanya came out of her office to greet him.

The receptionist who now goes by the name of Shante, stared Chino up and down.

"Uhm, chile, he is something else!"

"Thank you Shante." Tanya replied.

"Does he have a brother or something? Hook a sister up!" Tanya brought the conversation back. "Did you pull the Emerson file?"

"Yes, I did." Shante handed Tanya the file. "When would you like to schedule him in? For a meeting, of course."

Shante sounded as though she was insinuating Tanya met with more clients than Chino in this manner.

"Shante, don't play. I take my business very seriously, as should you, if you'd like to continue working here." Tanya made her position clear.

"I'm sorry Ms. Charles. I didn't mean ... " Shante tried to clean it up. Tanya's office door slammed shut.

Chino sat in the chair next to Tanya's desk. He actually cared a lot for Tanya, but there was nothing and no one that would change his plan.

"What the hell is up with her, she new?" Chino asked.

"That her, used to be a he, Shane Lewis, now Shante Lewis, and he, I mean she, just gets a little testy sometimes." Tanya came over to Chino, positioning herself onto his lap.

"I should go break his ass off somethin' since he, she, or whatever the fuck it is, wants to be a goddamn clown."

"Now baby, be nice, but for real you could break me off a lil' somethin', somethin'. I need you right now."

She was wearing a navy blue miniskirt suit, which was a definite contrast to her high yellow skin tone. Tanya was very attractive. She was mixed. Her mother was Black. Her dad was Irish. It didn't hurt that she had eyes as green as emeralds. Hair, long, sandy brown, of course.

Tanya took Chino's hand and slid it between her thighs. Chino felt the warmth. He situated her on his lap and began to unbutton her jacket. Chino looked into her eyes as he removed her jacket. He unhooked her navy blue lace bra and began to suck her breasts. Tanya loved the way Chino paid attention to all of her. Watching her closely, touching her gently, he knew a woman's body. He knew how to make a woman feel beautiful, inside and out. That was a gift.

He stood her up in front of him and unfastened the hook on her skirt. Sliding it down, revealing a navy blue lace thong to

69

match. Tanya was always coordinated. She removed her thong. Her second set of lips were staring at Chino, swollen, throbbing, waiting. Chino loved to eat Tanya's pussy. She was bare, never had hair there for as long as he could remember. He dove right in, tonguing her pussy as if he was kissing her lips.

"Ooh, ooh yeah, lick that pussy, baby, lick that pussy, ooh yeah, suck my shit, suck it, ooh"

Chino tapped her clit continuously with one finger, while his tongue danced in, out and around.

"No, baby, I don't want to come yet ... you're not getting away with that shit. You better act like you know and give me mines." Tanya was a bad bitch. Chino had to admit that.

"Give you yours huh?"

"Yeah" Tanya said, whimpering like a child.

"How you want it?"

"You know how I want it baby. You know exactly how I want it!"

Chino grabbed Tanya's neck, squeezing hard and plunged his tongue down her throat. Tanya was grasping for air. Chino warned, "Uh uh, bitch, you told me to give you yours, so here, take it!" Chino slapped Tanya. He grabbed her by the neck again, he threw her to the couch. Chino began taking his dick out.

"Miss Charles are you ok in there?" Shante asked.

"Just fine Shante, just fine uh, isn't it time for your break?"

"No, not yet."

"Well take it now!"

"Are you sure?"

"Look! Fuck this shit!" Chino rushed to the door and flung it open. Exposing a naked Tanya and himself hanging low.

"You satisfied? What you wanna come in and suck my dick? You he/she motherfucka or you wanna fuck my girl? You still got a dick or you done had all ya' shit swtiched?"

Shante stood still, mouth wide open.

"Chino!" Tanya was not shocked, but very perturbed.

Not only had he insulted Shante, but he was totally exposing her. This was her place of business.

"Look, Shante, go on a break, a long one. And trust me, keep this one between us!" Tanya gave her a look to confirm her cooperation.

"Ok, Miss Charles, only for you, but tell your man don't offer me no dick to suck, cause I will suck it dry!" Shante looked directly at Chino, turned around and sashayed out, slowly closing the door behind her. Tanya locked the door.

"Baby, that was uncalled for!"

"No, what was uncalled for, was her/him/whatever the fuck it wants to be, playin' motherfuckin' games. You know I ain't for that shit. He lucky I ain't punch his ass in the jaw and bring the man back out his ass."

"Look, I ain't got no time for this shit Tanya. I came here for some serious business and we are gettin' totally off the real reason I came here." Chino retrieved the mystery call from the phone's memory and handed Tanya the phone.

She placed the phone into a digital cradle and pressed three digits. A recording came on: "Your return call number is: 718 555 6625." It was that easy. Chino took the number down.

"Why are you writing the number down?" Tanya asked.
"Cause,"
"I can get you a name and an address, hold tight." Tanya,

71

still buck naked, went to her desk and dialed. "Yes, this is
Tanya ... fine and you, ... I need a favor, can you give me a
name and location for 718 555 6625 ... Great, Thanks!"
Tanya hung up. Chino was dying to know who it was. "Who is
it Tee?"

"What's in it for me?" Tanya teased.

"Look Tee, you really are not gettin' it. This is real shit.
This ain't no game, now stop fuckin' with me and tell me who
the fuck is associated with that number!"

"It's a James Murphy out of Queens, 111-44 Linden Blvd,
#11A."

"Lil' James!" Chino was mad at himself. "How could I not
have known?—I must be fuckin' slippin'. Na, he disguised his
voice. He sounded like a bitch. That's cool though, he needed
to be eliminated anyway."

"Chino, what's going on?" Tanya asked.

"Not a thing you need to be worrying your pretty little head
over, now come here, let me finish what you started."
Chino grabbed Tanya by her neck. That was her thing. "You
like it rough huh?"

"Yeah, that's right" Tanya said, gasping for air.

Chino used more pressure "That's right huh, well here, take
this shit!" Chino shoved his dick in Tanya's pussy so hard she
couldn't help but scream. "Shut up, shut the fuck up!" He
fucked her hard and good. Just like she liked it. Tanya was
straight. Chino did his thing, as usual.

"Are you coming by tonight?" Tanya whined.

"Na, don't look for me tonight. I got mad shit I gotta' do.
I'll call you tomorrow."

"Damn Chino, why do I have to take a back seat all the
time?"

"Tanya, do you be listening to me? Didn't I say there is some serious shit going on?"

Tanya bitched, "I'm just going to have to explore my options. I don't have time for this shit Chino. I can't be wasting my time waiting for you and you're not even trying to include me in your life!"

"Ok." Chino calmly stated.

"Ok! What the fuck do you mean, ok? What the fuck is that supposed to mean Chino?"

"It means what it is, 'Ok'—I told you I got some shit going on, all you care about is when I'm coming to fuck you—I don't have time for your shit, Tee!"

"I'm sorry baby, I—"

"Na, na that's how I want it, I'm out! Go ahead and find some other nigga to beat the shit out of you, I'm out!"

"Chino don't go, I'm sorry, please baby, I'm sorry, don't do this Chino," Tanya whined.

Chino walked out. He passed by Shante, who had returned from her break and probably heard everything that went on. He backtracked in his steps and said, "Now you know how she likes it, why don't you revert back? She's gonna need a man to fuck her!"

73

THE HEAT IS ON

"I don't give a fuck what you heard. Chino ain't give me shit he don't normally give me." Kareem glared at Lil' James. "And he wouldn't appreciate you goin' around askin' no bullshit ass questions neither, that shit is suspect man."

"Look, you bitch ass, not knowing how to hustle, young punk ass motherfucker. I don't give a flying fuck what Chino would appreciate. Somebody fucked over Shark and ain't nobody seen Blue and Gauge since this shit went down, so something tells me them niggas can no longer talk for themselves, which leaves your employer." Lil' James walked to his car, "Be careful who you work for young'n, shit'll get you killed." Lil' James drove off.

Kareem immediately two-wayed Chino and let him know what had just went down. 'Lil' James just came by shooting some foul shit- said you took Shark off. –Watch your back.'

"I'll be damned." Chino checked his two-way. "How could I not have known? Damn! Don't tell me I'm slipping fo'sho'? I still can't believe that little motherfucker is the same nigga who called me talking that bullshit. I should have thought of that!" Chino thought, to himself, 'I just got too much shit going on, but I gotta' tighten up. This shit is way too important for me to get caught out there.' Chino two-wayed Knees. He let him know to put the word out with the troops about Lil' James, if he came snooping around, handle it, and keep him posted.

Chino began his search for Lil' James. He decided to pull Lil' James' card. He called Shark.

"Yo Shark."

"Yeah, who this, Chino?"

"Yeah man, look, my worker Kareem just hit me saying some shit about Lil' James asking around about me."

Shark was silent.

"What's up with that shit, Shark?"

"He's just trying to find out what happened to my shit Chino."

"I can dig that man, but I hope he ain't planning on fucking up my small time shit in the meantime. I mean, I ain't big time like you Shark. I can't stand to lose my one little worker. Lil' James threatened to kill him, got him all scared up an' shit." Chino loved playing the role. He felt like an actor writing his own script.

"Don't worry Chino, Lil' James ain't killin' no kids, but don't nobody seem to know nothin' 'bout what went down."

"Shark, you know all the shit you've done for me, I would never do no snake shit like that to you man. You ain't done nothin' but good for me Shark!"

"That's what me know, an' me also know that Blue and Gauge could've plotted some shit and got me, but I gotta' do what I gotta' do to find out, that was a million dollars worth of my shit, sien!"

"I know, I had a connect set up for a straight deal on that shit too. I would have had my money and your money back in no time. Them niggas fucked it all up!"

"Who was your connect?" Shark asked.

"Uh, man I can't say, them niggas ain't tryin' to have no heat on em' Shark. You start fuckin' with them, they might try to come see me on some shit–not only that- they didn't know where and when shit was goin' down. I was supposed to meet up with them the next day." Chino was thinking fast. Shark caught him off guard with that one! "They was heated like a bitch when I told them I ain't have they shit."

"Chino, shit just ain't addin' up."

"Yo Shark, you find Blue and Gauge and I'm tellin' you man, you'll find your shit. I already got my niggas out lookin' for em', and if we get to em' first man, I don't think we gon' leave nothin' left for you dawg. These niggas got you thinkin' I fucked you over and that shit ain't cool man."

"Look, if you do find em', don't kill em', bring em' to me!" Shark hung up.

Chino headed straight to Brooklyn to collect his paper. Fuck what Kareem had, that was just a front.

Chino took the West Side Highway to the Brooklyn Bridge. He was in the middle of the bridge when he checked his rear view and noticed a money green vehicle that seemed to be following him. Chino started the test. He exited the bridge and proceeded to Atlantic Avenue, his plan was to stop for gas. Chino pulled into the Exxon and got out of his SUV. He looked around, but saw nothing.

Chino felt like someone was trying to bait him. He pretended to pump gas into his already full tank. Looking into his passenger side mirror he saw a green car, which looked to be the same car that was following him. The car slowly passed the gas station. Chino two-wayed Knees...

'Chino- Exxon/Atlantic/send heat.' Chino went into the store associated with the gas station. He watched out of the window to see the vehicle come back around, but it didn't.

Knees rounded up the crew. He told all the boys what was

going down. Buck and Free volunteered to go to the gas station, they were usually the junior hit men of the crew. Knees gave the rest of the crew instructions to give him all the money they had and to hurry up and work off what they had left. He collected the money from all of the troops, locked everything in the safe in the apartment and told everyone to be careful and lay low until Chino sent word.

Buck and Free got their driver, Bones, to take them to Chino. Bones was their official driver. Chino had to make sure if he needed his boys to travel, they would have a way.

They neared the gas station. Bones spotted Chino's Escalade. He pulled up at the pump in back of his. He noticed Chino was not in the vehicle. He looked to the store and saw Chino waving for them to come inside. Chino never carried a weapon in his vehicle if he didn't have to, which was smart, but this time he wished he had one. He could have been caught out there. As they approached the store, Chino spotted the car again. "There it goes, the green joint!" Bones turned quickly to see the car, he spotted a green Mazda, looked like a 626, but it could have been a 929.

"That's a Mazda, Chino. You know anybody with a green Mazda, man?" Bones asked.

"I'm trying to think." Chino said, "I ain't never see Lil' James in a Mazda, but that don't mean shit, and fuck all the bullshit about if I know someone with that shit or not. Them motherfuckas done followed the wrong nigga."

"Give me the shit! Follow me! Get em' in a sandwich!" Chino went back to his vehicle concealing the 9 millimeter in his waist by pulling his large shirt over it. He pulled off with

Bones, Buck, and Free right behind him. He drove down Atlantic Avenue. He didn't see the car. Bones beeped his horn and immediately made a left. Chino watched in his rearview as Bones took a different direction. Chino knew exactly what he was doing. Chino made a right went down two blocks made a left and came down Fulton. He spotted Bones and just as he thought, the green Mazda was headed in Chino's direction with Bones directly behind it.

The driver of the Mazda realized what was about to happen, but it was too late. Chino was on the left side of the two-way street, heading straight for the vehicle. He opened fire, shattering the front windshield, as well as the drivers' side window. He saw blood splatter inside and outside the Mazda, but he still could not tell who was driving. Buck and Free lit the back of the Mazda up. Both vehicles sped away. They had no time to stop. The streets were crowded with patrons, mostly of Jamaican descent, shopping for everything from clothes to weed. They would find out who was in the car later. Chino's adrenaline was pumping, he loved the thrill of the chase, he could almost bet that Lil' James was in that car. "Fuck that nigga, he don't even know who he fuckin' wit!" Chino said out loud to himself. Bones, Buck and Free took off in a different direction. He would catch up with them at the crib.

TO THE HOSPITAL

"Hey Mari, what's up?" Lisa decided to surface.

"Hey Mari, what's up? Where the hell have you been Lisa?"

"I had to clear my head. I just had to break out for a minute."

"Do you know your man is here, sick as a dog?"

"My man is there? What is Donell doing at your house?"

"Chino brought his ass here last night talking some shit about coming right back. I ain't heard from the nigga since."

s"What! Chino didn't say any- ... " Lisa caught herself.

"When the hell did you talk to Chino? Hold the fuck up! You mean Chino knew where you were, but you didn't bother to tell me or return my page? What the fuck is going on Lisa? I know you not fuckin' wit Chino?"

"Camaria, what's the matter with Donell?" Lisa ignored her question.

"He's sweating, shaking, throwing up, he's a mess!"

"I'm on my way!" Lisa hung up.

Camaria stared at the receiver in disbelief. Chino knew where Lisa was. That was it. She wanted to know what was going on. Camaria had a complex with her lovers, past or present being involved with her friends, especially her best friend. They both were acting too strange. What about Donell? How long had it been going on? Camaria unconsciously blurted out, "Shit, when that nigga gets well, he'll kill the both of them."

Lisa arrived in less than an hour. "Where is he?" barely

crossing the threshold.

"Hold up, I know you don't think you're going to just come in here and act like nothing happened."

"Look Mari, now is not the time to deal with minor bullshit, Donell needs me."

"Shit! He needed your ass yesterday. I paged you and you didn't even respond. Now you come rushing in here like you give a damn. You didn't even tell me where you were, ME!"

"I just needed to get away. I needed to get some shit straight within my own mind. Is that a fucking crime?"

"No it's not, but that man in there has been going through it! I don't know what he has, but he looks like shit!"

"Why didn't you get him to a hospital?" Lisa asked.

"Why didn't I? Bitch he ain't my fucking man! I don't fucking believe you. I didn't have to do what I did!" Camaria yelled.

"Look, I know, I'm sorry. We don't need to be doing this right now Mari. Where's Donell?"

"He's in the guest room!"

Camaria was heated. The thought of Lisa and Chino fucking, was fucking with her. She didn't want Chino anymore, but still ...

Lisa stood in the doorway of the guest room. She was shocked. This was the man who was just cursing her the other night. Donell was in a fetal position on the bed. He was shaking. The sheets that wrapped his body were soaked with sweat and urine from him not being able to get himself to the bathroom. Lisa could not believe Chino didn't tell her Donell was sick like this. Where was his heart? He couldn't have one. This was his best friend! She knew one thing, she could not leave Donell, not like this. She would stay with him and get him well before she would make any rash decisions. If Chino could treat Donell this way, how could she leave everything for him? 'Na, Chino would never do anything to hurt me, not me. He didn't want me to know because he knew I would come.' Lisa attempted to rationalize with herself.

Lisa entered, "Hey baby."

Donell looked up weakly, "Lis, whe..re y..ou be..en?

"I just went away for a minute baby. I'm sorry, I didn't know you were sick. I would have never left you."

"I di..dn't m..ean an.y of..th..e thi..ngs"

Lisa hushed him, "It's ok. I know you didn't mean them."

"Don't....lea..ve me, pro..mise yo..u'll nev..er lea..ve me."

Lisa couldn't block out Chino's voice playing in the back of her head "Four weeks, Baby Girl, I'm out!"

"I promise I won't leave you baby. I promise, but baby you don't look so good and I'm taking you to a hospital."
Lisa called for Camaria and asked her to call an ambulance. Camaria immediately dialed 911.

Donell began asking Lisa to forgive him for everything he had done. Lisa was worried. She had never seen Donell like this ever. "What could be wrong with him?" She asked Camaria, who was now standing in the doorway.

"Damn if I know, but I'm very curious to find out!"

Lisa gave Camaria a look in which to say, 'I already know what you think!'

The paramedics arrived. It seemed like forever, but they actually only took twenty-five minutes, which was a miracle in New York City. Camaria led them to the guest room.
One of the paramedics, who introduced himself as Kyree,

began to question Lisa. "How long as he been this way? What are his symptoms? Has he lost consciousness?"

"I, uh, don't know, uh----Mari!" Lisa was overwhelmed. She had no clue, not one answer to the questions he was asking her about HER man.

Camaria was busy on the telephone keeping Karen up to date on the developments. Karen felt she knew why Donell was sick. She had told Camaria the rumors, but Camaria vowed she would not tell Lisa. She would let Donell tell her. It just wasn't her place. Even as her best friend, she still felt it was a rumor until proven true.

"Mari!" Lisa called again.

Camaria gave Kyree all the information he needed. She told him Donell had been this way for the past two days. He had been experiencing chills, sweat outbreaks, and had been vomiting and apparently his bladder was weakening.

As Camaria was explaining Donell's situation, Lisa realized Camaria had not left Donell's side. Despite how she felt about him, she took care of him, for her. Lisa felt bad about keeping her and Chino's relationship from Camaria, but she knew how Camaria felt about the issue and she didn't want any beef. Lisa decided she would tell her and maybe once she described how things, "just happened" maybe, just maybe, Camaria would find her way to understand.

The other paramedic, who never introduced himself had been busy checking Donell's vital signs.

"He's not doing so good over here. We better get him to the hospital now."

"Mari, please call Donell's mother, the number's in this book ... " Lisa handed Camaria her pocket-sized phone book.

"No...no...do..n't ca.ll my...moth....er, plea...se." Donell was getting worked up.

"Please calm down, Sir," Kyree pleaded.

"You're going to need all of your energy."

"Ok, baby, ok, we won't call your mother until we come home, ok."

Kyree asked, "Which one of you are riding with him?"

"I am!" Lisa responded.

They lifted Donell onto the gurney. He reached out for Lisa.

She told him, "I'm here baby. I'm here. I'm coming with you."

"Mari, I promise I'll call as soon as I know anything. If Chino calls you back, tell him what's going on."

"Why don't you just call him and tell him?" Camaria shot back. "Don't think you're off the hook on this one! Don't think I don't know what's goin' on!"

Lisa didn't confirm her suspicions. She chose to ignore Camaria and tend to Donell.

On the way to the hospital Lisa thought about her feelings for Donell. She had given him all she had to give. Years of her life, she could never get back, waiting for him. She loved him. He was always in her corner, pushing her to get her education, telling her she could strive to be anything she wanted. Donell always believed in her. From day one he was always showing her off, always so proud of her. He bought her anything she ever wanted before he got locked up. She would boast to Camaria that the initials in all of her furs wouldn't have to be changed because both she, and Donell's last name began with an "S". They had been through a lot together, good and bad. She wondered what could be wrong with him. She didn't remember him mentioning not feeling well before. The ambulance pulled into the emergency entrance of Bronx Lebanon Hospital. Kyree had already called ahead so they could take Donell straight in. He ran down Donell's vital signs and gave the head physician what little he did know.

The head physician came over to Lisa. "Has your friend ever been tested for HIV?"

"What? What the hell are you saying? Donell doesn't have HIV! Why, 'cause he's been locked up, he has to have HIV? He has flu symptoms, not no goddamn HIV!"

"Look, I didn't mean to upset you, Miss ... Miss."

"Miss Spencer, Lisa Spencer!"

"Sorry, Miss Spencer, I didn't mean to insinuate that he absolutely had HIV. I just wanted to know if he had been tested. I had no knowledge of him being incarcerated and I don't stereotype individuals."

"I'm sorry too doctor, it's just that everything is fucked up. I mean, things are just going real crazy right now."

"I'm sure. Why don't you go over to the intake department? They'll be plenty of forms that will keep you busy until we have some news for you."

"Thanks, doctor, I'm sorry what's your name?

"Dr. Brennan," he extended his large hand to Lisa.

"Thanks, again I don't usually behave in this manner. I'm just totally stressed right now."

"It's ok," Dr. Brennan couldn't help but admire Lisa's good looks. He actually thought he had met her before, but he couldn't put his finger on where.

Lisa asked, "Is he going to be alright?"

"I'm going to do my best. Beverly," Dr. Brennan called to the nurse handling the Intake Department.

"Yes, Dr. Brennan?" Beverly responded.

"Please make sure Miss Spencer has all the necessary forms she will need to complete. Help her in any way you can." Dr. Brennan gave Lisa a warm smile and walked to the back where they had taken Donell.

"Come this way dear." Beverly was an older caucasian woman, who looked to be somewhere in her early sixties. Beverly gave Lisa everything she needed to complete and told her to have a seat in an area that was away from all of the drama of the emergency room.

Lisa's mind was racing one hundred miles per minute.

"HIV—I know this nigga ain't give me no fucking AIDS!" Lisa panicked. "If this motherfucker was up there fucking niggas and came back and fucked me like it wasn't nothing and gave me some shit, they don't have to worry about him dying from AIDS cause' I'll kill the motherfucker myself!"

Lisa suddenly thought about Chino. "Oh my God, Chino ... I slept with him."

DO THE MATH

Chino made it back to the Roosevelt Projects around seven p.m.. Things seemed normal, the usual crowds in the usual places. He spotted Knees in the front of the playground with some other dudes.

"Yo Knees!"

Knees saw Chino and immediately maneuvered his way to meet up with him.

"Yo wha's up, how'd things go?" Knees studied Chino. He could tell he was troubled.

"A'ight, we smoked that nigga. I told his ass not to fuck wit' me!" Chino lit a cigarette and took a long pull, "What'd the troops bring in?," he asked, exhaling little to no smoke.

"So far, we got a hundred thou. I locked it up in the safe. I re'd everybody up and put em' out for one more run about an hour ago. That's gon' be it for the night. I'm a' shut it down."

"That's gon' be it! Nigga it's mad early out here. The real fuckin' fiends don't even come out until the wee hours of the mornin' nigga----fuck that! You ain't shuttin' shit down. We pumpin' all motherfuckin' night!"

"Chino man, I'm tellin' you, I been scopin' shit out and it just don't look good to do no more business after this run. Niggas is watching, noticing we got mad work. I thought we was supposed to be keepin' shit on the low?" Knees looked at Chino with a serious face, "Yo Chino man, you know I got mad respect for you, mad mad respect, but trust me yo', shit ain't cool tonight. Niggas is sheisty. They seein' us get too much money right now. I was even thinking of takin' shit to

86

another borough."

"I don't have time to take this shit to no other borough I need to pump this shit now, right now!"

Chino was feeling like he was about to be closed in on. It was just a matter of time.

"Look, Baby Boy, you know I trust your instincts, but with me killin' this nigga today, Shark is not gon' stay off of this shit fo' sho. So, we gotta' come up with another plan, cause he's definitely gon' be hot over this shit. We need to work off all this shit asap. Let me get y'all straight, then I can slide off!"

"Cool, no problem. We'll come up with another plan. Let's go." Knees led the way to the clubhouse.

A few of the troops were already there. Buck and Free were among them. Chino pulled them to the side and gave them props for helping him out earlier. He told him they were his right-hand niggas and whenever shit went down, he would not hesitate to call on the two of them. They were proud. Chino instructed Knees to page the troops and have everyone come in with whatever they had.

All had arrived except for one. Pork was missing. They called him Pork because of his chubbiness. Knees two-wayed him, but he didn't respond.

"He's not answering, Chino."

"Call his house. He might have gotten caught up with his moms." Chino said.

"Hello, may I please speak to Michael?" Knees switched up. Pork's mother was strict. It was a wonder why Chino let him be down. "Ok, thank you. He's not at home either."

"What the fuck is going on? Where the fuck is this little

nigga at?" Chino was thinking of all kinds of shit. "I know this motherfucker ain't try to get me for my shit. I'll kill that little fat motherfucker!"

"Hold tight, Chino. Pork ain't on no shit like that." Knees was also concerned. He two-wayed Bones to look for him.

"A'ight my soldiers, shit has changed and we gon' have to do a one eighty. When I call you out let me know what you made on your second run, Knees already told me what we made on our first run. Slim?"

"I got eight" Slim responded .

"What you got left?" Chino asked.

"A half a brizzo."

"Put in on the table."   Slim placed the remainder of his work on the table.

"Weasil, what you got man?"

"Y-zo I g-zot tw-zelve s-zon" Weasil was on some new shit with some slang he picked up.

"Nigga, give me the rest of yo' shit and please stop talkin' that bullshit. It's hard enough to understan' yo' ass as it is-.and definitely kill that son shit!" Chino really wasn't feeling that. It was almost like pig-latin, but more ridiculous.

"Dolla Bill, Wha's up?"

"I'm workin' wit' fourteen Chino, I was almost done, but y'all called us in." Dolla Bill was the fly one of the crew. He had to have on new shit everyday. He was only thirteen, but he seemed much older. All of Chino's soldiers appeared older, due partly to the life they chose to lead.

"Scoop?"

"I got twelve, with a quarter of a brizzo left." He didn't wait for Chino to ask. He immediately placed his work on the table.

"Mick?"

"I'm working wit' about fifteen, duke. I be doin' my thing!" Mick always held his own secret competition as to who would bring in the most money. Since it was his secret competition, he usually brought in the most money 'cause nobody else was competing, but him.

"Word, I'm proud of you Mick," Chino stroked him. He knew that's what he wanted. "Now what you got left?"

"I'm through, right Knees?"

"Yeah man, good work, good work!" Knees confirmed.

"Everybody had fifteen. We should have been coming in with a hundred fifty thou' this run." Knees started collecting the leftover work.

"Shorty?"

"Yeah, yeah, I'm working with thirteen. I was almost finished Chino. Here, I ain't got much left." Shorty handed the rest of his work to Knees.

"Good job Shorty. Good job man!" Chino praised him.

"Buck I ain't expecting you and Free to have a whole lot 'cause I know y'all got side tracked with our little job this afternoon, but wha's your tally?"

"I got seven, Chino." Free chimed in, " I got nine nigga, now, ha I told you I was on yo'ass!"

"Whatever nigga." Buck took his boy's comment in stride.

"Now tell me something. How did Buck pull in seven, Free pull in nine and Slim, yo' ass been out pumping all day and all you got is eight? What the fuck's up wit' that?" Chino quizzed. Knees interjected, "Chino, Slim knocked off his whole fifteen, plus brought me five before his second package. So all in all he brought in twenty his first run. Shit could have just been slow."

"Yo, what the fuck are you the peacemaker all of a sudden?

89

Everything has a logical explanation, huh? Well tell me where Pork is wit' my shit!"

"I don't know Boss. I just hope it ain't a bad reason." Knees was getting worried.

"What you got, Dip?"

"I got twelve, Chino." Dip replied, giving up the rest of his work. They called him Dip because when shit went down, he was the first to dip and you wouldn't see the nigga for about a week.

"We gettin' there slowly but surely. Yo' Baby Boy, you might be right, I might have to call one of my connec's uptown and see if we can move the rest of this shit up there. I'm only at a lil' over two hundred thou'. Still way under the half way mark, but my soldiers, we did excellently! Keep up the good work. Knees will have your envelopes, don't spend it all in one place."

"Dolla Bill, stop givin' all your fuckin' money to these lil' bitches out there. I see I have to teach you how to make them bitches trick on you!"

"No doubt, Chino, I'm ready man. I know I could be a playa just like you!" Dolla Bill was pumped.

Knees and Chino were two-wayed simultaneously by Bones. Word was out. Some niggas robbed Pork. They stabbed him up real bad. He was taken to the hospital.

"Damn!" Chino exclaimed, "Motherfuckas' just can't let a nigga operate his business without pullin' some pussy shit. Hopefully Pork'll remember who did this. We gon' straighten it!"

"I told you Boss, I smelled shit wasn't right." Knees gave him that "I told you so" tone.

"Yeah, yeah, nigga that you did, that you did."

"His moms is gon' bug out, Chino." Shorty said. Shorty and Pork's mothers were close.

"Fuck his moms' buggin'! I wanna know who got my shit! That nigga had fifteen thou' on his ass. That ain't no bullshit. I'm gon' see a nigga."

Chino's cell phone rang, "Talk to me."
"Chino, this is Camaria."
"Yeah uh, Camaria, yo I'm sorry I ain't been back to deal wit' Dee. I just had some real important shit I had to handle, matter a fact, I'm still handlin' it baby. How's our man doin'?"
"Fuck you Chino. You're so full of shit, it's ridiculous. Don't bother coming back to get Donell. Lisa came and took him to the hospital."
"Lisa! Who told her he was sick? I thought I asked you not to say nothin' to her about that?"
"Come on, Chino! Spill it! Are y'all fuckin' or what?"
"You on some shit! I ain't fuckin' Lisa. If she told you some shit like that she's just tryin' to fuck wit' you. Shit, I'm trying to fuck you again."
"Nigga, hell no! Not if your dick was the last on earth. I'd masturbate first!"

"Hell no? Come on now, don't front. You know you love the way Daddy lay that dick down. Now say it!"

"Nigga, you trippin! I know you fuckin' Lisa. Y'all been acting too strange. She already told me Chino, so you may as well just go on and admit it."
"If she already told you, what the fuck you need me to

91

admit it for? You claim you don't give a fuck about me, so what you askin' me for?"

"Cause I just have to hear it from you. I just can't believe you did that shit to me. And that Lisa did that shit to Donell!"

"Did what shit to you? You ain't my fuckin' woman!"

Chino felt Camaria was fishing. If Lisa had told her, she wouldn't have to call him to get his side of the story, unless she still wanted to fuck him.

"Look, Mari, I got some real shit goin' on, so if you got something to say that I wanna hear, like, um, I can, uh, come over there and you gon' give me some head and let me fuck the shit out you, then talk to me, if not, you wastin' my minutes."

"Alright, I do want you to come over here, I do want to ... "

"Aahh shit, I don't believe it. You serious Mari? "

Camaria didn't know why she was doing what she was doing, she was just doing it. "Yes, I'm serious."

"A'ight, I'll be over there, just let me finish a couple of things up, get a couple of things squared away and I'll be right over. Damn I ain't had your pussy in a long time. I'ma' love fuckin' you."

"Yeah, I know, me too. Just hurry, Lisa might come back with Donell at any minute."

"Shhiiit, I just thought about that shit. Hell no! You meet me at my house."

"Why? Why you can't come over here Chino?"

"You know what? You ain't got nothin' but game wit' you. I ain't even fuckin' wit' you!" Chino hung up.

Chino two-wayed Lisa, 'Call me right now Baby Girl'.

Lisa got the page, but decided she wouldn't answer. She needed to find out what was going on with Donell before she talked to Chino, or anyone for that matter.

Chino talked with Buck and Free and let them know to do
what they do best. The thieves should be found within two
hours. Everybody ran their mouths in the Roosevelt. It was a
natural 'ghetto heaven'. There wasn't anyone rolling like
Chino.

'It had to be some small time niggas that did this shit, they
must have had Pork outnumbered,' Chino thought.

Chino two-wayed Lisa again, 'I really need you to holla, hit
me back.'

Lisa got the page, but still, she did not answer.

"Yo Chino, you gonna go check for Pork? " Knees asked.

"Na man, but I want you and Shorty to go down and check
him and if his moms need anything, find out and just let me
know on the low, and I'll handle it. I don't want his moms'
flippin' when she sees me. She might try to call po-po on me."

"True dat, I got it covered," Knees assured Chino.

Chino was trying to figure out his next move. Shit was
happening a little too fast. He still hadn't gotten word about the
murder on Atlantic and Fulton, now this shit with Pork. Lisa
was with Donell. Camaria was trying to set him up. What next?
Chino knew he first had to secure another location. He had to
get the rest of this coke cooked, bottled up, and distributed.
Chino felt he would rather find another section of Brooklyn to
get his shit off. Harlem was just too close for comfort. Shark
was too well known in Harlem.

"Yo Knees, don't you have a cousin that be movin' some
shit?" Chino inquired.

"Na, tha's my uncle, he in Fort Greene, but he can't see us

man. He's only fucking wit' eight balls here n' there."

"That's straight. As a matter of fact that's exactly what I need– I need him to loan us his territory. I can easily pay him double, fuck that, triple what he's used to makin'. We just need to get this shit off." Chino continued, "If we were able to make two hundred thou' in a day, all we need is one - two more days, tops!"

"I don't know Chino, that was with the fiends we know. We don't know what Kendu is workin' wit' on his side, but what I'll do is get that straight right now." Knees knew that would be Chino's instruction, so he just thought he'd save him the words.

"Cool, handle that. That's why you the leader of the crew Baby Boy!" Chino warmly assured Knees.

Knees hit his cousin Kendu up on his cell.

"Yo' son wha's goin' on? ...Yeah, yeah, maintainin'. Look dawg I got some real shit for you if you can handle it, but I can't go into details over the line. You know what I'm sayin'?" ... "No doubt, I'll be at the clubhouse, just come through." Knees concluded his call.

"So he's on his way?" Chino asked.

"Yeah, he was trippin cause' I'm his nephew and here I am tellin' him I got some real shit for his ass, and askin' him if he could handle it." Knees laughed.

"I feel him on that. Man he should have got down with us before. He could have been doin' way better than some bullshit eight balls. Niggas ain't ready, I'm tellin' you man." Chino replied.

CASUALTY OF WAR

It had been business as usual for Shark, even with the big loss he took. His operation was so strong, that the deal going wrong with Chino didn't slow his movement one bit. He had mad players in his game. All over the boroughs of the Bronx, Queens, and especially Harlem, Shark ran shit.

He was chillin' in his penthouse on the balcony overlooking Central Park West. Shark's shit was straight on some celebrity, out of a magazine type shit. He had a bad ass crib with five bedrooms, three baths, equipped with an indoor pool with an adjoining jacuzzi. He wanted for nothing.

Shark had called in a few of his men. He needed to get to the bottom of this shit. Lil' James and Shelly weren't producing answers fast enough. He was being laughed at by someone and that was not permitted.

The men Shark called in were all cold-blooded murderers. He was tired of playing.

There was Goo. Goo had at least twenty bodies under his belt. The shit turned him on. He would actually jerk off on a motherfucker after he killed them. He knew Shark from being locked up with him back in the days. Shark looked out for Goo and told him he definitely had a spot in his organization when he got out. Shark was a man of his word.

There was Hench. Hench liked choking motherfuckers to death. He liked to watch them die slowly. He would talk to his victims, explain to them why they had to be eradicated, while squeezing the life out of them. Hench was Shark's first cousin.

He had nothing but love for Shark. He wanted to be just like him. He idolized his older cousin. Hench didn't carry a Jamaican accent. His family had arrived in the states early on. He was born in Brooklyn.

There was Butch. Butch used to be a member of the Black Mafia that operated on the Lower East Side. They were heavily tied into the Italian mob. He was a killer for both organizations. Butch had no preference of how he eliminated his prey. The sight and smell of blood simply made his dick hard.

Basically, Shark had some sick motherfuckers on his team.

"Pay attention. Y'all already know what the fuck went down, sien. I need some real answers. Lil' James ain't come back wit' shit. Now I know somebody got my blood clad coke. Check out Blue's girl. Put some pressure on her. Make the bitch talk. Me know say she know somethin'!"

"Where she stay at?" Butch asked.

"I know where that ho stay, I fuck wit' her somewhat." Goo replied.

"Go head, stop playin' nigga, you fucking Blue's bitch?" Hench questioned.

"Yeah man, she got that shit. She a young bitch, redbone bitch. I don't fuck wit' her all the time, but you know, I could get it when I want."

"Well, take it from that angle and get you some pussy while you at it. Just find out if she knows anything about that pussyhole's whereabouts. He may have contacted her by now." Shark went to the bar. He poured himself a glass of straight Hennessy.

"Pour me some of that shit, Playa." Hench was always lit.

He stayed blunted and sauced up, but he stayed on top of his game. So Shark went ahead and blessed him.

"Spread the love, dawg." Goo wanted a little too. Shark just poured four glasses and looked at his men as if to let them know he poured it, but he damn sure wasn't passing them out too.

They all separately retrieved their glasses from the bar. The men made a toast with Goo leading the speech, " This is to us, the Henchmen, may we continue to serve and do what the fuck we gotta' do for our nigga Shark, cause the nigga looks out, and whoever done fucked wit' my nigga, is about to catch a bad one, thun, word up!"

"Word!" they all replied.

"Alright then, Goo, you got Blue's girl covered, sien. Hench, I want you to keep an eye on Chino. I just gotta' keep all my bases covered. I ain't been seein' him, he's up to somethin', an' if that blood clad buoy is the one behind this shit, he'll wish he never thought the muthafuckin' thought to fuck wit me. Straight up!"

Shark poured another glass of Hennessy and downed it.

"Butch, I want you to find out wha's up with Chino's buoy who just came home. They call him Dee. He's fresh out the pen, but Chino may have convinced him that this would have been worth the risk."

Shark poured another glass of the smooth cognac and sifted the liquid around in the glass. He looked intently at his men.

"Somebody got my fuckin' coke. I want the son of a bitch in my custody by nightfall! Sien!"

His men nodded in agreement. They concluded their conference and went out on their assignments.

It had been a minute since Shark had heard from Shelly or Lil' James. Neither one of them had checked in since Shark sent them out to find out what happened with Blue and Gauge. Shark dialed Shelly's cell phone, her voice mail came on, "I'm unavailable to accept your call at this time. Leave it at the beep for me." -- (beep), "Yeah baby it's me. I ain't heard from you. That ain't like you. Shantel was lookin' for you too. She said she got some function at her school you were supposed to go to. Baby forget that shit about lookin' for Blue and Gauge, just come on in. I put ---------(beep)-(You have eight more seconds of recording time.) Yeah, uh just come on in Shell."

Shark proceeded to call Lil' James, when he, himself got a call.

"Yo Shark!" It was Lil' James.

"Yeah, where you been? I ain't heard from you in a whole day!"

"I've been following Chino, Shark."

"So what did you find out?" Shark questioned.

Lil' James was silent.

"So what you sayin', you got proof he took me off?"

"Shark it's worse than that."

"Worse, what the fuck you a' talk 'bout'?"

"It's Shelly ... "

"I just left her a message. Where the fuck is she at? Both of you have been missin' since yesterday, don't tell me you gon' tell me you fuckin' my old lady. That would be the funniest shit ever."

"Shark!" Lil' James yelled.

"What?"

"They killed Shelly."

"What? Who killed Shelly? You betta' be blood clad jokin'! What the fuck are you tellin' me?"

"It was Chino man. I told you, you needed to watch that motherfucka man!"

"Are you tellin' me that Chino killed Shelly?" Shark was in shock. He was used to dealing with the craziest shit, but this was not expected at all.

"You got to be crazy. When? Where is she? Where the fuck is he? "

"Look I know this shit is crazy. I think he thought it was me following him. He thinks it's me that he killed, but I was following Shelly because I knew she would lead me to him. She was defending him too much. I knew she was going to warn him that we were watching him." Lil' James continued, "He's out in Brooklyn. I don't know exactly where because I stayed after I saw what happened. She took Shantel's car. I guess she figured he wouldn't suspect that car, but he did. I know he thought it was me, because I was on to him. I warned his worker, Kareem. I knew he was going to call him, but it wasn't supposed to go down like this!"

Shark was listening, but he wasn't hearing a word. He stopped hearing as soon as Lil' James said they killed Shelly. What was he supposed to tell Shantel? She would not be able to handle this. He could not handle it. In Shark's world, it was always a possibility that one of your family members would be the sacrifice for your doings. He just couldn't believe what he was being told. He had to see her for himself.

"Where is she?"

"She's at the morgue in St. Claire's hospital."

That made it all too real. She was in a morgue. He could

not digest this information. This could not be happening.

"Where the fuck is Chino and how did this happen?"

"I was about three cars behind Shelly. We followed him all the way to Brooklyn, but he noticed her, I'd say while we were on the Brooklyn Bridge. He went to a gas station and held up there."

"I should have let Shelly know I was there at that point, but I didn't want her to blow up. You know how she reacts to me. Chino is somewhere out here in Brooklyn. I stayed behind to make sure Shelly was handled properly." Lil' James was flustered.

"Handled properly! If you knew she wouldn't survive, you should have followed Chino. Now I have ta' search the whole fuckin' borough of Brooklyn to find this blood clad buoy, me a' kill his bumba rass, but me a' kill him slowly, oh so fuckin' slowly. You still out there, so you already know what the fuck you betta do!"

"Yeah, Shark, I know. Yo Shark, I'm sorry man." Shark hung up without a reply.

What the fuck was he just told? Shark was really not comprehending the fact that Lil' James just told him the mother of his child was dead, lying in an unknown morgue in somebody's hospital.

Shark operated his drug business away from his home. He never brought even a gram of coke passed his threshold. He didn't allow anyone else to bring drugs in his home either. His daughter rested her head there and he would never jeopardize her safety, nor the image she had of her mother and father. Shantel had heard rumors of whom and what her father was, but she never saw that side of him, to her he was just Daddy.

And Shelly, well Shelly loved Shantel more than anything and anyone, besides Shark, even though Shark and Shelly never married, they were a family, a deep, longstanding family. What would he tell his daughter? How could he explain?

Shark immediately put calls out to his men to inform them of the new developments. Word was out: Chino was a wanted man, alive and only, alive.

Shantel came home earlier than usual. She saw her father on the balcony and called to him. Shark, submerged in his thoughts and his sadness, didn't even hear his only child.

"Daddy, what's the matter?"

Shark looked at Shantel, with the saddest look, she had no choice, but to assume something was terribly wrong. "Daddy, what happened?"

"Shan Shan I really don't know how to tell you this sweet pea, but Mommy's been in a terrible accident."

Shantel, the spitting image of her mother, was just like Shark upon hearing this news, in shock.

"What kind of accident Daddy, a car accident?" Shantel's fear was rising.

"Come here baby." Shark motioned his daughter to his side. She came, hesitantly.

"Mommy was killed." Shark having to say it for the first time, took it in completely, but had to be strong for his daughter.

"Killed!" Shantel began crying hysterically. "What do you mean killed? What happened to my mother?"

Shark wanted to spare Shantel the horrid details. He merely explained that Shelly was just in the wrong place at the wrong time.

"Where was she? And where is she? I want to see my mother now, right fucking now!" Shantel cried, yelled, cried and yelled some more. The grief was overwhelming her. Her mother was mad cool with her. She could tell her mother anything and she would understand. She was like her best friend. Someone killed her best friend and her mother. Oh God! Shantel began to feel nauseated. She threw up.

Shark vowed as he watched his daughter that Chino would pay so dearly it would be unimaginable to the human mind. Shark called his mother to come and care for Shantel. He had to give the horrible news over the phone.

"Moma," since Shark was originally from Jamaica, when he spoke to his mom, the real Daverton Marshall Cornelius came out.

"Daverton?"

"Yeah Moma, Look me'a need you fi come ovr and look afta Shantel na'."

"A' Shantel almos' grown (ee) a' wha me'a hafa look afta her fa?"

"Moma, a somepin' terrible happened, a' someone killed Shelly ya know."

"Whoaa! A what de blood clad, bumba a gwon up dere Daverton, mea' tell you about de evil youa' deal wit. Ah so it come for you."

"Moma, mea' need fi' you fi' come look afta Shantel, you comin?"

"I'm on my wey" Mrs. Cornelius, Connie was her first name, was no joke. She had seen it all. Shark's father had been caught up in the drug scene heavily back in Jamaica. He was gunned down right in front of her, which was why she detested

102

the fact that Shark followed right in his footsteps.

Connie couldn't help but wonder what terrible mess could have caused the death of her granddaughter's mother. Shelly wasn't Connie's favorite person, but she didn't hate the woman. She was very sorry that she had been killed. No one deserved a violent death, except for those who killed violently.

Shark continued to console Shantel. He really didn't know what to say or do. He had never been in this situation before. He never thought he would be.

His mind kept darting back to Chino. He knew all along. He played him like a bitch on the phone, talkin' like he was gonna' set it on Blue and Gauge. Well guess who shit was gon' get set on?

THE RESULTS

Lisa had been waiting patiently for Dr. Brennan to return with some news regarding Donell's condition. She had completed literally forty forms for his admission. Donell had no insurance, so most of the forms entailed background history, such as employment, next of kin, etc.. Basically they were going to get their money from somebody.

Lisa noticed Kyree as he brought in another emergency victim. He noticed her also.

"Hey, you still here huh?"

"Yes, Dr. Brennan hasn't come back yet, it's been over two hours already. What could be taking so long?"

"It could be just about anything. He may have gotten called away to another patient. I'll see if I can find him for you."

"No, no just leave him. I'm sure he's very busy. He'll come out when he's done." A part of Lisa didn't want to know what was wrong with Donell.

"What'd you have this trip?" Lisa inquired, trying to take her mind off of her fears.

"Gunshot victim, he's pretty banged up."

"I'm sorry to hear that. Is he going to make it?"

"I don't know. I don't even know if it matters, they'll probably finish the job the day he gets out of here. These kids are taking no prisoners these days."

"I hear you on that."

Lisa's heart suddenly began to pulsate rapidly and her palms began to sweat. She saw Dr. Brennan walking in her direction. It didn't look good. Kyree didn't know if he should stay to offer Lisa support, or leave so she could have her privacy with Dr. Brennan. He looked to her for a signal, but she gave none. Lisa was immobilized, resembling a mannequin in a boutique window.

"Miss Spencer," Dr. Brennan's tone, solemn. Lisa wasn't ready to hear the dreaded results.

"Wait, wait, don't tell me anything just yet, not yet. I'm not ready."

Kyree looked at Dr. Brennan, who returned his glare, the two had worked together long enough to read the others' facial expressions. It wasn't good.

Kyree made an excuse to leave. He had decided he didn't want to be there for her reaction. "Lisa, I have to check on the patient I just brought in. I'll be back to check on you, ok?"
Lisa had a blank stare. She had no response.

"Miss Spencer, I understand your fear, but I really do need to share Donells' circumstances. If not with you, then maybe you'd better call his next of kin to come on down so I can speak with them."

"I'm sorry, Dr. Brennan. I must sound totally selfish right now, but I'm really scared. I can't deal with this."

"Lisa, is that your first name?"

"Yes."

"Well Lisa, Donell has a rare form of Leukemia."

"Oh no! Is he going to be alright?" Lisa was relieved it wasn't what she'd assumed, but this was really just as serious.

"I really can't say. It could go either way. It all depends on if we've caught it in time. How long he has also depends on if he can afford the necessary treatment, it's pretty expensive. I'm not surprised his doctor didn't recognize the symptoms. It appears as if it's a bad flu."

"Donell's been locked up for six years Dr. Brennan. I'm sure they didn't care to bother finding out if and why he was sick. In all the years I had been visiting him, he never told me he was sick."

"He probably didn't want to alarm you." Dr. Brennan studied Lisa. She was a beautiful young black specimen of a woman.

"Did you want to see him?" he asked.

"Can I?"

"Sure, but I still need to notify his next of kin. We will probably need to keep him here for a while to run some additional tests."

"I wanted to call his mother before we came, but Donell was adamant that I didn't tell her anything."

"Well I'm sorry Lisa, may I call you Lisa?"

"Sure you can."

"It's imperative that I speak with Donell's mother, Lisa. She may be able to answer some questions that will shed some light on why Donell never knew or let on that he knew he's been sick for some time. This may very well be hereditary."

"I promise to call Donell's mother as soon as I leave him. I really rather I didn't call her. She can be right rough and I wouldn't want you to go through all of that." Lisa thought that Dr. Brennan looked awfully young to be a doctor. He couldn't be more than thirty, or at least that's the impression she got.

"No problem, just let her know she needs to get down here or call me as soon as possible." He handed Lisa a card with his pager number. "Donell is in the third room on the left after you go through those big doors. I'll be admitting him into room 504 which is on the fifth floor, but that'll be a little later on." Dr. Brennan added.

"Thanks." Lisa slowly shook his hand. He cupped her hand with both of his. Very nice hands, she noticed, strong, big, warm hands. "Thanks a lot, Dr. Brennan."

"Thanks is really not necessary, Lisa. I haven't done anything to save him. I should be thanking you for getting him here in time, so that we may try. "

Lisa found herself staring at the doctor. And he didn't mind one bit. "I may need to reach you as well. There will be some things you will need to know about Donell's condition as far as care giving is concerned."

"Oh, ok, well here is my home number. I'll most likely be going back there, but here, take my cell phone number too, just in case." Lisa jotted her numbers down on a small piece of paper she retrieved from her purse. "I'd better go check on Donell. "

Dr. Brennan watched as she walked through the doors, 'Damn, it's something about that woman', He thought to himself.

*   *   *   *

Lisa really didn't know how to act. She didn't want to worry Donell or scare him. He was probably already scared. She entered his room slowly.

"Hey baby, how you feeling?"

Donell was hooked up to several machines. Some looked to be monitors, some looked like they were pumping Donell with fluid and literally blowing him up. He appeared to be floating in and out of consciousness.

"Lis ... " Donell was out of it.

"Don't try to talk baby. The doctor says you will need to stay put for a few days. They need to do some more tests and I know how you feel about hospitals baby, but you don't have a choice."

Lisa held onto Donell's hand. She kissed his forehead and stroked her fingers through his hair. She thought to herself, 'Damn, leukemia, I'm sorry baby. All of those awful thoughts I had and terrible things I said when I thought you had AIDS, I'm sorry'. All Lisa could do was cry.

"Don..'t cr..y L..is..." Donell managed to say.

"I'm sorry baby. I know I shouldn't be crying. I have to be strong for both of us. It's all good. We're not going to let this get to us. Were you sick in prison baby? You never said you weren't feeling good. When did you start feeling bad? Never mind, don't talk, save your strength. " Lisa realized she just asked about five different questions in one breath. Her mind was racing. She needed to call Mrs. Stephens. Lisa watched Donell as he drifted off to sleep. He apparently was given a sedative so that he could rest. Lisa retrieved her cell phone from her Fendi purse and dialed Donell's mother. There was no signal. She remembered her phone doesn't work in hospitals. She stepped out to the pay phone.

"Mrs. Stephens ... "

"Yeah! Who is this? I ain't got no goddamn money, and you can't get what I ain't got?"

"Mrs. Stephens, this is Lisa."

"Oh Lisa baby, how you doin'? Wha's the matter, they ain't lock my baby up again did they?"

"No, no Mrs. Stephens, Donell is here with me."

"Oh thank you Lord, Jesus, I can't take it no more with that boy!"

108

"Mrs. Stephens, I have some not so good news."

"What is it? Oh my God, they done hurt my baby!"

"No! Mrs. Stephens, please nothing like that, but Donell uh, he's here in Bronx Lebanon Hospital."

"In the hospital? What happened chile? Wha's wrong with my Donell?"

"Well, the doctor is actually requesting that you either come on down here or for you to call him. Now if you want to come, you let me know and I'll be waiting outside with your cab fare. If you'd rather call him I have his pager number."

"What does he want with me?"

"Mrs. Stephens, Dr. Brennan says that Donell has Leukemia…"

"Leukemia?"

"Yes, and I guess he wants to ask you questions about your family history maybe to see if anyone else in your family ever had or has the disease."

"My son don't have no damn disease. Who the hell has been tellin' you this bullshit?"

"Mrs. Stephens, Donell is very very sick. They are going to be keeping him here for some more tests. Now if no one else in the family has been or is sick with leukemia, fine, I'll tell the doctor, but if there is anything and I mean anything Mrs. Stephens that you can think of, please tell me. You don't have to tell a stranger, you can tell me and I'll take care of everything for you."

There was silence.

"Mrs. Stephens?"

"I'll be there. You better be downstairs. I told you, I ain't got no goddamn money!"

"Yes, Mrs. Stephens."

Lisa felt there must have been someone in Donell's family other than Donell affected by this menacing disease.. Mrs. Stephens was acting strange, not that that was unusual, but Lisa knew her quirky common law mother-in-law. Something was up.

Donell was still knocked out from the sedatives he had been given and would be for some time. Lisa headed outside to go wait for Donells' mother. Her two-way went off. 'Baby girl, Mari wants me to fuck her'.

Lisa dialed Chino's cell phone.

"Talk to me." Chino answered.

"What the fuck did you just page me with?" Lisa fumed.

"Oh, so now you answering?" Chino asked with an attitude.

"Look Chino, I would have gotten back to you sooner, but I've been held up in the hospital with Donell. Which your selfish ass neglected to tell me that my man was sick as a dog and you dumped him at Camaria's house. What the fuck is up with you? How fucked up are your morals? Oh wait, I forgot you don't fuckin' have any!"

"Look, I'm sorry Baby Girl. I knew you'd find out Dee was sick. I ain't wanna worry you. I told Camaria I was coming back and I was. And I hear you callin' the nigga your man. So what, you done told him you going back wit' him Lisa?"

Lisa didn't answer his question.

"Chino, Donell is very sick. I'm not discussing anything else right now. All that other shit that's going on is just going to have to wait."

"All what other shit? I told you I'm out of here in a few weeks. Did you make a decision?"

"Are you hearing me Chino? What is your problem? Why

110

you acting like you don't give a fuck about Donell?"

"I give a fuck, but ..."

"But what Chino? How could there be a but? This man is supposed to be your dawg. Forget the fact that we've been fucking around behind his back all these years, that's fucked up enough, but now you want to just leave him while he could be on his deathbed?"

"Deathbed. What are you sayin'?"

"I'm saying that Donell may be dying Chino!"

"What the fuck is going on?"

"The doctor is saying that Donell has Leukemia. His mother is on her way down here now. That's what the fuck is going on, but you're too busy with your fucking deals!"

"Oh shit!"

"Yeah, oh shit. And what's this shit about Mari wanting to fuck you?"

"Yeah, your girl is buggin'. What'd you tell her?"

"I ain't tell her shit. She was askin', but I didn't say a damn thing. So now she wants to fuck you huh? I tell you bitches are a trip, even if they claim to be your best friend."

"You comin' wit' me Baby Girl?"

"Chino, Donell needs me right now. How can you not acknowledge the fact that this man is fatally ill? Are you heartless for real?"

"Na, it ain't even like that. I just got a lot of shit goin' on right now. Dee is my boy, my number one mufucka, our shit don't get no thicker, and as far as me askin' you if you comin' wit me, I just wanna know. Where's Dee right now?"

"He's in a temporary room asleep. Oh my God! His moms is probably here already and heated. I'm supposed to be out front to pay for her cab."

Lisa started to jog from the emergency entrance to the main entrance.

"Look, I don't know if I'm going to be able to go with you Chino. I got a lot of shit I gotta' take care of before I think about going anywhere."

"Come see me tonight, meet me at my house."

"No Chino. I'm a' stay here tonight. I'm going to the house and get a few things and I'm coming back here. Donell needs me and I'm going to be there for him, unlike your trifling ass."

"It ain't even like that Lisa. You should understand the game by now."

"Oh I understand the game, and the game ain't shit!"

"Ok, I see you need to see me. You done flipped on some ole' other shit. I understand Donell is sick. Just do what you gotta' do by him for the next four weeks. That's more than enough time."

"More than enough time for what?" Lisa asked.

"For you to get all your shit in order Lisa. I'm tellin' you, you comin' wit' me."

Lisa hurried him off the phone. "I'll call you back later. Let me go check for Mrs. Stephens."

"Baby Girl?"

"What Chino?" Lisa asked as if she no longer wanted to hear his voice.

"You comin' wit me!"

"I heard you Chino."

Lisa made it to the main entrance of the hospital, but not quite soon enough.

"I ain't tryin' to rob yo' dumb ass. What I look like tryin' to jump out of yo cab? I'm damn near sixty-five years old.

Where the hell am I gon' run to? I hate you damn foreigners.
You don't trust no damn body? Well go the hell back to yo'
own damn country if you don' trust no damn body here!"

Donell's mother was laying the cab driver out. Lisa went to
his window and asked how much was the fare. The driver
stated it was twenty-seven dollars.

"Twenty what? You mus' be out yo' damn cotton pickin'
mind!" Mrs. Stephens yelled. "You think you got you some
dumb ass black women in front of you don't you? Don't you!
Think we just fell off the fuckin' turnip truck, huh?"

"Don't worry Mrs. Stephens, I got it." Lisa gave the cab
three tens. Instead of offering her change, he just pulled off.

"See chile. I told you. They too damn rude. After that damn
bombing they all should have been shipped the hell out of this
damn country. All of em!"

"Yes Mrs. Stephens. "

They went into the emergency room. Lisa was on her way
back to Donell's room with Mrs. Stephens when Dr. Brennan
called to her.

"Yes, Dr. Brennan, I was just on my way back to check on
Donell" Lisa put her hands on Mrs. Stephens's shoulder. "This
is Donell's mother, Mrs. Stephens."

"What the hell y'all done to my baby?"

"Mrs. Stephens, Dr. Brennan has been taking excellent care
of Donell since we've arrived." Lisa knew how Donell's
mother could be. She didn't want her flipping on Dr. Brennan.

"Donell ain't been sick a day in his life and don't nobody in
this family got nothin'."

Dr. Brennan questioned, "What about his father's side?"
Mrs. Stephens had a strange look on her face. She knew
something. Lisa felt it. Why would she keep it a secret?

113

"I'm going to go check on Donell. Mrs. Stephens you stay here and talk to Dr. Brennan. It seems to me like you do have some things you'd like to discuss with him. I'll come check for you in a few, ok?"

Mrs. Stephens hesitantly agreed, "Yeah, ok."

Lisa left the two of them standing, watching her as she walked through the doors.

"Mrs. Stephens, Donell is very ill. I know he's been away for some time so he doesn't have a medical record that I can refer to, but with the tests that I've run so far, we have determined he has a rare form of leukemia."

Mrs. Stephens had a lost look on her face.

Dr. Brennan continued, "Now many doctors mis diagnose this disease and that may have been what happened when he was incarcerated, but did his father or anyone on his father's side show signs of this disease or complications of any kind that may give me some background information?"

It seemed as though time had suspended itself and it took Mrs. Stephens forever to answer the doctor, but she finally divulged the information Dr. Brennan was searching for.

"Donell's daddy had some kind of trouble. Yes he did, never went to a doctor though. Kept tellin' me he jus' rather die in the house wit' me an' the kids there wit' him."

"When was this Mrs. Stephens?"

"Oh I'd say about four years or so. Ain't been that long since my Harry passed. At leas' it don't seem so to me."

"Did your husband ever go to the doctor at all? Did you guys have a family physician?"

"Dr., my husban' couldn't afford no famly' doctor for us. He did go to the free clinic over on 161st and Sheridan. We all went there when we needed to see a doctor."

114

"Mrs. Stephens, I don't know how to tell you this, but Donell's expectancy isn't that long."

"I'm sorry, but can you talk to me in plain English? I don't understan' no fancy doctor talk."

"Excuse me Mrs. Stephens, I didn't mean to –"

"No, no that's quite alright. Now what's wrong wit' my baby?"

"Donell has a disease that unfortunately may take him away from us, probably within the next three to six months, if we don't find a bone marrow donor."

Mrs. Stephens looked at Dr. Brennan like he was crazy. Not her Donell. Take her other son, the no good son of a bitch that spit in her face when she tried to steer him right, thought she was trying to control him, but not her baby, not her Donell.

"There mus' be some mistake Dr, uh, Dr."

"Brennan, Mrs. Stephens, Dr. Brennan."

"Yeah, uh, there mus' be, see my baby jus' came home and uh, he was jus' fine." The tears were building up in Donell's mother's eyes.

"I'm so sorry Mrs. Stephens. I wish there was something I could do, but there really isn't. All we can do is make his days as comfortable as possible."

"I don't believe you. Where's Lisa? Where's Donell? Where's my baby at you !@%$#" Mrs. Stephens lost it. She called Dr. Brennan every name in the book. He realized it was anger. He'd seen it too many times before.

"Come with me- I'll take you to see your son."

A FAMILY'S PAIN

Shark's mother had reached the penthouse. She hated that her son lived way up in the sky. Where they were from in Jamaica, a two-story home was a rarity. Imagine living on the 35th floor with a balcony overlooking the whole of the city! She had to take Dramamine to maintain because she was afraid of heights. Visiting her son gave her the same effect as flying on an airplane.

Connie was hurting inside. She knew her son was steering himself into an early grave. Now, Shelly was dead. She saw that as a warning. Sharks' mother dabbled in the spirits. She felt she could sense what was due to happen. She saw a death, but she thought for sure it was to be her son. Thank God it wasn't, but the soul He took, was just as unprepared. Connie had been announced before being allowed to go up. Shark awaited her arrival.

"Moma!"

"Daverton," Connie embraced her son.

Shark held his mother very dear in his heart.

"What a g'won'?," she asked.

"Me no know, a somebody a' rob me an' dem kill Shelly ya know?"

"So you'a' know who fi blame?"

"Yeah, me tink say me a' know, no, me a' blood clad know fi' sure, sien ... "

"And so what, you'a gwon go an' kill him too!"

"What else can I do?"

"Violence doesn't solve violence Daverton! You never

116

learn a ting from ya fadda ?"

"Yeah, me learn me hafa watch my back every step a' de' whey. Never trust anyone as far as the eye can see 'im."

"Daverton, please, just stop all this foolishness and mind ya'self ya' know. Jah na like this behavior ya' know!"

"Moma, me can't just lie like a wounded dog and them a kill my Shelly, ah my daughter's mudda ya' know!"

"Me know, Daverton, a' me know!"

Shantel came into the living room. One look at his daughter and Shark made up his mind, despite his mother's wishes. He had no choice. Chino was a dead man.

"Shantel, come here baby." Connie attempted to console her granddaughter. Shantel obeyed her grandmother. She just couldn't contain her grief. Once Connie wrapped her in her arms, she began to sob.

"Shh, now there, a'me know it's hard sweetie. Me know say that you loved your moma' and me know say she loved you as well a' dat me know."

"Why, why my mother?"

"Jah was ready fi' her Shantel. There is no reason udda (other) than that!"

"It's not fair! It's just not fair! My mother was so cool Grandmoma. She was like my home girl. I could tell my mother anything and she would listen to me. She would never judge me. She would just listen. I can't take the pain. It physically hurts."

"I know it chile', I know it all too well."

Shark went over and held his daughter tight. "I know I can't bring your mother back, but I swear to you I will see to it that the person responsible pays dearly."

117

"Daverton!" Connie yelled. "Don't you feed that trash talk to my granddaughter ya know! A mi a' tell you that is not the whey to handle this crisis, but you never did listen and me a' tell you me feel say the worse of this is not over yet! You need fi' stop all the bullshit you a' deal wit' and I mean now Daverton! Sien!"

"Look, Moma I know me asked fi' you fi' come over here and look afa' Shantel, but I feel say it's a better idea if you two go to your house and lay low. Wit' tings the way they are trouble is liable to come here and me can't take it if someting else a' go wrong. "

"Shantel go and collect your tings. Your fadda won't listen to his own moma an' me feel say evil a' comin', an' me don' want you around here."

"I don't wanna go! I wanna stay here with my father!" Shantel lost control. She was beginning to hyperventilate.

"Shantel!" Shark shouted, "Please calm down. Don't do this. Go with your grandmoma."

"No! No! No!" Shantel was screaming.

Connie slapped the shit out of Shantel. Shantel stood still, mostly from shock. She looked at her grandmother. Eyes wide open in disbelief.

"That was jus' to calm you down. Now g'won an' get your tings, an'me' na' g'won say it again!"

Shantel looked to her father and back to her grandmother. She saw a blank stare on her father's face and for the first time since he told her that her mother was dead, Shantel realized this was deeply affecting her father.

"I'm sorry. I'm so sorry." Shantel grabbed her father's waist and clung tightly, "I'm sorry Daddy."

118

"You have no reason to be sorry. I'm sorry. I'm sorry you are going through this." He hugged his daughter and kissed the top of her head.

"I'm going to get some things. I'll be ready in a little while." Shantel told her grandmother.

Connie knew Shantel's actions were not directed toward her. She knew her granddaughter loved her. She understood her actions and reactions totally. When Connie slapped Shantel, it was out of love. She didn't want her granddaughter to have an anxiety attack, which Connie saw was coming had she not slapped her.

"Daverton, you take this time to straighten this mess out. Me don' want this chile' comin' back to this, because me won't send her back, sien!"

"Yes Moma."

Shantel was in her room packing some clothes to take to her grandmother's house. She couldn't believe that her life had changed literally, in one split second. One minute she was chilling. She had everything a teenage girl could want, and the next, she was motherless and miserable. She didn't know who Jah was or God was, but as far as she was concerned there was no superior being. If there was, how could he or she allow her to hurt so. Shantel went into her dresser drawer to get some pajamas and things. She looked up and saw a picture with her and her parents at her eighth grade graduation. They were so proud of her, especially her mother. Shelly shared with her daughter, the life she had. Shantel knew exactly how her father and mother met. She found it quite comical. She felt they were meant to be together forever. Even though they never married, to Shelly that was just a formality, she knew who had Shark's heart, she didn't need a piece of paper to prove it. Shelly actually relayed to her one and only daughter that marriage can ruin a relationship. Therefore, Shantel never really planned to look for a husband, like so many mothers train their daughters to do.

Shantel was a strong female. She was very much a combination of her parents. Half Jamaican, half African-American, and a whole lot of attitude. Never disrespectful though, just confident, extremely confident. Shantel knew that her father would take care of the person who killed her mother, but she would rather stay home. She couldn't take the thought of something happening to her father as well.

Knowing Connie the way she did, she decided to continue packing and obey her father's wishes. Shantel loved her grandmother very much, but since she was from Jamaica, she had a different way of handling things. Had it been great-grandma Shirley, she would have convinced Shark that it would be best for the family to stay close together. "Oh my God," Shantel just thought, 'no one had told great grandma Shirley'.

Shantel came back into the living room with two suitcases. "Daddy, nobody has called great grandma Shirley!"

Shark said, "I know, I was going to wait until we actually identify ... "

Connie cut in, "We'll tell 'er when the time is right Shantel. Do you tink say you have everyting? Did you leave any clothes in your closet?"

"Yes, but I need to talk to my father, please... Alone. No disrespect Grandmoma. "

"No problem, I have to go to the ladies' room." Connie left

120

the two of them alone.

"Daddy."

"Yes Shantel?"

"Daddy, please be careful. Can't you have somebody else take care of this and you come with me to Grandmoma's house?"

"No baby, I really wish I could, but I can't do that. I must make this right Shantel."

"But Daddy, there is nothing that can make this right, not even killing whoever killed Mommy."

"Shantel, I know you may not agree with what I'm doing right now, but one day you will understand."

"I know you truly believe that Daddy, and I love you ... "

"I love you too, Shan Shan." Shark's eyes were bloodshot.

He'd been distraught ever since Lil' James told him the dreadful news. Shantel had never seen her father this way. It scared her. She felt sorry for the person who was responsible for her mother's death. Her father was sure to devour his very soul, but she also felt a lot of hatred for them too.

"Daddy, please promise you'll call me every hour to check in."

"Shantel, I promise you will know where I am at all times, now please don't give your grandmoma any trouble. Mind her, hear me?"

It was funny how Shark switched up his dialect when he wasn't upset or talking to his mother. You would never guess he was a native of Jamaica. He'd been here in the States since he was a teen-ager. Connie made it a point that they stay familiar with their roots. Shark and his two siblings, one brother, one sister, visited Jamaica quite often. Shark thought it was a beautiful country, but he felt America was the only place

121

he could truly capitalize on what his father taught him and that was the drug game.

Shantel hugged her father as if it was the last time she would see him. She looked at him long and hard. He was so sad. "I'm so sorry Daddy," was all she could find to say.

"Shantel!" Connie called on her way back to the living room.

"Yes, Grand-moma, I know. I'm ready. "

"Me don't mean to rush you, but you know how traffic can be in this "Manhattan". Me don't know see why so many cars a' come up and down these streets dem, like dem in a race or' someting."

Shark pulled some money out to give his mother. "Take this Moma, jus' in case."

"Jus' in case what? Daverton, me don' wan' hear no foolishness ya' know. Me don' need no money for notin'. You know, me been tinking... We should g'won and go back home where tings are a lot simpler. We can get along fine wit de money we have now, eh'? Me tired Daverton, hear me, me tired!"

"Sien, me hear you Moma." Shark kissed Shantel on her forehead and gave her another hug. He then kissed Connie on both her cheeks and he hugged his mother, like a little boy clinging to all he knew.

"Don't forget your promise Daddy ... "

"I won't, Shan Shan."

THE LAST RUN

Chino was rolling a blunt. He was waiting for Kendu to come so he could put him up on what he was trying to accomplish. Knees had gotten all the soldiers envelopes together, including Pork's. He was packaging the remainder of the work into ten thousand dollar bundles. He thought it best to wait a while before they went to go check for Pork. The way Shorty described Pork's mother, he didn't want to feel her wrath either. He did say a prayer for his little stickman. He hoped he was doing alright.

Chino knew it wasn't smart to cloud his senses with weed, but he was under a lot of pressure and he needed an escape. He puffed hard on the blunt, inhaling the thick smoke through both his mouth and nostrils, absorbing every ounce of the effect and aroma of the potent lime green skunk buds. He was silently mapping out his next move. He would move one hundred thousand worth of work and just take the rest with him. He would go to Virginia, where he had family and he also had some niggas he knew who would definitely get the rest of the shit off in little to no time. He would hit them off and then call to send for Lisa. Chino wanted to see Donell before he went out of town, but only if conditions permitted.

Bones two-wayed Knees to alert him that Kendu was on his way up. Knees let Chino know that Kendu had arrived.

"Yo, you sure this nigga can be trusted?"
"This is my blood Chino. I don't have no doubts. I know

123

some people family be shady as a bitch, but my family is a family. Blood is all we got!

"I feel you. I wish I could say the same."

Kendu knocked on the door. Knees went to the specially made peephole, which was lowered to his eye level. He identified Kendu and slowly opened the door.

"What's goin' on thun?" Kendu was definitely thugged out.

He had on a jean suit by one of the infamous rappers who now had a clothing line. Kendu's whole mouth was gold fronted. He could pick up several radio stations and televisions, he had so much metal in his mouth. He wore a dual-colored doo-rag, too tight around his head and his Timb's were wide open with no strings, which left the tongue flapping all around.

"Wha's up baby?" Knees asked. They gave each other dap. Knees performed the introductions. "This is my boss and mentor, Chino."

The two men acknowledged each other, giving pounds.

"I always wondered who the cat was that had my nephew caught up in the game I been trying so hard to keep him out of."

Chino didn't have time for bullshit. "Look man. This here is some real shit. I'm not for no games. Your nephew chose to be on my team, I never asked him, so that's that. Now are you here to get in on what I got or you here to play uncle?"

Knees felt Chino getting uptight, so he interjected, "Look Du don't come in here on no "save the children" shit. I been down wit' Chino for a long time and he's had my back without a doubt, so you just playin' yourself wit' that shit man."

"I'm just saying, you blood and I had to speak mine. That's just how I feel."

124

"Yo, you know what? Fuck that. Forget it. I don't even want you handling no shit of mine. You ain't ready playa, go 'head back to your eight balls."

"Oh it's like that?" Kendu asked.

"Yeah nigga, what the fuck you think?! This is some real shit. You think this is some pussy operation we runnin' here? Yo' mothufuckin' nephew got more sense than you do nigga. You don't come in my house talkin' some shit about me havin' your nephew caught up in some shit. You here for business purposes. He told you what this was about when he called you. You said you was ready, but now I see why you ain't never hit into no big time cake, you's a soft-ass nigga!"

"What!" Kendu was a lot of shit, but soft he wasn't.

Knees saw shit was getting way out of hand. "Yo, Du man chill man. Let me talk to you."

Chino was through. There were no more decisions to make. He wasn't giving this man shit, unless he did a complete one eighty.

Knees pulled Kendu into the kitchen and explained to his uncle that Chino had been nothing but good to him. He reasoned with him in a way in which that his uncle could plainly see that Knees was content and trusted Chino with his life. Kendu humbled himself and went back into the living room.

"Look man. I was totally off about you. I apologize, man-to- man."

Chino looked to Knees. He truly went for this kid. Knees' eyes were pleading. He wanted Chino to put his uncle on, for whatever reason Chino still didn't know, but he knew Knees and he let Kendu in on what he needed.

"Yo, you think we can move about five kilos in two days

where you pumpin'?" Chino questioned.

"Hmm, that's a lot a' fuckin' work, yo," Kendu replied.

"Yeah I know that! That's not an answer to my question."

"It's possible, anything is possible, no doubt, all things."

"Look, I ain't looking for no "footprint" poem about shit being possible! Can it be done or not?"

"Yeah it could be done. I got my block on lock. If I say it's Christmas, niggas gon' spread the word for everybody to come and get their presents. You know what I'm sayin?"

"Yeah, see now you talkin' my language," Chino replied.

"I'm gonna send three of my best wit' you as well as your own nephew. I know you'll take extra precaution with him there, and he's my right hand. He oversees all my operations."

"That's cool." Kendu said.

Knees handed Kendu a package. He turned to Chino, "You let him know the terms, Boss."

Chino looked at Kendu, "Yo Dawg, no matter what happens, that package you got there is your pay. You work it off however you like. That's a fifty thousand dollar bundle your nephew just hit you off wit'. That's just to show my appreciation for you lettin' us work your territory, you know, make up for some lost business on your part. Know that we'll need you on the scene at all times, reason being, your people don't know my boys. It's your job to let them get to know them. Feel me?"

"I feel you man." Kendu was pumped.

"I think I need to send a few more of my soldiers to look out too. What's your situation where you at? You paying the police or you hidin' from em'?"

"I ain't got no extra money to be payin' a mufucka!"

"Yeah, that's what I thought. Knees you know what to do."

Knees immediately began to holla at the six soldiers he wanted involved. Buck and Free was a given. Knees decided he would include his best workers. All he had was two days, which was more than enough time, if the clientele was right. He paged Shorty, Dolla Bill, Mick, Slim, Buck and Free to come back to the clubhouse for instructions.

Kendu watched in awe as his nephew handled the business of a man twice his age with so much calm and ease. Chino had to be doing something right.

"Yo man, I just want to say good lookin' out wit' my nephew an' shit." Kendu continued, "And I'm feeling how you do business. You just looked out for a nigga for real." Kendu was referring to his payoff for the use of his territory. He never had a fifty thousand dollar anything, except for a bond out of jail, which we all know only ten percent of that was needed.

"No problem. If my man here says to cut you some slack, then that's wha's up. You feel me?"

"No doubt!"

"We may have gotten off to a rocky start, but I feel where you comin' from. I mean, if that was my blood I probably would have come at me the same way." Chino admitted.

Kendu responded, "It's all good though. As long as he's straight, I'm cool. I can see he's down for you no matter what yo'!"

Knees maneuvered his way between the two men. "Y'all talkin' about me like I ain't even here."

Chino started feeling Kendu a little more. He realized he needed to keep him cool, seeing as though he was about to put him onto some big shit. "Yo Du, for real my partner just landed himself in the hospital. I know I got my junior army intact, but I was thinking about expanding."

127

"No doubt, Chino, I'm ready. Whatever you wanna do man." Kendu had been waiting for an opportunity like this.

"Yeah, we'll see nigga, we'll see." Chino stated.

The requested soldiers, including Bones, started arriving back at the clubhouse. Soon everyone was present. All the boys were introduced to Kendu and advised as to what phase two of the plan would be. Everyone was ready. This wasn't new to Chinos' boys. Kendu seemed a little overwhelmed with the larger operation, but he was very excited by all of the activity going on around him. In all his days of hustling, he'd never been quite in the thick of things like he was right now. Chino was on another level. The level he was dying to get to. Kendu wanted to know what he was doing wrong. Why was his operation considered bullshit? After all, he had been at this for at least two years.

'No thing,' he thought. With the package that Chino gave him he was well on his way. Kendu vowed to make sure he studied these young soldiers so he could duplicate what Chino was doing.

"A'ight, check this out. Bones will follow Kendu. Knees I want you to ride wit your fam man." Chino continued, "Bones you take everybody else. Four collections will be done. Four runs is all we need. Feel me?"

Chino had already established where they would hold up. He had a chick named Vetta in Fort Greene that he fucked with from time to time. She was down for his cause whenever he needed her. He called and told her to find somewhere else to chill for the next two days. Once his soldiers reached her crib, they would hit her off with enough money that if shit turned

128

and went the wrong way she could easily replace everything she ever owned, plus some. Kendu's spot was two Projects away. That was more than enough space.

"I'll be checkin' in. Knees, you know to holla if something unexpected goes down. We need to be out. I know Shark got word that shit is on. He probably got niggas trying to scope me out as we speak. We'll use the escape route."

"Kendu, take Knees out the front of the building and meet up with Bones in the back of the building. One more thing, I want this place cleared out. I mean nothing left. Knees, you have the majority of all the work with you. I'ma' take the rest with me. I want you to two-way Dip and Weasil and have them get rid of everything in this apartment and lock it up. This is it for the clubhouse, so y'all say your good-byes. Four runs. Four collections. Knees, get everybody paid up. Once that's all done, I'll advise."

"Oh yeah, y'all make sure to check for Pork. Make sure he's ok and Knees, see to it that he and his moms got what they need some kind of way! Got me?"

Knees nodded in agreement. "Where you gon' be Boss? That nigga Shark ain't gon be movin' alone. Let me at least send Buck with you."

"Na, Baby Boy that ain't gonna be necessary. I got me. It'll be better if that's all I have to look out for right now. I want my soldiers to move together and protect one another. If something should happen to me, y'all know who to see and that's wha's up!" Chino strapped up, as did everyone this time.

"After we make this cake, y'all goin' on a long break. We had a great streak. Whoever wants to expand with what they've learned and mastered, cool. My advice to you would be just do it together, like you been doin'. Don't let no outsiders and I mean no one get between what we've built, which is unquestionable trust and faith in one another. You feel me!?"

A host of "no doubts", "that's wha's ups", and "true dats"' followed Chino's mini speech.

"Yo boss you soundin' like you ain't gon' see us again." Mick squealed.

All of the boys agreed and started asking a whole bunch of questions.

"Look, all I'm trying to say is that I want y'all to be prepared for anything this time. If y'all don't see me again, just know that y'all are and always will be my lil' niggas. Down for whatever! But this is reality and I want y'all to be aware and alert. You're going into a territory that's truly unknown to you, and yeah it's only for two days, but two minutes, fuck that, two seconds is all it takes for a nigga to catch you out there." Chino gave all of his present soldiers dap and a half hug.

Knees watched Chino very closely. He knew this was it. He would maybe see him when he came to collect, but that would be it.

"Let me holla at you for a second Knees," Chino said, as if he had read his Knees' mind.

"You know what I'm up against. You my nigga. They don't come no better than you dawg. That's from the heart man. I need you more than ever to lead this operation. I'ma' be real wit' you. I'm out. I'ma' go to VA to get the rest of this off and lay low for a while. I want you to have my cut by tomorrow at four o'clock. Straight pump for mines first. Then the second day is all you and the boys cake right there. I will keep in touch with you man, but what I really want is for you to chill with your uncle. Oversee him now, 'cause with his new found fortune, he needs to hold his head and I can't think of a better man for the job of making sure he does that, cause' you damn sure did it for me man." Chino didn't let anyone see how he embraced Knees. He kissed each of his cheeks and just held his face for a few moments. It was as if he was saying good-bye to his own son.

Knees knew exactly what it was and he let Chino know by holding his fist out to him. They united fists and nothing else needed to be said.

YOU CAN RUN,
BUT YOU CAN'T HIDE

Chino knew damn well he'd better show his face at Bronx Lebanon hospital. There was no question about that. He knew Lisa had to be heated with him. He couldn't have that. He couldn't blame her either. He replayed their conversation in his mind and he did sound uncaring and cruel regarding Donell's condition. That was his boy, for real, regardless of all the extracurricular shit that was going on.

Chino decided his vehicle wasn't a good thing to be in, especially since Shark would be looking for it. He had every bit of his cash and the remainder of his work in a duffle bag, slung in a criss- crossed fashion over his chest. Chino walked up the stairs to the roof. He assessed the distance of the jump to the next roof over. It seemed like a crazy-ass thing to do. He'd seen it in countless movies, but now he thought the motherfuckers must have been out of their minds, actors and stuntmen alike. They devised this emergency plan quite some time ago, but up until now, it had never been put it into effect.

Chino heard a cluster of gunfire. He looked down from the roof. He couldn't see the faces clearly, but he saw several people standing around his truck. He thought he saw Shark's black Denali parked in front of it. What he could clearly see, were weapons in the hands of the men surrounding his vehicle. They began to fire, lighting it up. If he had been inside of it, there would have been no chance of survival. Chino was stumped for a split second. He wondered how Shark found out exactly where he was so quickly. No one knew. He had killed

Lil' James, or so he thought, something was fucked up.

Chino finally came out of the clouds and reacted. He ran to the opposite side of the roof, backed up and told himself, "This is it! Ride or die motherfucka!" He ran with all he had to the edge of the roof and jumped. He felt his body hit the ledge of the adjacent roof. He grabbed the top of the ledge with one hand, his other hand slipped, leaving him dangling. He realized he should have thrown the duffle bag over first, but it was too late now. Chino could hear a lot of people down below. He didn't want to look down to see what was going on. He heard additional shots. He heard sirens. Chino took a deep breath and swung his other arm over as hard as he could. He pulled himself up over the ledge and fell over onto the roof. He got up quickly and thought to himself, 'they may have seen me hanging, they may know I'm up here'. He didn't feel safe leaving out of this building either. There was one more roof, but it seemed further than the one he just jumped. 'Oh hell no, fuck that!' Chino thought. He knew these buildings very well. Shark had no idea of all of the escape routes set up for the lawbreakers of the Projects.

He went down two flights of stairs, then switched stairwells. He did this all the way down to the sub-basement level. Chino entered the laundry room. He quickly removed a large vent above one of the washing machines, climbed up and in. A woman folding her clothes watched in disbelief, but knew to mind her business. This vent connected to Marcy Projects. He would leave out of Marcy and catch the train all the way to the Bronx.

Chino wondered if Knees and Bones got everybody out safely, then he thought 'yeah, they should be straight. They

133

went out the back. Shark and his crew was in the front shootin'
up my shit. Damn! I loved that truck. Shit! Luckily I wasn't in
that bitch'.

There were undercover police officers in the train station,
nothing out of the ordinary. They were in their usual positions,
waiting for someone to hop the train (attempt to ride for free).
Chino hadn't taken the train in a while. He wasn't used to the
long lines that were at the token booth. He was growing
impatient. He thought about taking a cab, but you really needed
to call a cab in the Borough of Brooklyn and he couldn't take
the chance of being seen waiting for a cab. Chino's two-way
pager went off , 'Yeah, we all good!'. Good. At least that was
going according to plan.

Chino paid his money, got his token and paid his fare. He
eyed the undercover officers, but since he had complied with
paying his fare they looked at the patrons waiting to buy
tokens, and a few homeless beggars that plagued the station.
He went to the elevated platform and waited for the train. Once
he got on the "J" train he would take it to Fulton, then catch the
number 4 train to Mt. Eden Avenue. Chino hated taking the
trains, especially New York City Mass Transit. He couldn't
have been happier the day he had purchased his first car.

It seemed like forever before the train had come. Chino
rode the back of the train as he always did when he used to ride
the trains. There was just something about the last car. Chino
didn't want to be noticed. He should be in the first car with the
driver of the train. Nothing ever goes on in the first car. Chino
started to make his way to the front of the train. He had gotten
pretty much to the middle of the train, which had quite a few
people on it. He decided it would be good enough until he got

to Fulton.

There was a man sitting in the corner by the doors. By looking at him you would assume he was homeless. He definitely smelled homeless. He eyed Chino curiously. Chino felt someone staring at him. He turned to see why he felt someone's eyes on him. The man stood up and began to walk toward Chino. He began to shout loudly, "No! John Stringer, you can't have a cigarette, sit down and eat your food!" He repeated this over and over, all the while walking in Chino's direction. Chino was buggin' off the dude. He was thinking to himself that he was crazy and had probably escaped from Bellevue or some other mental institution, but as he drew closer Chino realized this man was coming straight for him ... not that he had the slightest idea as to why. Shit was really beginning to be "off the wall".

"Yo duke, you better back up! I don't know you, man." Chino tried to rationally explain to the man.

"No John Stringer, you can't have a cigarette! Sit down and eat your food! Oh no! Shoot the dog!," the man shouted.
The people that were on the train couldn't help but to laugh. Chino didn't find this funny. The last thing he needed was for attention to be drawn to him.

"Look man, I'm telling you, my name is not John Stringer and I ain't got no damn cigarettes!" Chino saw the man reaching into his pocket.

His instincts made him react. He reached for his gun, but when the train stopped and the doors opened, Chino pushed the man out of his way and exited the train. As the doors were closing, Chino saw the man merely take a cigarette out of his pocket and light it up.

"Damn! I hate taking these motherfuckin' trains!" Chino

exclaimed, as he sat waiting for the next one.

*   *   *   *

Chino had finally made it to the Bronx. He had one more stop to go and he would be at his destination. He thought about what he would say to Donell. What could he say? He was very sorry for his illness. He had no idea of how to comfort his best friend, but he knew he had to make things right between them. He told him he would be back to Camaria's and he had lied, not that he'd meant to lie, but he lied all the same.

The train arrived at Mt. Eden subway station. Chino exited the train and proceeded to the hospital.

Paranoia was getting the best of him. He continuously watched his back and looked over his shoulders. He went through the doors of Bronx Lebanon Hospital and walked up to the admission's desk. "I'm here to see Donnell Stephens," Chino stated.

"I'm sorry Sir, but visiting hours are over,   " said the heavy-set attendant sitting behind the admission's desk.

"Look. I just took a two-hour train ride to get here. I need to see Donell Stephens. I won't be long, but I've got to see him." Chino attempted to reason with the attendant, unfortunately she looked as if she could care less.

"Sir, I'm sorry you traveled all this long way, but I cannot allow you to visit anyone. Visiting hours are over at 8pm and it is now 8:27."

"Do you have a supervisor I can speak with?" Chino asked.

"Yeah, I have a supervisor, but she will tell you the same thing! " The girl snapped.

136

"Well I would rather her tell me. So would you get her for me?" Chino asked, now smiling as if he was never refused entry.

The girl got up and walked to the back. Chino grabbed the yellow visitors' pass and swiftly walked to the elevators. He had planned to check every floor and every room until he found his best friend.

As the elevator doors opened, his mouth opened as well. Lisa was on the elevator. She was apparently coming from the hospital cafeteria. He entered the elevator.

"Chino! What are you doing here?" Lisa had a look of sheer surprise. Chino was the last person on earth she expected to see at the hospital, let alone in the same elevator.

"Hey Baby Girl, I don't believe I'm running into you like this. How's my lady doing?"

"Chino, chill with that bullshit right now, ok?"

"Chill with what? Yo what the fuck is up with you Lisa? You ain't in front of Donell! Why the fuck you actin' like you ain't happy to see me? I been through some shit to get the fuck up here!"

Lisa eyed Chino more closely, she noticed he didn't look his usual self. "What did you get yourself into now, Chino?"
The elevator stopped at the fifth floor, the two emerged from the elevator.

"Yo Lisa, I'm not feeling the way you be flippin' when we're out in public. I'm telling you I'm ready to give up everything for you, but you stuck on this scene here."

"Yo Chino, I'm not feeling the way you be flippin' when one minute you want me to go away with you, then the next minute you're propositioning my best friend to fuck."

"I know you're not jealous of that bitch Camaria?" Chino tried to keep his voice low. He didn't want to draw attention to the two of them.

They arrived at Donell's room. Lisa grabbed Chino's arm before he opened the door. She looked deeply into Chino's eyes. She wanted to tell him that she wasn't going. She had no intention whatsoever of leaving her family, her life, everything she knew that was good. Instead, she chose to give him a quick kiss with a touch of her tongue. He just knew, or shall we say assumed that she was coming with him, without a doubt.

"Let me go in first Chino," Lisa said, "I don't want you to startle him."

"What?" Chino asked.

"I don't want him to be surprised to see you."

"Yo Lis, I'm not even supposed to be in here, forget about all that, come on," Chino led Lisa into room 504.

Chino was not prepared for what his eyes were a witness to. His best friend of more than twenty years was lying amidst a cluster of machines and tubes. He looked back at Lisa solemnly, as if to apologize for his negligence in caring for Donell. He could have gotten him to a hospital and he would have, had he known his condition was life-threatening.

Lisa saw Chino drifting.

"Look, don't blame yourself. Apparently his father had a trace of this disease."

Chino stared at Donell. He reached out to touch him, then hesitated. Chino looked at Lisa. He thought about everything that was going on and he was suddenly exhausted. His two-way went off, 'oki doki- Knees'.

Lisa sneered at Chino as he checked his pager. "You just can't get away from your business, huh Chino."

"Baby Girl you know I got a lot of shit ridin' right now. Why you keep stressin' me about shit?"

Donell, was sure he had not heard what he thought he just heard. He knew he recognized the voices, but the dialogue ... No way ...

Donell tried hard, but could not ignore the tickling cough that was lingering in his throat. He wanted to remain silent. He was sure he was hearing things. The sedatives had made him hallucinate, or so he'd hoped. What he was now hearing with his ears, could not actually be a possibility, could it? 'Oh God, NO! What the fuck?' Amazingly, he concealed it.

"Oh I'm not stressin' you, but I know one thing, I can't leave Donell like this. He needs me- I won't leave with him in the condition he's in. That's my motherfuckin'word." Lisa was adamant.

"I'm not going to get into that right now, because I know this is all fresh. I'll give you some time to decide what you're gonna do. I'm leaving for Virginia in about a day or so. I'll hit you from there. You let me know what you decide. I got too much ridin' on me right now. I can't get caught up in this shit with you or with Dee over you. I'm a wanted man right now. "

Donell was definitely awake and aware now. He wanted to hear it all. He was already partially numb from the sedatives, possibly dying from a disease he knew nothing about, and now the voices of two people that he loved and trusted, were killing him softly.

"I told you not to fuck with Shark, but you wouldn't listen. You never listen to me, but yet you claim to love me."

"Don't fuck wit' me Lisa. You know goddamn well how I feel about you. I never listen to anyone, including my moms, who I love with everything I got. It ain't got shit to do with not listening. I just know what's best for me. The decisions regarding me, need to be made by me, and that's that!"

"Whatever Chino."

Donell couldn't listen to anymore. He knew all he needed to know. He let out the overdue cough he had been holding in. Lisa and Chino looked at each other, realizing they had took for granted Donell was still knocked out from the sedatives. They both scurried toward his bedside.

Donell's eyes fluttered. He could not muster the strength to open them. He just twisted his head slightly to the left. Lisa spoke, "Baby, can you hear me?" Donell didn't respond. Chino tried, "Yo Dee, it's me man, It's Chino ... " Still, no response. They assumed he was still sedated. Donell appeared incoherent. Lisa and Chino continued their conversation.

"Look, I just came to holla at Dee one more time before I left for VA. I wanna see you one more time before I go. Is that gon' be possible?"

"No Chino. I'm not leaving Donell. I'm going to go get some more things from the house and come back here. Donell's mother should be back in the morning."

"So let me take you to do that."

"You just said you're a wanted man right now. You expect me to let you take me somewhere? That's your meaning of love huh!"

"Come on Baby Girl, you know I would never get you caught up in this shit. Shark has no clue that Donell is in this hospital and he doesn't know where you live."

"You never know. Who knows where the hell those niggas are? I'm not going to be anybody's statistic or in the wrong place at the wrong time. I don't have time for that street shit anymore Chino. That's what fucked me and Donell up and it's going to fuck you up too! Shit, it already has. What the fuck was all this for? A million dollars that yo' ass may not even live to spend! It's just not worth it Chino."

Donell listened to his girl speak to his best friend. They were engaged in a conversation that would have emanated between the two of THEM. He just couldn't fathom the concept. The deception was amazing. Donell really would have never truly believed they would have betrayed him this way. The two people he trusted more than anyone in the world.

"When Dee wakes up, just let him know that I did come to check for him, a'ight?"

"So that's it Chino?"

"Lis, what do you expect me to do? You want me to stay here and get killed, while Dee lies there dying? What exactly are you saying?"

"I don't even know what the hell I'm saying anymore Chino. I'm tired. I'm confused. All of this shit just came out of nowhere."

Chino looked at Lisa. She looked tired. "Come here Baby Girl."

Lisa looked over to see if there was any motion or sign of consciousness in Donell. There was none. She knew that she should in no way be intimate with Chino in this room, but God himself knew, she needed to be held. Lisa walked to Chino and let him embrace her. He held her, inhaling the essence of her being, the fragrance of her body. He really loved her very

141

much. Lisa had all the qualities that delighted the eyes and mind of any man. She was succumbing to Chino's touch, as she always had.

"So. When were y'all going to tell me that my dawg, my number one dawg, was fuckin' my lady?" Donell spoke, no longer feeling weak and helpless after being funneled a host of treatment intravenously.

Lisa quickly broke free from Chino. Both of them looked to each other in bewilderment. There was no way out of it. This was the moment that was destined to be upon them since the commencement of their betrayal.

"Yo Dee man, it's not like that man. I'm not even gon' get all into it 'cause you not feelin' well, but it's not like that man. I never meant to do you dirty man. " Chino wanted to be anywhere else right now. He always wondered how they were going to break it to Donell, and it happened to be unknowingly.

Lisa had a very perplexed look on her face. She just didn't know what to say. She looked from Chino to Donell, back to Chino, back to Donell.

"You lucky I'm in this bed motherfucker, 'cause I'd kill you," seethed Donell.

It all began to replay in his mind. Chino staring at Lisa as she went for their drinks. Lisa tellin' him to ask "his boy". The conversation they had when Lisa initially left. Chino blaming him for everything, telling him Lisa probably didn't want to be found. Now he understood. While he was sick, discovering he had a life threatening illness, his best friend was discovering a life with his woman.

Donell looked to Lisa. She couldn't look at him. "Lisa," Donell called. She still had the same look on her face. Lisa was

142

undeniably in shock. "Lisa, baby," Donell called again. Lisa turned to him. Her face was soaked with tears. Donell asked, "Why?" Chino went to reach for her, to comfort her.

"Don't you fuckin' touch her!" Donell yelled. Lisa sprang to his side. "Baby, please take it easy, you're not well. I'm sorry, now isn't a good time for this. Chino is not even supposed to be in the hospital this late, so we really need to be careful."

Donell interjected, "No, he needs to be careful!"

Chino knew Donell was upset and he had every right to be, so he remained silent as Donell took jabs at his manhood. They both knew this was killing the very fiber on which their friendship was built.

"You need to go on and break out Chino." Lisa said, requesting that Chino leave the hospital.

"I need to holla at you first, then I'll go, but not without talking to you!" Chino insisted.

"She don't have nothin' to say to you man, neither the fuck do I, so do what she said and break out Chino." Donell attempted to get up, but the tubes restricted his ability.

"Look man, I know this shit is comin' out real fucked up right now. Shit, you may not ever talk to me again, but it wasn't like we set out to deliberately hurt you man. You need to really understand that," Chino tried to explain.

Lisa again looked from one to the other. She still didn't know what to do or say.

Donell studied her. He noticed she resembled a lost child. When she looked to him, he looked at her curiously. What was going on? Had his best friend infiltrated what they had built in eight years? He knew damn well she couldn't love him, could she?

143

"Lisa you need to let Chino know that he should leave before I alert the hospital that he's here and have him arrested." Donell decided to pull rank.

"So you gon' take the pussy way out huh? Look I know you sick man. I just came here to say good-bye. I'm not going to cause no shit. This ain't the place. When shit calms down I'll contact you ... both." Chino looked into Lisa's eyes and said, "Baby Girl, if you have any feelings left for me at all, just step into the hallway for thirty seconds, please?"

Chino exited the room. Lisa looked at Donell. He knew. She didn't have to say anything. He turned his head. She rushed out the door. Chino waited. He knew she would come out to talk to him.

"Chino, it's over now. You need to make shit right with Shark so we can figure all this shit out." Lisa pleaded.

"Look, I need to see you one last time. I swear you won't get into no shit and I promise you won't regret it." Chino held Lisa's face close to his own. He breathed his breath in her ears, followed by soft kisses. "Please Baby Girl, if something happens to me, if I could be with you just one more time, I don't even think I would give a fuck."

"Meet me back at the Marriott. I still have the room." Lisa knew at that very moment, she was either crazy or absolutely caught up in this man.

"Let me get your key. They ain't gon' let me up there without you. Just tell them you lost your key, they'll give you another one. " Chino said.

Lisa noticed a nurse coming their way. She swung Chino into the stairwell and leaned against the door to prevent anyone from entering. Lisa dug for her key. She hated the fact she always had so much shit in her bag. She could never find

144

things as quickly as she needed. She finally came across the key, which resembled a credit card. She gave it to Chino. Chino looked at Lisa and smiled. "Don't make me wait too long." Chino dashed down the stairs.

Lisa emerged from the stairwell. She rushed back into the room, only to find Donell's room swarming with nurses and a security officer.

"Tell them Lisa!" Donell demanded.

"Tell them what?" Lisa questioned.

"Tell them that we just had an intruder in my room. Chino Wells. He's probably still in the hospital," Donell continued. The security officer was jotting down something on his pad. He then said, "We had a report from the front desk that there was a gentleman inquiring on Mr. Stephens' room number. He demanded a supervisor, but then disappeared. Now Mr. Stephens has alerted us to the fact that a, Mr. Wells came in threatening him."

"Donell, what are you talking about?" Lisa was not going to play along with this. Chino had enough people after him already. "Mr. Wells was very concerned about Donell. Mr. Wells is leaving town tonight and wanted to make sure he said good-bye to Donell."

"You gon' lie for that motherfucker!" Donell was disgusted. He couldn't believe what he was hearing. Not only did she rush out after him, but she was standing in front if his face lying, defending him. He already knew the answer to the question of her feelings for Chino.

"Mrs. Stephens, regardless of Mr. Wells coming to visit for a harmless reason, he was on the hospital premise unlawfully, and we must report it." The security guard could sense there was more going on, but decided not to pry.

"My name is Miss Spencer. Donell you know you shouldn't let this happen. He risked his life coming to check for you." Lisa wanted Donell to retract everything he said, but he wouldn't. That was the least he could do for what he felt Chino had done to him.

"I don't feel safe. He might try to come back to finish the job!" Donell complained.

"I really don't believe you Donell. You know damn well Chino wasn't trying to hurt you. What the hell are you trying to do?" Lisa realized Donell was hurt and upset, but she felt he was acting like a "bitch".

"I'm leaving ... " Lisa looked at Donell. He was still filling the security guard with information or should we say misinformation about Chino.

"Where you going? You goin' back to your boy Lisa?"

"I'm going to get some things and then I was coming back here. Now if you don't want me to come back Donell, say the word, because I'm tellin' you I'm tired of all of this bullshit."

"Oh I want you to come back. We have a whole lot to talk about. Don't you think?"

Lisa just looked from him to the security guard, nodded in agreement and left the room.

GOODBYE FOR NOW

Shark was fed up to say the least. His soul mate had been murdered in cold blood by a man whom he had, and would have given almost anything. And he couldn't get his hands on him. He called Lil' James to let him know he was now in Brooklyn and to get directions to the hospital where Shelly's body still remained. He still didn't believe he was ready to see her, but he could not allow the mother of his only daughter, the love of his life, to stay at a morgue in an unfamiliar hospital any longer.

"Yeah Lil' James, it's me. I'm out here. Where are you?" Shark asked.

"I'm still here at the hospital. They won't release her to me. They say I'm not her next of kin and I don't have no identification to say I know her," Lil' James explained to Shark.

"How the hell do I get there from Stuyvesant Avenue?" Shark was losing his cool. He hated Brooklyn. Ironically, he lived in the borough the first half of his years in the States, but for some reason he never vibed with the cats in Brooklyn. He felt they were always out to get something for nothing. Nor did he learn to navigate his way around this complicated borough.

Lil' James gave him the best directions he could. Shark advised his men of what his next step was. Chino had obviously eluded them this time, but the more he slipped away, the more furious Shark became. Goo drove to the hospital. Shark ranted and raved in his native tongue with a vengeance.

147

Why had Chino done this? What did he have to gain? Surely he knew the money wouldn't last forever.

"Boss I'm telling you when we find him, he'll wish he never fixed his twisted mind to fuck you over!" Butch attempted to calm Shark, but it wasn't working.

"Me a kill his bomba rass, me a kill im' me say! Him a kill my 'oman an a g'won as if him never did a ting, me say me want his blood clad head !!!"

They pulled up to St. Claire's hospital. Shark couldn't move. Lil' James was waiting outside in front. He saw that Shark was not in good shape. He rushed to the vehicle.

"Hey Shark, come on man." Lil' James tried to help him out of the SUV. Shark's eyes pierced through Lil' James with a venomous glare. He looked at Lil' James as if he was his worst enemy.

"It was you he was looking to kill, not my Shelly!" Shark was in a mood that no one had ever seen in him. He was in the game too long not to know that your closest loved ones could at any time serve as your enemies' casualty.

Lil' James backed off and let Butch and the others handle the situation. He did and didn't understand why Shark was reacting in the manner in which he was. 'Who told Shelly to take it upon herself to involve herself in a man's business anyway?

Yeah she could have asked all the questions in the world, but to actually follow someone to unknown territory. Lil' James did know one thing, it was supposed to be him in that morgue and Shark knew it too.

Hench held Shark up, "Look man, I know this is hard as shit, but you got to go in there and have them arrange for

Shelly to be moved to Harlem man."

Goo pulled Lil' James to the side. "You know he's just uptight right now. He'll be alright. This shit is just getting a little out of hand. Now we know Chino was in Roosevelt Projects 'cause his vehicle is through. We lit that shit up like the Christmas tree at Rockefeller Center, but he wasn't in it, so he's still out there somewhere and I'm telling you we need to find this motherfucker, it's crucial!"

"Yo, you don't think I know that man. I've been out here tracking this motherfucker's every step. I know he was running something out of the Roosevelt, but word is that his boys ain't pumpin' no more. I got connects everywhere, but right now, don't nobody seem to know nothin'."

"Well we better comb these motherfuckin' streets until we find something. This shit can't go down like this." Hench said. He felt for his cousin. Shark was going through it and naturally so, he and Shelly had been together for as long as he could remember.

"I'm on it man. I never got off of it!" Lil' James was determined to find Chino and bring him or his body to Shark.

"I'm out, y'all know how to get back right?" Lil' James asked.

"We'll be a'ight, go on and do what you do." Hench told Lil' James.

Lil' James didn't bother to try to talk to Shark, he knew what he had to do and words didn't have shit to do with it.

*   *   *   *

Butch decided he would stay in the vehicle and leave Shark and the others to deal with the matter. Butch never did favor

149

hospitals. His mother went into a hospital one day and never came back out. That was nearly ten years ago, and he's never gone into a hospital since. He vowed if he was sick he would treat himself, if that didn't work, oh well ...

Shark mustered up every ounce of strength he had left in his body and led his men into St. Claire's. He stopped at the front desk and requested assistance. He explained why he was there. He was given a pass to the sub-level and told that he could go, but he could only take one additional person with him, preferably a family member. Hench immediately agreed he would accompany his cousin. Goo went back to join Butch.

The elevator ride down was a solemn one. As soon as they got off of the elevator, signs with arrows spelled out their direction. What was a ten second walk to the large steel double doors labeled "morgue", literally took Shark and Hench fifteen minutes to approach.

Hench looked over at Shark. Shark looked wounded, like he himself had just taken a bullet in his gut. He didn't want to see her like this. He didn't know if he could. The coroner came out from behind the doors.

"Hello gentlemen. Are you here to identify someone?"
Hench expected Shark to answer, but when he didn't hear anything he looked over again to see why. Shark had such a blank stare on his face, it was as if he was not there. He definitely hadn't heard the coroner's question. Hench responded, "Uh, yes, we are here to identify Shelly, uh," Hench realized at that moment, that in all the years he knew Shelly, that's the only name he knew. "Shark, man, I don't, I don't know Shelly's last name."

"We are here to identify Michelle Marshall." Shark spoke as if a spirit entered into him to bring him back from the daze he had been in. He knew Shelly would not understand him behaving in such a weak manner, even if it was due to the loss of her life. She had always been attracted to the power Shark possessed. She always commented to him that she loved his strength. Shelly felt as long as she was with him, she had nothing to worry about or fear. Shark felt her now, empowering him to do what he knew he had to do.

"I see. Come on inside." The coroner backed his way through the door and held it open for Shark and Hench to enter. Hench immediately noticed the smell. It was a mixture which reeked of iodine and death. The walls of dim chrome that held a portion of the citys' newly deceased were unnerving. The gray floors appeared black in color. This room did nothing, except emanated the vertigo which Shark was experiencing.

The coroner introduced himself. "I'm Humphrey. I can show you the body, or really in this case, what's left of her."

Sharks' insides were in knots. There was no feeling to describe what he was feeling. All he knew was that he had never felt this bad in his life.

"Are you sure you wanna do this man? We can have her sent to Unity on 124th St and let them take care of her, maybe they can fix her up real good," Hench suggested.

"I doubt she'll be able to have an open coffin," Humphrey said with no regard. He did this day in and day out and showed very little compassion. To him this was just a job.

"I want to see my wife!" Shark yelled.

"Sure. No problem. Come this way." Humphrey led Shark around the wall of refrigerated corpses to a mass array of chrome columned rows. He walked to the second row, and looked back at Shark who was all of a sudden stuck, "Mr. Marshall, if you'd rather come back another time I

151

understand." Humphrey noticed Shark was acting a bit odd. He'd seen people hesitate before, but he seemed downright petrified. Hench knew something had to be wrong because Shark didn't bother correcting the coroner regarding his name. "I'm cool mon'." Shark began walking to where Humphrey had been standing. Humphrey then disappeared from his sight into the long row of chrome refrigerators. As Shark was turning in to follow, he stopped again when he saw Humphrey pulling open one of the large drawers. He saw Shelly's foot. She always kept her feet done with an exotic design on her toenails. He approached the open drawer. He noticed the foot looked nothing like Shelly's, until, he saw her toes. Humphrey looked at Shark. He could tell a positive identification had already been made. "I'm warning you Mr. Marshall. You may not want to see her like this."

Shark had seen many gory sights. He had been an instrumental part in a lot of them, but there was nothing that could prepare for him for what he was about to witness. Humphrey pulled the drab blue sheet from what was left of Shelly's body. Shark was immediately sickened when he saw what was left of the woman he loved with all of his heart, the mother of his child, and his only true friend. Shelly's entire right side, from her head down to her torso, had been stripped away, literally mutilated. If Shark hadn't seen her toes, he may have questioned her identity altogether, but he had to accept and deal with the fact that he had made a positive identification of Shelly and arrangements needed to be made.

"You can cover her now."
Shark walked slowly back to where Hench had been standing. Hench hadn't moved an inch since entering the

152

stench filled room. One look at Shark was all he needed to know that it was in fact Shelly. Shark told Hench to give Humphrey the details regarding the location of the funeral home and to call Scotty. Scotty was the mortician at Unity Funeral Home. He knew Shark very well. Shark kept him in business. Scotty would take care of everything. Shark was in need of air. He opened the large double doors, coming into what seemed like a new life. He breathed a deep breath. This all seemed to be one big nightmare he hoped he was about to wake up from.

Shark called Lil' James, "I need to find Chino now, me can't wait no blood clad more. A' my baby mudda a lie in a morgue wit' half her face there upon a slab, me a kill his blood clad rass a right fuckin now ya know!" Shark was beyond the point of being fed up. "I want a contract on his head. Fifty thousand dollars. Anybody that sees him, fuck keepin' him alive, kill him! I will curse his blood clad corpse sien! A me want him!"

"The word is out Shark," Lil' James replied.

"Where is his sidekick, the blood clad boy who just came home, a Donell me think say him real name?"

"I haven't seen him at all Shark. He wasn't with Chino out in Brooklyn. Maybe he's not fucking around with Chino, seein' as he just came home."

Shark replied slowly, "Yeah, maybe, but check his whereabouts. Check out his bitch. Check all of Chino's bitches that you know. He couldn't have fuckin' rass clad disappeared into thin air!"

"I'm on it." There was a long silence. "Shark."

"A me already know what you fe' say and me know, jus'

find him."

Lil' James was going to tell Shark once again how sorry he was. He would have taken the bullets had he known, even though his feelings for Shelly were what they were. He would have never wished this for her.

Lil' James placed several calls. The word was out! There was a bounty on Chino's head on a first come, first served basis. However, Lil' James was determined to save his boss some money on this one, as well as do what he should have done from the moment he suspected Chino. If he could only find him. .

TIME TO PAY THE PIPER

"I don't know what Camaria was talkin' about," Karen said. "All I know is Donell is sick in a hospital."

"Well, what the hell else do you know? I know you got to know more than that petty bullshit." Lil' James probed.

"No I don't. That's one hundred percent of what I know. I ain't got no time for this bullshit James. Camaria and me are tight. She ain't fucking with Chino. She used to, but that was a long time ago. Camaria said Donell had been taken to a hospital, but she didn't say which hospital or for what reason. I'm getting as much info as I can."

"Fuck all that! I know you can get something better than that for me."

Karen had been a friend of Shark and Shelly's for a long time, but she had been friends with Camaria for a long time as well. "I'm just tellin' you the info I'm gettin' back. Donell was brought to Camaria's house and then taken to a hospital. I don't know which one."

"I'm going to ask you one more time. What the fuck do you know?"

"I know something ain't right. Camaria told me that they had to take Donell to a hospital to have him checked out. He was vomiting and pissing all over himself an' shit!"

"Did she say Chino took him to the hospital?"
Karen saw where this was heading. She didn't want to get anybody into anything. She knew Chino had brought Donell to Camaria's. She also knew that Lisa had been fucking Chino.

155

Being that, Camaria was nice enough to share it with her during their last conversation, but she didn't want to implicate Camaria or Lisa, or Chino for that matter. Karen always played the neutral role. She felt it was the best way to stay alive in the game.

"Look when I talked to Camaria, she didn't say how Donell got to her house or who took him to the hospital, but if you want to me call her and ask her all of these questions, scare her and make her suspicious, I'd be more than happy to."

"Shit just ain't addin' up. I don't get it! This shit ain't even that complicated, but yet every day the answers are slipping further and further away, except for the known fact that Chino killed Shelly."

"What did you say?" Karen was blown away. "Chino killed who?"

"That motherfucker killed Shelly, thinking he was shootin' at me out in Brooklyn. Shark got a motherfuckin' bounty on his head, but I want that motherfucker. Now I'm gonna ask you again...What the fuck do you know exactly!?" Lil' James' eyes represented slits of piercing anger.

"Oh my God! What in the world?" Karen was still absorbing the dreadful statement that had just been made.

"Karen, you know we go back. I know Shelly and you were mad cool at one time. If you know anything, you owe it to her to tell me so I can make this shit right. "

Karen didn't know what to do, nor what to say. Shelly was dead, that was a horrible thing, but if she gave any information, more people would die, that blood, she didn't want on her hands.

"James if I knew where Chino was I swear on my mother, I

would tell you, but I don't! Now what I can do is try to see who knows what. Maybe someone has seen or heard something by now."

"Yeah alright Karen, you got my number, make sure you use it." Lil' James gave Karen one last questioning glance before leaving.

*   *   *   *

Karen immediately called Camaria, "Mari, Lil' James just left here talkin' about Chino killed Shelly, and asking me if I know where he is and do I know who brought him to the hospital and, and ... "

"Karen, slow down, hold up! What?" Camaria couldn't believe her ears. "Chino did what?"

"He killed Shelly. He thought it was Lil' James he was shootin' at, but it was Shelly and he killed her. Shark put a contract out on Chino, but Lil' James really wants to find him first!"

"What in the fuck is going on?" Camaria's head was spinning. "Last week everything was normal, now all hell is breaking loose. Does Lisa know all of this?"

"I don't know! He didn't mention Lisa and neither did I. James doesn't know Lisa like that."

Camaria said, "I know one thing. I better call her and let her know what's up. Chino may or may not have put her up on shit!" Camaria was wondering exactly how much Lisa in fact, did know. After all, she was being very secretive about the whole situation. Was she in on this shit with Chino?

"Karen I'll call you back. Let me call Lisa and see what the hell is going on."

Camaria decided even if Lisa had been in on it from the beginning, she owed it to her best friend to hip her to what was going on. She called her cell, no answer. The machine came on, playing the late Aliyah's "Can I Talk to You?" Camaria left a message, "Lisa, I really need to talk to you. I just got some disturbing news and I need to advise you as to the particulars of the mishap. Please call me as soon as you get this message. I know you know who this is."

She two-wayed Lisa, "Shit is hot as hell-- call me asap, Mari"

Camaria didn't know what to do. She figured Lisa was still at the hospital with Donell and maybe turned her phone off, but then again Lisa had not been answering lately. Camaria decided it couldn't hurt to try going to the hospital, but then realized visiting hours were over a long time ago.

Camaria then thought to call to see what room Donell was in. Lisa surely arranged for him to have a telephone in his room so that his family and friends could call him. She dialed information, "What city and state?" The automated voice requested.

"Bronx, New York." Camaria replied.

"What listing?"

"Bronx Lebanon Hospital." Camaria replied .

"Please hold while the operator retrieves that number ... " A live operator came on line, "Would you like the general number or a particular department?"

Camaria was about to take her frustration out on the operator but decided against it, "Can I have the number to admissions, please?"

The operator questioned, "Admissions?"

Camaria stated sarcastically, "Yes, admissions, you know when someone goes to the hospital and they are actually admitted?"

The operator detected the attitude, but decided not to feed into it. "Sure dear. Is there anything else I can help you with?" Camaria snapped, "Anything else! You haven't even given me the first number I just asked you for, Goddamnit can I please just have the fucking number to admissions?" Camaria regained her composure, "Look, Miss! No thank you. There is nothing else I would like, just that one little itty bitty number, ok?"

The operator shifted Camaria's call back to the automated format, she then heard, "That number, 555-4040 can automatically be dialed for an additional charge of thirty cents by pressing "1" now." The phone rang five times before a voice answered, "Bronx Lebanon."

"Hi, I am trying to locate my brother. His name is Donell Stephens and he was brought there earlier today?" Camaria knew they would not just give the number to anyone, so she laid on the "sister" act.

The voice responded, "Hold on." Easy listening music played in Camaria's ears as she held. The voice returned moments later, "Uh, we do have a Donell Stephens, he was admitted earlier today, but I have been told by my superiors that he is under guard and that no information is to be given regarding his actual room number."

"Under guard?" Camaria became worried immediately. "Did someone try to hurt him?"

The voice spoke, "Again, I am not able to furnish you with that information. I was told there is a list of people who are able to see Mr. Stephens. If you give me your name I can check

159

and see if you're one of the lucky ones." Camaria thought for a moment, Donell definitely didn't think to add her name to his list, they were ok now, but still, "Uh, my name is Lisa, Lisa Spencer. Spencer is my married name. "

"Well I do see a Lisa Spencer, but it says that you are actually his fiancé. I thought you said you're his sister? "

"Uh, well I," Camaria was stuck. "Well I am his fiancé, but I don't really like telling everyone that, as you said yourself he's under guard. There is a lot going on right now, and I myself am trying to stay safe, if you know what I mean." Camaria figured she didn't have anything to lose at this point, so she went for it "Look, why I'm calling is, I ordered a phone for Donell's room, but the number they gave me isn't working?"

The voice asked, "What number did they give you?" This wasn't going to be easy.

"They gave me a number that is ringing to a Chinese restaurant." Lisa grabbed a take out menu that was on the table and read the number to the woman on the other end of the phone. Camaria knew this was a long shot, but again, she didn't have anything to lose. There was silence. "I show his number to be 555-0504, the last three digits represent the patients' room number." Camaria couldn't believe it was just that easy.

"You know they did say something about that, thank you, sorry to trouble you."

The voice on the other end had begun to say, "no trouble at all", but unfortunately, heard a very loud click after the first two   words.

Camaria immediately dialed Donell's room. She was about to give up and hang up after the sixth ring, but he finally picked up. "Hello." Donell said.

"Dee, this is Mari. What the hell is going on? Karen called me saying that they put a contract out on Chino because he killed Shelly and that Lil' James is looking for Chino, you, Lisa and me too!, " she continued, "Then when I try to get information on you, they tell me you're under guard. Is everything ok? Is Lisa with you?"

"No Camaria, she left, she ... " Donell couldn't get it out of his mouth.

"She what?" Camaria asked.

Donell was quiet.

"She what? Donell did something happen to Lisa?"

"No, nothing has happened to her, not that I know of anyway."

Camaria heard the disdain in his voice. "Donell what's up? First of all, how are you? I'm sorry for not asking that first."

"I'm alright. I do have some rare form of leukemia, but they're pumping me with some shit that's making me feel better, I guess."

"Did Lisa go back to the house? I tried to call her on her cell, but I got voice mail. I also two-wayed her, but I have yet to hear a word. Sound familiar?"

"I'm surprised you don't know." Donell said.

"Know what? I seem to be the one who doesn't know shit, but I know one thing, if a motherfucker got my name in his mouth to hurt me from some bullshit that Chino did, somebody better fill me in quick!"

"Mari, Lisa and Chino, they," Donell just could not bring himself to say it, especially to Camaria. She had to know, of course she knew. She was making him feel like an ass, like she always did. "You mean to tell me that you didn't know they were fuckin', Camaria?"

Camaria looked at the receiver, then put it back to her ear, "Uh, well, no, I mean not until earlier today. I tried to get it out of Lisa, but she wouldn't admit to it."

Camaria was shocked, "So you tellin' me that she told you that?"

"Well she didn't volunteer the info. They were nice enough to give me a front row seat for the Lisa and Chino show." Donell surprisingly didn't feel awkward talking to Camaria about it. She apparently had just started to put it together herself.

"I couldn't get away from the conversation if I had wanted to, they thought I was knocked out from the medication, but I heard every fucking word they said!"

"Oh no! I don't believe this. So what, they left together?" Camaria asked, trying to make heads or tails of all the drama that was now unfolding.

"They didn't leave together, but they are probably together right now." Donell had an uneasy feeling in the pit in his stomach just thinking of what Chino and Lisa were doing.

"Do you know why Chino killed Shelly?" Camaria asked.

"No, I don't, but I don't think Chino meant to kill her. Him and Shelly were tight." Donell revealed.

"Well that doesn't make much of a difference." Camaria needed to know more. "What is really going on Donell?"

"Look Mari I don't feel comfortable talking over the phone. You just never know. I'll put your name down as a special visitor. Come first thing in the morning and I'll be able to put you up on what's going on."

"I don't feel safe staying here. I feel like a sitting duck." Camaria was passed worried. Shit was just getting out of control and she still didn't know what the fuck was going on. Camaria heard her doorbell ring. "Somebody is at my door. I am not expecting anyone. Who the hell would be at my door at this time of night?"

Donell heard the uneasiness in her voice and tried to calm her, "Maybe it's Lisa."

Camaria walked to the door and peeped through the peephole. She ran into the kitchen, "Oh shit Donell, Lil' James is at my door! I don't know shit! Why the fuck is he at my door?" Camaria was nauseated. All she could think of was Lil' James being dissatisfied with how much she didn't know and losing his temper, and hurting her to prove a point, if she was lucky. She knew how the game worked.

"Calm down Mari. Just don't open the door. Act like you're not there, or tell him you have company. Make him think that a man is in the house with you and call the police." Donell tried to offer any suggestions he could.

Lil' James heard activity in the apartment. He began to bang heavily on the door. "Open the door!"

Camaria marched to the door and yelled back, "Open the door? Who are you? I don't know you! Hell no I'm not opening my door. You better get the hell away from my door. I called the cops and they'll be here any minute!"

"Bitch if you know what's good and you want to stay the fuck alive you better open this fuckin' door!" Lil' James was tired of the bullshit. Somebody knew something and they'd better start talking. Shelly had been a casualty, so he didn't give a fuck about the female on the other side of the door.

"Look, I don't know you. I don't know what the fuck you

want with me. I already spoke to Karen and I told her and I'm telling you I don't know shit about any of this, so please take this shit somewhere else !" Camaria pleaded.

Donell felt useless listening to what he was hearing, he was also scared for Camaria. "Mari call the cops right now!" She did as she was told. Donell called the security officer from outside his door, "Yo, I need police dispatched to River Park Towers, building 40 apartment "G"!"

The officer utilized his walkie talkie and radioed for police. Donell began to pull himself up out of the hospital bed, but was restrained by all of the intravenous tubes that were still connected to his body. He started pulling feverishly at the tubes, trying to remove them. He wanted to help Camaria, after all, she was the one who truly looked after him when he got sick. Lisa and Chino were too busy trying to connive to be together. The security officer took notice of what Donell was trying to do, "Whoa man, hold on. You can't leave."

"Yo I gotta' get outta here man! My friend is about to be hurt. She may even be killed. I gotta' go yo!" Donell was out of control. The night duty nurse came barging in, "What is all the commotion about in here? Boy, what are you trying to do, kill yourself?" The nurse asked Donell, while simultaneously trying to get a hold of him to secure the tubes and place him back into his bed. She requested the security officers' assistance. By this time, the entire staff on the floor was in Donell's room.

"I gotta' get out of here, tell them man!" Donell looked to the officer, but the officer fronted. His job came first. As a man, he understood where Donell was coming from, but he had already called for the police to go check out the situation. From what he was witnessing, Donell would not have made it out of the hospital without collapsing. "I have to agree with the nurse man. You're not strong enough to go anywhere."

While Donell was trying to convince both of them that he was absolutely capable of leaving, an orderly snuck up and stuck a needle in his forearm. Donell went ballistic. "What the fuck are you doin'? What the fuck did you just give me? Don't give me that shit! I told y'all motherfuckers I gotta' go!" Donell felt himself getting heavier. His speech began to slur. They had given him a sedative. He was trying to fight it with all of his might, but it was useless. Twenty more seconds and he would be out for the count for at least an hour or two. All he could do was envision what was going on at Camaria's right now.

ENOUGH IS ENOUGH

"I gotta' call Chino and let him know we good." Knees was counting out. Shit couldn't have been sweeter. Fort Greene was new territory for him, but he was thoroughly pleased at how easy it was to move the work. It was pretty much impossible to do what they had just done, especially in unfamiliar territory. Knees vowed at this moment that he would change that unfamiliar to familiar in no time. He thought to himself, 'Like Chino said, as long as we stay together, it's all good.'

"I just can't believe we turned the fucking block out! Motherfuckers are still coming back! Yo we need more work!" Kendu was open. He had never been involved in such a large operation and he was truly intrigued. Shit, at this point, he was addicted to the flow of the money and the power. After all, everyone thought it was his shit that was on the block.

"Ain't no more work. We even did the shit Chino gave you for your own personal. So what we got to work with?" Knees asked.

"I got somebody who can get me some work. I got plenty of money so he'll be more than willing." Kendu was not going to stop the flow while the gettin' was good. This was his chance.

"Well Du, you do what you gotta' do, but our work is done here for right now. I wouldn't mind coming back up here to pump, but right now I gotta' get Chino straight."

"No doubt, no doubt," Kendu agreed.

Knees hit Chino on his two- way, 'shit is gold, already done, call me'.

166

Chino, chilling in the hotel room waiting for Lisa to arrive, received the page. He immediately called Knees. "Yo what up?"

"Like the message said nigga, we done. What's up? Where you want your load dropped?"

"Shit, bring that shit directly to me. That's what's up. I'm tellin' you man, you my mufucka! They don't come no damn better." Chino was proud.

"I'm at the Marriott on 59th, room 417. I want you to call a cab to bring you here. I don't want Bones and the rest of the boys knowing where I am, for their own safety. Just tell them you'll be right back. I'll fill you in when you get here, just get here."

Chino's head was spinning. There was just a little too much going on right now. In his mind, the best thing was that Lisa was on her way to him. The money came secondary. That's how he knew he was completely gone. He thought about Donell, and the look on his face when he discovered the truth. It hurt him that after all they had been through, it had come to this, but it was too late now, way too late.

Chino heard Lisa coming through the door.

"You wouldn't believe how Donell sung like a canary to the hospital security guard! He told them that you threatened his life, and to watch out for you, because you may come back to finish the job! Do you believe that? I know he is sick and I know we hurt him. But," Lisa paused. "Maybe I don't know." Lisa actually had to catch herself and imagine herself in Donell's shoes.

Chino added, "Na, I feel you, I mean I know this is some off the wall shit, but he didn't even want to hear how it went down."

"I could see why he would want to be spared the details Chino."

"Fuck all that! I got other things on my mind, come here," Chino had that sound in his voice. He wanted her.

"Chino how can you think of sex right now with everything that's going on?"

"All I want is you. All I need is you. As long as I have you, I'm good, you hear me?" Chino came up behind Lisa and slipped his hands around her waist. He rested his chin on her shoulder. "I love you Lisa."

Lisa was mentally exhausted and confused. She had waited so long to hear Chino say those words to her, yet under the circumstances, it seemed meaningless. Lisa turned to Chino, "I love you too, but we've crushed Donell. I don't know what I was thinking. Here he is sick, maybe dying and we're in his room, in each other's arms. It's just not right Chino."

"I know, it's not right, but what if we were in there as friends? Would it be odd, us hugging due to our mutual attachment to Dee?"

"No, the hugging we could have explained, but if only I had known he was not completely out of it.. I wouldn't have went on and on the way I did."

"Well there was no way to know so just forget it, it's over. We knew this day would come and it came. Now come here." Chino placed a wet kiss on her neck.

He continued, and she let him. Chino thought if this would be the last time he was to be with Lisa, he was going to make it well worth it. Lisa still had her jacket on. Chino removed without removing his eyes from hers. Lisa couldn't help but blush. He always gave her butterflies in her stomach when he looked into her eyes.

Chino slipped his tongue into her mouth slowly. Lisa returned the gesture. Chino sensuously sucked her tongue as she held it out for him. He ran his fingers through her hair and cupped her neck gently. Chino stopped to again look deeply into Lisa's eyes. He guided her head on a slant to be adjacent with his, and ever so passionately, deeply shoved his tongue into her mouth, kissing her feverishly. Lisa moaned in ecstasy.

"Do it Daddy, do it to me, fuck me."

Chino placed his hand over her mouth, "No Baby Girl, I'm going to make love to you. I've never done that with anyone."

Lisa knew what Chino meant. She knew he never cared about any of those women he was with. He just fucked them. He wanted to make love to her.

Chino lifted Lisa off of her feet and carried her to the bed. He slowly removed Lisa's clothing, planting soft kisses on her creamy chocolate skin as he peeled away her garments. He took in every morsel of her scent. Chino whispered into Lisa's ear, "You will always be mine," he followed that statement with a hot wet tongue, he smothered Lisa's ear with heat and moistness sending her into a minor frenzy. He traced his finger down to her hot, wet, awaiting pussy, already creaming from the pleasure she was receiving. He slowly fingered her soft cushiony mound of tight flesh. Chino had to taste her. He kissed and licked his way down to her volcano of liquid and dove his tongue into her. He went downtown as if this was his last trip. Chino looked up at Lisa, her face expressing sheer joy, his soaking wet from her juices, he didn't want to leave her behind.

169

"Baby Girl?"

Lisa wrapped up in the moment, didn't hear Chino. "Baby Girl!?"

"Uhhmm, yeah Daddy, yeah."

Chino decided he would save what he had to ask until after they made love, not that it would have any more influence on the outcome, of course.

"You like the way Daddy do his pussy?"

"Ooh yes, I love the way Daddy do his pussy." Nothing else seemed to matter when they were in "their world".

Chino came up to meet his ebony beauty. He tongued her deeply, running his hands softly over Lisa's smooth skin. He was drowning in her very being. He couldn't leave without her. He suckled her breasts. Chino lifted himself slightly and gently placed the head of his penis at the very tip of Lisa's awaiting tunnel of pleasure. "Oh please, put it in Daddy, put it in please."

"Put what in Baby Girl?" Chino teased.

"My dick, Daddy, give me my dick." Lisa was totally ready for this extreme pleasure. She secretly craved it.

Chino thrust his hot thick penis into her. He made long slow strokes, savoring every morsel of Lisa's deep, hot love cavity. She was so wet, always. Chino loved this pussy. He couldn't see himself being without it.

"Come with me tonight." Chino couldn't wait any longer.

"Uhm, Daddy don't, not now," Lisa didn't want her orgasm spoiled by Chino's demands.

"Yeah now." He started stroking her pussy with more force. He shoved his tongue into her ear.

"Daddy, don't, please, I can't, don't ask me now." Lisa knew she was putty in his hands. He wasn't playing fair.

Chino tapped his forefinger against her clit. The combination of the three drove her absolutely nuts.

"Come with me Baby Girl. You know you can't be without me. You're addicted to me. I'm addicted to you. I gotta' have you. "

Lisa began to climax, "Ooh, ooh, shit."

"You coming with me Baby Girl?" Chino breathed into Lisa's ear.

"Oh, you fuck my pussy so fucking good." Lisa came all over Chino. She was on cloud eighteen, fuck cloud nine.

Chino was high off of the feeling of his lover coming all over him. He shoved his tongue back into her mouth and made love to Lisa until he came.

"Say you'll come Baby Girl. Say you'll come with me." Chino repeatedly asked through gasps of breath, sweating from his spectacular performance.

Lisa lay naked on the bed, staring into space. Chino just stared at her. He admired this woman for many reasons. He wanted her with him always. Chino wished for a split second that he would have never gone through with this whole mess with Shark, but since he knew there was no going back, he quickly shook the feeling.

Chino kneeled at the bedside, in front of Lisa. He began to stroke her face lightly. "You are so beautiful Lisa. Inside and out. If something happens to me, I want you to know that I have never loved anyone except you, and that's some real shit I'm tellin' you right now. I want you to know that."

"Chino, you know I want to be with you, but everything is so crazy right now. I just don't know. I can't leave right away. I need to be with Donell right now. Maybe in a few weeks I can come down. You said Virginia right? I can meet you. You can pick me up from the airport or the train, whichever one I decide to take, ok baby, but I have to do what's right. It won't sit right with me if I don't. Can you understand that?"

"I understand. I don't like it, but a few weeks is cool." Chino lay back on the bed. He stretched himself out, pondering, a few weeks. The phone rang.

Lisa was startled. "Who could that be?"

"It's Knees. He came to hit me with the rest of the cake."

"Why did you have him meet you here Chino? What if he was followed?"

"Na Baby Girl, it ain't like that," Chino responded as he picked up the receiver and placed it to her ear. Lisa gave him a hard, yet playful nudge in the stomach, "Yes," Lisa answered,

"Sure, you can send him up."

Lisa gave Chino a slip of tongue as she got up. She gathered some articles of clothing and headed to the bathroom. She was startled a second time by an abrupt knock on the door. "Damn he knocking like the Goddamn police. Check him on that shit Chino. This ain't no Super 8 motel."

"Chill baby. This is my little man. He's cool."

Chino went to the door. He looked through the thick microscopic lens in the door to make sure there would be no surprises on the other side. He didn't see anyone. "Announce yourself!"

"It's me man, Knees."

Chino opened the door. Knees rolled in. "Yo, it was no joke getting in and out of that motherfuckin' cab man. That shit ain't for me."

Chino chuckled. "I apologize for putting you through that shit Baby Boy, but I couldn't take no chances."

"It's all good Boss." Knees was just happy to see that Chino was still in one piece. He handed Chino the duffle bag. Chino quickly scanned the contents. There was no need count it. He trusted Knees just that much.

"So what's up from here Boss?"

"Same thing Baby Boy. I'm out. I'll be leaving as soon as I can tie up a few loose ends and get to Penn Station."

"But we got everything off, why do you still have to leave?"

Knees really didn't want Chino to leave. He was all he knew as a father figure, without Chino, he would have no one to make him feel important.

"I know Baby Boy, but this shit is a little bigger than just the money right now. I crossed a partner of mine, as you already know. Them niggas are heavily on my motherfuckin' trail, so the best thing for me to do is breakout until shit settles itself a bit." Chino wondered why all of a sudden Knees acted as if he didn't understand "what is was". Then it dawned on him, he was all Knees' had.

"Man look, I know you don't think you can get rid of me that easily. I'm not ever going to be out of your life. We have our two-ways, cell phones, and when I get straight, ain't no doubt I'ma' holla so Bones can bounce you and a couple of our other soldiers down to check for me. You know I'ma' have shit pumpin' down there in no time.

Knees smiled, "That's wha's up!" He reached up and hugged Chino. Chino hugged him back.

Lisa emerged from the bathroom. She was taken aback by this youngster in a wheel chair. Chino introduced the two. "Baby Girl, this is Knees, Baby Boy, this is Lisa." He could tell that Lisa was surprised at what stood, or rather sat before her.

They traded greetings. Chino continued, "So my favorite girl in the world, next to my moms of course, finally gets to meet my favorite cat, even though he's a minor cat." Chino smiled.

Knees stared at Lisa. Lisa in return, stared at Knees. Chino looked back and forth between the both of them, grinning. His pager went off, 'Mari in tbl - D."

"Baby Girl, D pagin' me telling me Camaria's in trouble."

"Trouble? What kind of trouble? Goddamnit Chino! What the fuck is going on?" Lisa was hysterical. "I'm going to find out right now, enough is enough!" Lisa was at her limit. She dialed Camaria's. It seemed as though the telephone rang endlessly before it was picked up.

"Hello." A man's voice spoke.

"Hello! Who the hell is this? Where is Camaria?" What the fuck have you done with my best friend!?" Lisa screamed.

"Ma'am, I'm sorry. This is officer Boyd with the NYPD."

"NYPD, Oh my God! What happened? Where is Camaria, the resident of the residence you're in?"

"M'am please calm yourself. I am not able to supply you with the full details. We've pretty much just arrived here at the scene."

"The scene? What scene? Please God, tell me Camaria is ok!"

"Again I'm sorry M'am, but I'm unable to give you any pertinent information at this time. What I can tell you is that the victim has been rushed to Metropolitan Hospital. You may want to try calling them." The officer hung up. Lisa stared into the receiver in sheer horror. "Victim, he called Mari a victim. Oh my God!" Lisa instantly felt sick to her stomach. She didn't know how she knew, but she knew something terrible had happened.

"What happened Baby Girl?"

"I don't know what the fuck happened. They took Camaria to Metropolitan Hospital. He wouldn't tell me what happened. He called her a 'victim'."

"They call everybody "victims," Chino said.

"No the fuck they don't. They call victims, victims, and I'm sure she's a victim behind this bullshit you're caught up in." Lisa was hot. "This shit is way out of control Chino. Instead of you plotting your get-away, you need to be stepping to Shark and killin' this shit before somebody gets killed, if they haven't already."

"Once I breakout, Shark will just send the heat where he thinks I am." Chino replied.

"Are you listening to yourself? Who's to say just because you get away, one of us won't end up a fucking casualty? What about me Chino? That's how much you love me?" Lisa wouldn't let it go.

"Come on now Baby Girl, you already know none of this shit has anything to do with my feelings for you. I'll admit, shit is going a little off course, but a lot of unexpected shit was thrown in the game. I'm doing what I feel I need to do."

"Well what I need to do is call the hospital and check on Camaria. You need to call Donell and ask him if he knows anything since he's the one who paged you."

Chino frowned. "I'm the last person he wants to talk to and you should know that. He probably called me because he figured I may go over there to help Mari. You call him. I'll call the hospital."

"But then he'll know we're together ... " Lisa still felt

awkward even though Donell knew about the two of them. "He apparently doesn't mind talking to you. He paged you."
Chino agreed just to make peace. He dialed Donell's room. Donell answered immediately, "Hello."

"Donell it's me Chino."

"Yeah man, Camaria's in trouble, she said Lil' James was at her door."

"Lil' James. That's impossible." Chino's head was spinning.

"She said that Lil' James' told Karen that Shark put a contract on you for killing Shelly!"

"What?" Chino was in shock.

Donell was still feeling a little weak from the sedative. His voice began to sound faint. "How could you do that man? That woman ain't never been nothin' but good to you and for you man. What the fuck is happening to you dawg?"

"I'm good, man. I'm just shooting craps. Right now, shit's rolling a little offbeat. I ain't mean to kill Shelly! That's my word! I thought I was deadin' that little midget motherfucker. He caught on to what went down and he called me with the shit. Somebody was following me during my operation in Brooklyn and I thought it was his pussy ass. I didn't know it was Shelly. I would have never guessed that it was, man, that's my word. That was my motherfuckin' girl, man."

"I still ain't fucking speaking to you motherfucker," Donell said with venom in his voice. "I just wanted you to know what was going on. Is Lisa there with you?"

Chino looked at Lisa. She was on the hotel phone trying to navigate her way through the hospital's red tape. He didn't want to hurt his friend anymore. "Na man, I said my good-byes at the hospital. She must be going to take care of some shit for you. Maybe she went to check on your moms."

"Yeah, she said she was going to get some things and come back!" Donell wanted Chino to know his position. That he still had Lisa, and if up to him, that's how it was to remain.

"Alright, well I'm gone man." Chino attempted to end the conversation. Donell refused to let him off that easily. "Why, man?" Chino knew he would. He wished he didn't, but he did.

"Are you ready to hear this?" Chino asked.

"Hell no motherfucker, but I need to know!"

"She's the only woman I have ever loved. We didn't set out for it to happen, but she was alone for so long man. She needed somebody to listen to her, to hold her." Chino had to catch himself. He was surprised that Donell was still on the line.

"I just can't believe you did this shit to me man. This is me, man." Donell expressed his hurt.

"Honestly man, I'm just glad we're talking about it, just in case something does happen to me. I will at least be at peace with you."

"What you gon' do Chino?" Donell was still concerned for his best friend's welfare.

"Right now, I'm trying to break out for a while, but I gotta' find out what happened to Camaria."

"Shit man, all this talk I forgot!" Donell began to get excited.

"Calm down Dee. I got my lil' nigga here with me checkin' shit out. We already know that she's in Metropolitan Hospital. We'll know her condition in a few. You need to get some rest though. I'll handle shit."

"Chino,"

"Yeah man?"

"Be careful, man."

"No doubt. No doubt."

Chino hung up. Lisa was still on the phone. She was getting very agitated with the person on the other end.

Chino rubbed his forehead with his hands. He sighed deeply. He looked over to Knees. Knees was silent. He was curious as to what Chino was going to do. His back was pretty much up against the wall. There really was no way to kill the beef with Shark. It was way beyond that point. Things had gone too far.

"I have no choice." Chino spoke to no one in particular.

"Kill or be killed."

"Boss, why don't you let me call in the troops?" Knees wanted to help.

"It's bigger than our junior army Baby Boy. I don't want none of my lil' niggas' blood on my hands from some dumb shit I did. Even if I handle Shark myself, his boys are going to make good on the contract out on me. Shit, they would fatten the pot. The only way out is for Lisa and me to break out. I need to think about what I can do to make this shit right. Shit went totally off course. Shelly had nothing to do with this. That's why Shark is out to do me in. I could have gotten him straight on the money and the work, but this..."

Chino took a moment to reflect on the initial reason he started all of this. "Hold up, if it was wasn't for that bastard, my father would still be alive. I mean yeah, Shelly was a fucked up mistake, but what about my motherfuckin' father?" Chino became a different person all of a sudden. He had a deep seeded hatred for Shark in regards to the death of his father. That was the reason for his betrayal in the first place. "Ok, this

178

is what's up, I know he's not going to rest until I'm in a box. I'm putting a contract out on his ass too! Shit. I bet his own fucking family will try to blast his ass for the amount I'ma' put on his motherfuckin' ass, and if I should happen to get to him first, well, wouldn't it just be my lucky fuckin' day."

"I don't think you should try to hit him Boss. You're too hot right now. You need to just go ahead and break out." Knees didn't think Chino was thinking properly. He was acting on his emotions, which would be a major mistake and most likely a very costly one.

"I ain't gon' run from that nigga like I'ma' pussy. I was just going to lay low for a while until shit die down. Now if I go, I have to go and never come back. My whole family is here. I can't do that. I'ma' mufuckin' man. I ain't no mufuckin' bitch ass nigga! It's time we had our say with one another anyway. It's time he knows how the fuck I feel about what he did to my pops. Then, whatever comes, comes."

Lisa finally ended the call. She was in tears.

"What's up Baby Girl?"

She looked at Chino with madness in her eyes. "Camaria's in critical condition Chino. She was stabbed, Chino!" Lisa began beating on Chino's chest, screaming and crying. "Goddamnit Chino! Why? Why did you start this shit?"

Chino held her tight. He brought her face to his. She felt the heat of his breath. The dire need for her to understand and forgive him lingered in his voice. "I'm sorry Baby Girl. I didn't mean for Camaria to get hurt. You know that! I'm not going to let that motherfucker try to hurt you too so fuck all that going back to the hospital shit, you're not leaving my sight."

"Chino I have to go back to the hospital. I gotta' go check on Donell."

"Lisa, you're not going back to the hospital!" Chino yelled."Right now we are as safe as we can be and none of us are leaving this room right now until I figure out exactly how I want to handle all of this."

Knees nodded to Chino, rolled into the bathroom and closed the door.

"See Baby Girl, that's what I need you to do. Just go along with what I say, when I say it. This is some real shit we in. This ain't no fuckin' movie, you dig?"

"Look Chino, I know shit is way out of control ok, but we can't just stay up in this hotel room. We can't hide forever. Eventually Shark is gonna' find us. Then what?" Lisa asked, hysterically.

"We're not going to stay in here forever. I'm just saying that right now nobody knows where we are and that's the best position we could possibly be in right now. I'll call Shark and set up a meeting. Just the two of us."

Lisa looked at Chino. She loved this man. She didn't even understand the depth of their connection. She wanted to be with him, but was she willing to risk her very life?

"I don't think it's smart for you to meet with Shark alone. He's not trying to hear anything you have to say. You're a fucking dead man as soon as you're spotted."

"Ok Baby Girl, you give me a plan. I just want to stop all the bullshit. We can handle this shit like men. We'll just both go out, that's no doubt, cause I ain't goin' out like no bitch ass nigga!"

"Chino, I just don't even know right now. I need to pinch my motherfuckin' self because I would love to wake the fuck up from this nightmare." Lisa walked toward the balcony. She needed some air. "I have got to check on Mari. She looked after Donell while he was sick. I have to go check and make sure she's going to pull through."

"Hell no! You can't go anywhere to check on anyone until I contact Shark. Once I contact him and have him call off the dogs, you might be able to move. Until then, make a call or two, but you ain't goin' nowhere."

"Well then call him so you can put an end to all of this!"

CAN WE TALK?

Lil' James was no closer to finding Chino than he had been in the very beginning. He really didn't want to hurt the fragile female he'd left behind bleeding, nearly dismembered from thirty-two gashes in her once lovely, very lively physique, but she had to be taught a lesson. She knew how to contact Chino. He knew she did, but she just wouldn't talk. Lil' James figured Chino must have fucked her at some point for her to have been so loyal. He wondered if Chino's dick felt better to Camaria's than his own. She was just too pretty for Lil' James to pass up, so before shit got out of control he got himself a little taste of some sweet young pussy, unknown pussy, to him, that was the best kind.

'Maybe she really didn't know where Chino was.' Lil' James pondered on current events. Why would Chino stir shit up in this manner? Shark was nothing but good to him. He wanted to kill Chino just on the strength of him disrespecting Shark. Shelly he knew was a catastrophic mistake, but with the compelling burden his actions placed on Shark, there was one thing and one thing only that would suffice, and that was Chino's life.

Lil' James' cell phone rang. "Hello."

"This time ain't gon' be no mistake motherfucka!"

Lil' James instantly recognized the voice on the other end. "You the dead man nigga, not me. Save your weak ass threats." Lil' James ended the call. He immediately called Shark.

"Yo Boss! This motherfucker just had the nerve to call and threaten me."

182

Shark was calm, "Look, I'm tired of pussyfootin' around with this chump. Apparently I picked the wrong person to eliminate him. For real, he should have been dealt with by now. Straight up!"

Lil' James detected a difference in Sharks' tone, a difference he really didn't seem to recognize, nor appreciate.

"I'm doing the best I can Shark. I just came from some bitch's house that wishes she was dead right now for not assisting me with my search. If I'm doin' all this for nothing, let me know. I'll stop dead in my motherfucking tracks."

Shark realized this was not Lil' James' doing. He had been doing all he could, but the bottom line still remained, they were no closer to finding Chino.

"What did he say when he called?" Shark questioned.

Lil' James returned his question with a question, "Why haven't your boys found him yet? What. Ain't it about three or four of them? Have they come up with anything?"

Shark detected the irritation in his voice. "No they have not, but we both know that this shouldn't be taking so blood clad long!"

"I know Boss. I'm doing everything I can, believe me. He'll respond if he finds his homeboy dead in his hospital bed."

"What?" Shark was all ears.

"I did manage to get the name of the hospital that his boy is in," Lil' James boasted. "The nigga had the nerve to call and tell me-this time ain't gon' be no mistake! All his people are about to be fuckin' cancelled." Lil' James testified.

"A' what the blood clad is this boy thinking. Him crazy, a dat me know." Shark honestly wanted to talk to Chino before

183

he killed him. He really wanted to know why Chino chose to ruin all of their lives. He knew he was foolish and didn't think things through enough at times, but he really never expected him to go this far.

"He called you eh'? Him a' call me soon and when he does, him betta know what it is sien!" Shark's adrenalin was pumping. He smelled Chino. He strongly sensed his presence. Chino was very near.

"I'm headed to the hospital, I'm gon' do this nigga."

"No wait! I have a plan. He'll come if he knows we have his partner sien. Did she manage to tell you what room he's in?"

"No, but I'll find out."

"Just come to the penthouse. We'll take care of things from here."

"You sure Boss, I think it's best if I just go on and handle this shit now."

"Didn't I just say to come to the rass clad penthouse? A' wha'? My words don't matter no more? A' you the boss man now?"

"No. Hell no Shark! What the hell has gotten into you? You been coming at me like I'm the one who did you dirty! "

"Just come to the penthouse, Lil' James."

Lil' James did as he was told. He made a U-turn in the middle of street, plowed through a red light and proceeded to head back to midtown. He was mad as hell. He put his life on the line for this motherfucker who was now talking to him as if he was a piece of shit. As if he had something to do with this whole thing. Did Shark possibly believe he would have something to do with this crazy shit Chino was pulling? What would he possibly have to have to gain?

Shark was pacing the floor when the phone rang. He picked up on the first ring anticipating Chino's voice on the other end.

"Yeah."

"Daddy, why haven't you called me? You promised!" Shantel was almost hysterical.

"I'm sorry baby. I was so caught up trying to get things straight. I thought I asked Lil' James to check on you, but I see that he neglected to take care of that as well. You just can't get good help these days. I tell you."

"Daddy are you alright? You don't sound like yourself."

"I'm fine Shan Shan. Everything is going to be settled very soon and you'll be able to come back home. Where's Moma?"

"She's in her room. She's been in her room since we got here, praying. She has candles lit up everywhere. She's acting really weird too."

"Things are going to be strange for us for a while Shantel."

"Yeah I know, but Mommy came to me and she told me that she's ok."

Shark was taken aback by his daughters' statement. "Oh she did, huh?"

"Yep! I know you don't believe me, but she really did. She said for you not to hurt the person that did this to her because he didn't know that it was her. She said that she loves us both and that ..."

"Shantel, look I know you want your mother to come and tell you all kinds of things, but the fact is that she is gone."

"I know that Daddy."

"Shantel, are you alright?"

"I'm absolutely fine. My mother has come to me. She told me she will never leave me. She's my guardian angel."

Shark was worried about his daughter. He had seen this sort of thing on television before, but it was another thing altogether listening to it from his own daughter who had just lost her mother. His life mate. His soul mate. He wondered if Shelly did visit Shantel. Why didn't she come to him and tell him her last thoughts? Shark felt selfish and very lonely all of sudden. Shouldn't he be happy? His daughter's voice personified hope and strength when just a while ago she was inundated with grief.

"Well, you know what Shan Shan? That is the best thing I've heard all day. I'm a little jealous that Mommy only came to visit you, but I'm glad she eased your mind. You've just eased my mind."

"I love you Daddy, and Mommy loves you too. She told me to tell you that she loves you with all of her heart and always will."

Shark was silent.

"Daddy?"

"I'm here."

"It won't be easy, but we have to be strong for Mommy." Shantel indeed held a tone of tranquility.

Shark just couldn't get Chino out of his head. "Shan Shan I want you to know that I love you more than life itself, and ..."

"Stop, stop it right now!" Shantel yelled at her father as if she was scolding a child. "I just told you that Mommy wants all this foolishness stopped, and you're not even thinking of stopping are you?!"

Shark held firm in his position as a father and as a man who had just lost someone very near and dear to his heart.

"No. I will not lie to you. I never have and I never will. I will seek revenge on your mother's killer Shantel. I cannot rest until I do. Despite what she thinks, she will not be able to rest in peace until the matter is resolved."

"Daddy, if you go against what Mommy has come and said to me, I will never speak to you again. These are her wishes. You can't just disregard her wishes." Shantel was adamant.

Shark didn't want his daughter to be upset with him. She had just lost her mother, and now she was threatening to isolate herself from his as well.

"Ok, I will seriously think about letting Chino live."

"Chino!" Shantel couldn't believe it. "Are you saying, that…"

"Yes. Chino killed your mother. Shot and killed her in cold blood."

Shantel knew this could not be true. Chino was her protector. Whenever she had beef at school, Chino would come straighten it. No, not Chino.

"That's what she meant by 'him not knowing it was her'. Daddy don't you see? Chino would have never killed Mommy. Never!"

"Shantel this is more than mistaken identity. I can't just overlook everything Chino has done to destroy me and my family because he did it by mistake. Killing your mother may have been a mistake, but Chino started this on purpose!"

Shark heard a beep. There was another call on his line. He was very eager to cut over. Shark was sure it was Chino, but he didn't want to make his daughter more upset with him than she already was.

"Look, Shan Shan, what I will say is that I will think heavily about what we've talked about. You know your mother was very special to me, even though I never officially made her my wife."

Shantel interjected, "You regret that now I'm sure."

"Yes I do. I really do."

"Mommy knows that already, and she understands."

Shantel was really beginning to freak Shark out with all of this talk about Shelly telling her every thought, but if it calmed Shantel through this crucial time, so be it.

"Daddy whatever happens you have to be careful. I can't end up with absolutely no parents at all."

"You won't Shan Shan."

"But you can't promise me that can you?"

There was silence on the other end.

"Yeah, that's exactly what I thought!" Shantel huffed. The beep was back.

"I don't want to rush you off of the phone Shan, but ..."

"Yeah, yeah I know. You have to take care of business."

"Come on Shantel don't be like that with me." Shark didn't like it when his daughter was upset with him.

"I'm cool Daddy. You're not going to listen to me or Mommy. You don't even listen to your own mother!" Shantel hung up.

Shark quickly clicked over to catch the caller vying for his attention, but all he heard was a dial tone.

"Damn!"

Shark decided he needed to take it down a notch. He was very edgy. Not that he didn't have a right to be, indeed he did, but he needed to concentrate. He wanted to examine everything that had gone on since Chino took him off. 'He must have killed Blue and Gauge.' Shark thought to himself. 'Why in da hell did this blood clad buoy do this? Did the death of him fadda warrant all of this? No, it had to be more to it.'

The phone rang. Shark jumped at the sound. He picked up

immediately. "Yeah."

"I know you've been waiting for this call." Chino's voice was calm, mellow even.

"What I'm waiting fa' is fa' you to explain to me why you have killed my wife and why you felt the need to rob from me what I would have given you, had you only asked."

Chino really didn't know what to say. He didn't expect this reaction. He expected for Shark to flip his lid and go off so he could feel some justification for the disaster he had created.

"You know I would have never harmed Shelly. That is mainly the reason for my call. I just found out that it was Shelly following me. I thought it was that pussy midget that I'm still going to kill once I see him."

"A wha' the bumba wrong wit' you Chino? A wha' did I ever do to deserve for you to do me dutty?"

"I have looked out for you and your blood clad family since you were a yout', a likl' pickney, sien. A wha' fa your fadda! That is why you destroyed my family?"

"Didn't you destroy mine?" Chino was bland in his response. There was no emotion portrayed in his words.

"Your fadda wanted to do the job Chino. I didn't ask him. He asked me what he could do to make a quick score."

"But you set him up with the bank job. My moms told me. It was you who called our house at one in the afternoon July 26, 1990. That was the last time she saw him alive."

"Do you know what that was like for her? No you don't know because you never personally called her yourself to say shit! Money was your way of apologizing."

"So you take my money and kill my wife. Do you feel betta'? Does that make your fadda' happy now?"

189

"I told you Shelly was a mistake! The worse one I've made so far. You know how I felt about Shelly. I already told you, she is the only reason I made this call, other than that, you would have never seen or heard from me again."

"Do you really think it would have been that simple Chino?"

"It's as simple as I want it to be."

"What's that, a challenge Chino? You want to go to war wit' me still!? I should have your bomba clad head for this and you still want to talk cockt to me, uh?"

"Look I already know that you're gonna do what you gotta' do. There is nothing I can say tostop the contract out on my life."

"How do you know, Chino?" Shark himself couldn't believe the words that were coming from his mouth. It was as if it wasn't him speaking. Someone or something seemed to be speaking for him.

"What are you saying Shark that there's a way for me to make this right?" Chino knew this had to be a trick, a part of Shark's plan to lure him in. Na, he wasn't falling for that.

"My daughter seems to think that you would have never purposely hurt her mother."

"I wouldn't have. Me and Shelly were mad cool. She never had a bad word to say to me. She understood me. She always tried to keep me out of trouble."

"So did I," Shark added.

"Look I fucked up ok. I fucked up big time. I could have kept going if it hadn't been for this. I apologize from me to you. I know this ain't gon' change nothin', but I would have never hurt a hair on Shelly's head."

"Where are you?" Shark questioned.

190

"Come on man, now you know I ain't telling you where I'm at."

"Look Chino you're going to give back my blood clad money and we are going to try to find a way to deal wit' dis shit. A' you feel I was responsible for your fadda's death and I know you were responsible for Shelly's. Let's not forget Blue and Gauge."

"Yeah that shit all sounds good, but I just can't trust it Shark. I believe you're going to have me hit. That's how a true soldier would get down."

"Chino, I am damn near fifty years old. Shit gets old after a while. I have lost my heart with Shelly. All I have is my daughter and she wants me to change my ways, so think of this more from Shantel than from me."

Chino was hearing it, but he still wasn't buying it. " I just don't know man. I don't see how you can let all of this go?"

"Before I spoke to my daughter, I wasn't going to let it go. I was going to torture you, then murder your blood clad rass sien! That would have satisfied me for a moment, but then what?"

"So you're just going to drop it as long as you get your money back?"

"That's what I said," Shark stated, not even believing it himself.

Chino thought he would push his luck. "What if I can't get all the money back to you? You know a lot of shit has been going down Shark. I had to take care of a lot of people."

"A now youa' fuck wit' me Chino! Me swear to Jah, me can't understand why you continue to fuck wit' me! Get my blood clad money together sien. You have twenty-four hours. Not twenty-five! You hear me? Twenty-four rass clad hours!

I'll be in touch in twenty-three with the meeting place."

Lisa had heard enough. Listening to Chino and Shark on the phone infuriated her. Were they simply making up? Camaria had merely served as a senseless liability. Her attack could have been prevented if only Chino would have made this call earlier.

Knees was still in the bathroom, doing what, she had no idea. He had been in there for a while, but that really wasn't Lisa's main concern. it actually worked in her favor. Chino was engulfed in his conversation so he didn't even notice Lisa slipping out of the hotel room.

CLOSE CALL

'This shit is ridiculous. This man doesn't realize all the destruction his little vendetta has caused,' Lisa thought to herself.

She made her move. The elevator seemed as though it took forever as it descended to the lobby. Lisa wondered how long it would be before Chino realized she was gone. It really didn't matter to her. She could clearly see that Chino was caught up in a mental whirlwind right now. Shark was his main priority at the moment.

Lisa asked the hotel doorman to obtain a taxi cab. She was not going to desert her best friend no matter what had transpired between them about Chino. All the beef seemed so minimal at this point in time. All Lisa could think about was Camaria's condition. She shuddered at the thought of losing her girl. Lisa told herself not to think negatively. No speculating until she knew exactly what the deal was.

Finally, a taxi dropped off two passengers in front of the hotel. Lisa barely allowed the couple to exit the taxi before she scurrying into the back seat. "Metropolitan Hospital, please."

The taxi driver studied Lisa from his rear view mirror. She was obviously very troubled about something. He wanted to be of help if he could. He tried to initiate a conversation, which was unusual for cabbies to do in this particular area of Manhattan.

"Is everything ok, Miss?" The driver hesitantly asked.

Lisa was so immersed in her thoughts, that she didn't hear a word. The driver decided to leave her where she was. He'd seen that look before. He felt sorry for her.

193

Tears began to trickle down Lisa's face. The cab driver felt morally obligated to help her.

"Miss!"

Lisa's eyes fell upon the back of his head.

"Are you ok?" He asked again.

Lisa just stared at the back of his head. The driver watched momentarily though his rear view as this attractive, solemn being silently wept.

"Yes I'm fine, thank you."

"There is a box of tissue behind you."

Lisa turned around and grabbed the box of Kleenex in the pretty pink decorative box. 'How interesting', Lisa wondered how many people have cried in the back of this taxi, apparently enough to warrant a box of tissue.

"Thanks. That's very kind of you."

"Sure, no problem," the cab driver answered.

They suddenly encountered heavy traffic approaching the West Side Highway.

"I should have taken Central Park. It would have been much more peaceful."

Lisa spoke, as if being abruptly awakened, "I think it's closed to vehicles on weekends, especially at this time of night."

"Right, right. I knew there was a reason I didn't take that route." The driver smiled.

Lisa diverted her attention to the sights of the city. New York City was absolutely breathtaking at night. The lights scintillated in the sky and dazzled the naked eye. In the daylight, well, now that was a whole different story. Maybe she did need to get away. Maybe going with Chino would do some good. Her relation-ship with Donell would never be the same. Not that it was great, but at least he trusted her. He would never be able to live with the fact that she had been intimate with Chino, and frankly, Lisa didn't want to deal with the repercussions of her actions. She did however need to make sure that Donell would get the proper care he needed to fight this battle. Lisa made a mental note to call Dr. Brennan once she had the opportunity. Together, she was sure they could come up with something. She had a good feeling about Dr. Brennan.

"We're here."

Lisa was surprised. "Already?"

"Yes, once we hit the highway, it was smooth sailing."

"How much do I owe you?"

The meter displayed an amount of seventeen dollars and fifty-five cents.

"No charge. This one is on me."

"Oh no, I can't let you do that. Here you go." Lisa placed twenty-five dollars in the slot, insisting that he accept his fare.

The driver scooped the cash out of the bulletproof dispenser. "Thank you very much. I really appreciate your generosity."

"And I appreciate your concern and your kindness. Thanks for the tissue." Lisa exited the taxi, closing the door while waving good-bye to the sincere taxi driver. What a contrast he had been to the taxi driver Donell's mother had encountered. New York sure had a mixture of all kinds of people.

Now that Lisa was in front of the hospital, she was terrified to actually go inside. She had seen enough hospitals in one week to last her a lifetime. She knew it was way too late for her to be able to see Camaria, but she had to seize the moment she

195

had been given to get out of that hotel room. She figured she could at least get some additional information. She would just sleep in the lounge until the morning, which was not very far off. Lisa wondered if Chino even noticed she had left. Of course he did. He was probably two steps behind her, but that was the least of her worries.

Lisa went to the emergency room. It was flooded with people who were physically ill and from the looks of things, some were mentally ill as well. She spotted the intake section and made her way to the desk.

"Hello," Lisa said.

The woman at the desk seemed uninterested.

Lisa spoke again, "I said hello!"

The woman glanced up, then looked back into the literature she had been reading. Lisa decided not to deal with her. She walked around the woman's desk to the office behind her. Lisa knocked, then immediately opened the door. There were two males dressed in scrubs who eyed Lisa very curiously.

"Gentleman, I'm sorry. I didn't mean to barge in on you."
The woman from the intake desk stormed in behind Lisa. "Excuse me! You don't just walk into any office you damn well please around here. I could have you arrested for trespassing!"

"I believe I requested your attention, which you neglected to give me. Feel free to call your superiors or whatever officers you'd like. I'm sure they would be very interested to know how you totally ignored an inquiring citizen while reading, let me see, what was it? Oh yeah, "A Do Right Man"."

The woman looked at Lisa as if she wanted to strangle her. The men in the office had smirks on their faces a mile long, obviously enjoying Lisa's handling of the burly woman.

196

One of the men interjected, "Ms. Williams why don't you go on back out to your post. We'll take care of this young lady, whose name is ... "

"Lisa, Lisa Spencer."

"Hi, Lisa Spencer. I'm Dr.Raymond and this here is Dr. Murphy. Now, what has got you all in huff?"

"Again, I apologize for barging in here, but my very best friend was brought here sometime tonight. The police brought her. Her name is Camaria Rogers."

The doctors looked at each other. They knew exactly who she was looking for. Lisa noticed the looks between the doctors.

"Do you know who I'm talking about?"

Dr. Raymond glumly responded, "Uh, well, yes, we do have a woman by that name who was brought in a few hours ago."

"Is she alright? The officers wouldn't tell me anything except that they brought her here."

"Well, uh ... " Dr. Raymond looked to Dr. Murphy, a short bald pale man whose face became as red as a beet.

"Oh my God! Will someone please tell me what is going on?"

"Well Lisa, can I call you Lisa?" Dr. Raymond was hesitant. He hadn't quite seen anything like what had happened to this young lady. He'd read about it, but only in the goriest of novels. "Your friend Camaria has been hurt very badly."

"I know that already. The cops made that pretty clear! What I need to know is, will she be alright and if it is at all possible for me to see her?"

"Well, " Dr. Murphy replied, "You know its way past visiting hours for patients."

Dr. Raymond interrupted him. "She is in Intensive Care, Arthur. One of us could take her up there if she were family."

"But she said she's just her friend."

Dr. Raymond pulled the other doctor to the side and after a brief discussion, Lisa was on her way to the Intensive Care Unit to see Camaria.

"I want you to be prepared for what you are about to see. Your friend was severely stabbed repeatedly." Dr. Raymond led Lisa off of the elevator, to the Nurse's Station where they donned the necessary masks, scrubs and gloves that were required in this unit.

All Lisa could think about was the sheer horror Camaria must have felt while this heinous act was occurring. Chino was dealing with animals. She had no doubt in her mind that this was sent as a warning to Chino and those close to him. Yes, she was most likely next if she wasn't careful.

Dr. Raymond escorted Lisa to the last room at the end of the hall.

"Are you sure you want to go in?"

Lisa hesitated slightly. "Yes, I have to."

Lisa was not prepared for what lay before her-- if it was Camaria, no one that knew her would have recognized her. Her entire face and body had been sliced up. She was covered in bandages from head to toe. Remnants of blood seeped though the bandages. She was still unconscious.

"She was stabbed thirty-two times. She's very lucky to be alive." Dr. Raymond said.

Lisa was speechless.

He asked, "Do you know who did this to your friend Lisa?"

Lisa was in a daze. She felt nauseous. She wanted to throw

her guts up.

"No ... I uh ... when I called over to her house the police answered and they told me that they had brought her to Metropolitan. "

Lisa was not going to involve the police. She wanted to, but she knew that was against all codes of the street. She didn't feel Chino had anything under control. This was evidence enough that everything was definitely out of control.

"Did Camaria have any enemies that you know of?" Dr. Raymond asked.

"Not a soul. I'm thinking they must have been looking for someone else." Lisa tried to steer away from the questions.

"Someone else, like who?"

"I don't know who. I just know that Camaria never hurt a living being and this is some bullshit! I swear to God I'm going to ..." Lisa caught herself.

Dr. Raymond could sense that Lisa knew much more than she was letting on, but he wasn't going to press. What was important, was making sure this woman lived. He was sure she would want to let it be known who the culprit was that did this to her.

"Just so you'll know Lisa, she was also raped."

"Oh my Jesus." Lisa cried, "What the fuck is wrong with these sick ass bastards?"

Dr. Raymond consoled Lisa as much as he could. He thought it would be a good time to give it one more shot. "Don't you think as a best friend you owe it to her to help catch the maniac who did this?"

"Dr. Raymond, I'm going to be straight with you because you've been straight up from the beginning. The maniac who did this will do the same to me if I so much as breathe a name to anyone." Lisa looked into the doctor's eyes. "Do you see the position that puts me in?"

"Clearly."

"Then do you understand why I would rather not get involved, especially where the police are concerned. I would not live to see another day."

"They have protective custody Lisa."

"Ha, don't make me laugh. I would be dead within twenty-four hours."

"Ok, then just what do you plan to do, since you obviously know who did this!"

"I'm thinking, Dr. Raymond, I'm thinking. "
Camaria's body began to convulse.

"Oh no! Oh my God what's happening to her?" Lisa asked, panicking.

Dr. Raymond called for back up. Camaria's room was immediately flooded with hospital staff. Lisa had gotten lost in the shuffle. She was literally pushed to the back of the room. Lisa watched anxiously as the doctors and nurses did everything they could to stabilize her best friend. Lisa started praying aloud. "Lord Jesus I know I don't talk to you often, but you're always in my head and forever in my heart. Please, please don't let her die. I beg you. She doesn't deserve to die."

Lisa heard a beeping noise. It was her pager. She took it off and threw it at the door. She was furious with Chino for allowing this to happen. She had no words for him. She didn't know when or if she ever would.

"Ok. We've got her." Dr. Raymond said to his crew. "I

want to thank you guys for responding as quickly as you all did. As you can see, it can mean the difference between life and death."

There was a mutter of voices and mumbling. Lisa could feel that all eyes were on her. She looked up to meet several eyes, full of suspicion and curiosity. Dr. Raymond came to her rescue.

"Doctors. Nurses. This is Camaria's sister, Lisa. She will be staying at her side. Please accommodate her in any and every way possible. Lisa will provide a list of a few other family members such as Camaria's mother and so forth that will be allowed to look in on Camaria. That is all."

The staff seemed at ease once Dr. Raymond shed light on whom Lisa was. They began to offer their sympathy. Lisa was gracious to them all.

The room finally cleared.

"What happened to her?" Lisa questioned Dr. Raymond.

"She went into cardiac arrest."

"Isn't Camaria too young to have a heart attack?"

"Camaria's heart was missed by a quarter of a centimeter. Her body has suffered a tremendous shock Lisa. Cardiac arrest would be considered a common side-affect in this case."

"So she could still have a heart attack?"

"Let's just say the next twenty-four hours are crucial to her survival."

"I was serious about the list of relatives. I will accept three names from you."

"That's not necessary. Two is all that I know of. That's Camaria's mother, whom I'd rather wait to tell until she's out of the woods. If she sees Camaria like this, she WILL go into cardiac arrest. The other is her brother, and again, I'd rather not."

"Lisa, someone in her family needs to know what her condition is. I'm going along with the fact that you don't want to divulge who did this, but I cannot allow you to keep her condition from her next of kin."

"I'm sorry doctor. You're right."

Lisa gave the doctor both names and Camaria's mother's home telephone number. She would simply act as if she had no clue how this happened. She knew Camaria's brother Lamont would try to kill the world and that is just not what this situation needed right now.

Lisa had a change of heart, "Wait, I'll make the call. It shouldn't come from a stranger.

Lisa watched as Camaria fought for her life. She felt like shit. She wondered what she could do to possibly help in all of this.

What she did know was that Shark and his boys were some sick motherfuckers and she really didn't want to get too close. Lisa wondered why they came after Camaria. There was no direct tie in with her and Chino. Why not one of Chino's family members?

Lisa thought she may know who would be a good person to answer some of the questions she had. She dialed the number from the phone next to Camaria's bed.

"Hello."

"Karen."

"Hey Lisa. What's up? You finally surfaced huh ... Camaria told me you had practically disappeared."

"Oh yeah, what else did Camaria tell you?"

"Not much, just that you hadn't been returning her calls and that she was worried about you."

"Well it's not me that we should be worrying about right now, it's Camaria."

"I don't get it." Karen replied.

"Camaria's been stabbed Karen and raped by one of Shark's men. I think they call him Lil' James."

"Get the fuck out of here!"

"He didn't say he was ..."

"He what?-- Karen don't tell me you know something about this!"

"Oh shit! I don't believe this motherfucker! James came here asking all kinds of questions about Chino, asking me if I knew where he was."

"And what did you tell him?"

"I told him that I had no idea where Chino was. I told him I didn't want any part of all of this shit."

"You didn't mention Camaria to him?"

"Why would I?"

"Why would he even go there, Karen? It's not like he knows Camaria, but he knows you and you know Camaria."

"What are you trying to say?"

"Look Karen, don't play fucking dumb! That shit may work with those dumb ass goons, but I know goddamn well those jaws of yours done flapped some shit they shouldn't have."

Karen was quiet.

"I never thought he would go over to Camaria's house Lisa. I didn't know he even knew where Camaria lived."

"I told Camaria that James was sniffing around trying to find Chino, but all she wanted to do was warn you and let you know to be careful. She thought you may be with Chino."

"Oh, and why would I be with Chino?"

"Come on Lisa, who's playing dumb now?"

"Just how much do you know Karen?"

"Don't worry. I know what I need to know, but I didn't tell James anything about you or Camaria or even Chino for that matter because I didn't want to be involved in any of this shit."

"What do you mean, you know what you need to know? What the fuck is that supposed to mean Karen?"

"All I told James was that Mari told me Donell was sick and he had to be taken to a hospital. I didn't tell him which hospital and I didn't tell him how he got to the hospital. Is Camaria alright?"

"No she's not alright! That punk ass couldn't be a man and find a man to take his anger out on, so he butchered Mari and sexually violated her as well! "

"This is my fault."

"How? Didn't you just say that you didn't tell him anything?"

"Yeah, but still I mentioned Camaria's name. Where is she?"

"I don't think you should know that. The less you know, the better."

"What I need you to do, is to call her mother and her brother and break the news to them. I just can't find the words to tell Ms. Rogers. Lamont is going to go ballistic. I just can't handle that right now."

"Lisa they know you much better than they know me."

"No, they like me better. They don't know me any better."

"Don't you think it's the least you can do?"

Again, Karen was silent.

"You know what? Don't even worry about it Karen. I knew Camaria should have never trusted your ass in the first place.

Just like you said, Lil' James oh no, I mean James as you so politely call him, didn't know anything about Camaria, until YOU mentioned her." Lisa ended the call.

She didn't want to do it, but Lisa proceeded to make the call she dreaded to make.

FORGIVE & FORGET?

Lil' James had finally made it back to Shark's crib. He was announced and permitted to go up to the penthouse.

"Boss," Lil' James called out.

"I'm out here." Shark was out on the balcony overlooking the city. Dawn was approaching. To Shark, it was the most beautiful part of a new day.

"I checked on Shantel for you. She was talking crazy."

"Oh was she?"

"Hell yeah! She was saying that Shelly came to her and told her all kinds of shit. She even said that you were going to forget everything that happened because Shelly wanted you to." Lil' James continued, "I'm sorry Boss. I know you hate lying to Shantel."

"What did I lie to her about?"

"I know you're not saying that you're going to let this nigga live after all of this?" He looked at Shark in disbelief. " I know that's not what you're saying." Lil' James waited for an answer.

Shark continued to look out at the early morning sky.

"What the hell is going on Shark?" Lil' James asked. "This shit is starting to make no sense at all, like I'm fucking caught up in a fucking X-files episode or the Matrix or some shit."

"Shantel made me promise that I wouldn't retaliate against Chino. She said she would never speak to me again."

"Look Boss, I know a lot has gone down and I know Shantel is in a very emotional state right now, but this man destroyed your family. He shook your entire empire and you're

206

going to just look the other motherfuckin' way?" Lil' James couldn't believe his ears. "Let niggas on the street get a whiff of this shit! You'll lose everything. Man they gonna think you gone soft Shark."

Shark looked at Lil' James. He knew he could trust Lil' James with all that he owned, but if he was willing to let the shit go he didn't want to be questioned as to why.

"Lil' James tell me what is about Chino you hate so much?"
Lil' James didn't expect that question. "What do you mean man? I hate what the fuck he's done to you. Ain't that enough? This man has killed your girl. He's stolen fifty fucking keys of shit from you! Tell me what is it that makes you NOT hate his ass, because this shit isn't making any motherfucking sense to me."

Shark really didn't have an answer. His decision was made. He wasn't willing to risk his relationship with his daughter to get revenge on Chino. Shelly was gone. He needed a change for him and his family. This was his sign to get out.

"I should have gone ahead and did his boy, at least he would be mourning just like you. Na, I should have killed that bitch. I know she was fucking him. You should have seen her trying to protect his ass."

"Just what did you do to her, and who is she to Chino?"

"It's really a friend of Karen's, but she fucks with Chino, or at least she did at one time. I just shook her up a bit."

" I know you. What did you do to her?"

" Let's just say my blade was getting lonely."

Shark stood silently.

Lil' James wasn't sure what was wrong with Shark. He thought he may still be in shock from the loss of Shelly. This was not his boss, who he knew as one of the most ruthless men he'd ever met.

"I gave Chino twenty-four hours to return my money. He didn't mean to kill Shelly. I do believe that."

"What the fuck is wrong with you man?" Lil' James yelled.

"A who da blood clad youa' talk to Lil' James? A Shark dis! Mea' da same man understand! Me tired of the pussy hole bullshit, sien."

Lil' James knew Shark meant what he was saying. He wouldn't press him anymore. He also wasn't going to let Chino off that easy. After all, his life was also being threatened by Chino.

"Alright, alright, I got you. I don't know what's come over you, but if that's what you want."

Lil' James asked, "What I'd like to know is, how are you going to retract a contract that half the syndicate is hot on? Niggas are going to question it."

"I'm my own man, what I do is my concern, no one else's. I want you to get the word out that the contract is no longer valid."

"And what if he doesn't give you back your money?" Lil' James asked.

"He will."

"But Shark."

"No buts. Just do it!"

Lil' James did as he was told. He got on the phone and made as many calls as he could to get the word out. Everyone he contacted was both surprised and angered. Soldiers depended on money like that. Now the offer was taken away just as easily as it was received. And yes, the question was posed, "Why the call off?" Lil' James told them all that it was a business decision. Shark came into the den where Lil' James had just finished calling off the hit on Chino.

"Have you taken care of everything?"

"I was able to reach a lot of the people. I left messages where I could, but there are a few that I wasn't able to reach."
Lil' James had in fact reached all the men he had called about the contract, but this wasn't over. If Shark wanted to forgive Chino, for whatever crazy reason, that was on him. Once the deed was done, maybe Shark would have a different outlook on the situation. If not, well, that really wouldn't matter much now would it?

"Look Boss, I'm going to head back to my crib and take it easy for a while. There's just been a little too much shit going on with me and I need to chill for a minute. You know ... get my mind right."

"Yeah, yeah. I know."

"I'll give you a call tomorrow when it's close to my meeting with Chino, until then just take it easy mon'."

"That's exactly what I'm going to do, go on in and just take it easy."

Lil' James arrived at his apartment, which was decent, but nothing in comparison to the way Shark was living. Instead of doormen, his building had a security guard or a fake cop as the kids of the neighborhood liked to refer to them. He rode up to the eleventh floor and got off the elevator. As he approached his apartment, he noticed his door was slightly open.

Lil' James immediately pulled his gun and crept up along side the wall in attempts to slowly enter and surprise whomever was trying to surprise him.

He entered quietly. He looked around to find his apartment

totally ransacked. He remained silent as he checked the rooms, closets and the bathroom. Whoever it was had left. I guess not finding what they wanted, or in this case, who they wanted.

Lil' James was sure it was Chino or one of his boys that had been to his place. He wished he was at home when they paid their little visit. He would have been more than hospitable. Lil' James called Shark to let him know what had happened. He thought maybe he would change his mind, but he didn't get an answer. Lil' James thought maybe Shark had gone to bed, after all this shit, he needed some rest too.

Even though a new day was beginning, Lil' James was exhausted. He had a full day the day before, what with chasing Chino around town, disfiguring females, threatening up and coming hustlers, yeah it was time for a nice hot shower. What better way to reflect on yesterday's activities? Especially that tight pussy he was in earlier.

He figured he would try to begin straightening up his place after he got some sleep. "Dumb motherfuckers they ain't even take shit," he said as he thumbed through a wad of cash in his bedroom drawer.

He grabbed some clean boxers and tossed them on his bed. He grabbed a towel and headed for the bathroom.

Lil' James entered the shower just as the bathroom began to steam up from the hot water. He took several deep breaths, allowing the steam to clear his sinuses. A shower was just what he needed. Little did he know, it was just what Buck and Free needed as well.

The mini killers entered again as they did before, through the bedroom terrace door, courtesy of the adjoining terrace of the vacant apartment next door.

Buck went back to the drawer and retrieved the cash they

purposely left behind during their initial visit. He then went to the trunk at the end of the bed and copped all the jewels that had also been left behind, all a part of the plan.

Free walked toward the bathroom. He heard the running water and winked at Buck, signaling the location of their prey. Buck winked back and continued to help himself to Lil' James' belongings.

Free cocked his 9 millimeter, approached the bathroom and suddenly heard the water cut off. Damn, he would have rather gotten him while he was in the shower, but oh well. Suddenly he had an even better thought.

Lil' James started humming a tune as he groomed himself in the mirror. He decided what he needed was a shave. He was looking kind of scruffy. He really hadn't had a chance to take care of anything for himself since all the confusion began.

Lil' James was old school. He shaved with a razor and that thick ass cream. His homeboys always clowned him about it. They claimed he boasted about living in the new millennium, yet he acted like he was caught in the era of "The Color Purple". As he bent down to retrieve his shaving tools from the cabinet under the sink, he was hit by a sharp object ... to his ribs ... to his head ... he then felt a jab to his neck ... 'Oh no! Was it going to be over just like that?' He tried to speak, but the jab to his neck had him speechless. His voice screeched like a sick parrot. When he finally came to, he was taped to one of his dining room chairs from his neck to his feet with duct tape. His vision was blurry, but he could see well enough.

He screeched, "I see that bitch couldn't come himself! He sent some goddamn toddlers to do a man's job!"

Free burst out in laughter. "Well gaga googoo motherfucker, cause this here toddlers' about to send you back

211

through the birthing process. Yo Buck come check how this nigga is still popping mad shit, yo!" Free placed a piece of tape over Lil' James' mouth.

Buck surfaced. He had taken everything and anything of value. "Let's holla at Knees. Let him know we got this pussy. Let Chino hear his bitch ass voice before we do this nigga."

"Yeah bitch. You been threatening our boss. We here to kill you motherfucker." Buck was ready to do this. He wanted Lil' James' head on a platter and he was definitely ready to serve him to Chino as a highly anticipated main course.

Free cut in, "It's all gravy we ain't get you the first time baby. That's what's gon' make this time so sweet, ain't no missing' this time. We in yo' face motherfucker! Now what?"

Lil' James knew this was it. It was only a matter of time. How could he be so careless? He knew his apartment had been infiltrated. Did he believe he was invincible or was it him that was slippin' instead of Shark? What did it matter? All the contemplating in the world wouldn't change his current circumstances.

"What's up big man? Oh my bad, I mean little man. Cat got your tongue? What happened to all that live shit you was poppin'? What happened Playa? We don't look like toddlers no more, huh? Yeah, we looking like some grown ass men to you now huh?" Free prodded. He couldn't resist.

He recognized the look in Lil' James' eyes. Free knew, that he knew ... This was it!

IT'S CURTAINS

Knees just wanted Chino to stay-----no matter how----

"Boss, do you really think Shark would let this whole thing just blow over?"

Chino sat idly on the bed, inadvertently rocking back and forth. He resembled a scared and lost child. A look Knees had never seen on his face before.

"Boss?"

Chino snapped out of the daze he appeared to be in. "Where the hell is Lisa? I know she ain't been in the damn bathroom all this time."

"Boss, I'm the one who went to the bathroom. Lisa was gone when I came out the bathroom. I figured you gave her a job to do."

"How in the hell? I never saw her leave." Chino was frazzled. He wasn't sure in which direction he should go. Deal with Lil' James, or try to find Lisa? He did know that he had to find Lisa before Shark's people found her. He had a strong notion of where to look, but he didn't feel like dealing with that scene. He decided Lil' James was more important. After all, he was the reason all of this shit was blown out of proportion. 'If it had only been him in that damn car,' Chino thought.

Knees' two way went off. 'We got the duck in our clutches, ready to make him stop quacking'.

Knees smiled. His boys had done well. Knees knew Chino had too much to deal with, so he took it upon himself to use the authority given to him and ordered his junior hit men to find Lil' James and put an end to his shenanigans once and for all.

He wanted to share the good news.

"Yo Boss, they got him." Knees exclaimed.

"Got who?"

"That little motherfucker you been trying to get at!"

"Who got him?"

"Well I knew he needed to be dealt wit'. You remember you told me if I ever felt the need to bring on heat don't ask, you trusted me, remember?"

"Yeah Baby Boy, now who has him!?"

"Buck and Free. Who else?"

Chino's shoulders felt like a heavy weight had just been lifted. He knew if Knees said they got him, they got him. This was the best news he had heard all day.

"My little niggas!" Chino cheered. "That's what I'm talking about!"

"Where is he? Where do they have him?"

Knees requested their location.

'At his crib. Just wondered if Chino had a msg 4 his bitch ass b4 we send him 2 meet his maker'

Knees wanted Chino to read that response for himself.

"Oh hell no! This is too good to pass up." Chino replied. "Tell them I'm on my way. Keep him right there!"

Knees responded. "What about your girl Chino?"

"I know where Lisa went. She went to check on Camaria. I'll have plenty of time to deal with that later. Matter of fact, you chill here. Shit might get a little crazy and the wheel mobile ain't gon' cut it right now." He told Knees, "Lisa might come back and if and when she does, tell her she better stay her black ass right here. Shit ain't totally safe yet. I ain't gon' try to page her because she don't want to be paged. I know her like the back of my hand."

214

Chino went into the bathroom to freshen up a bit. He still had the scent of pussy on him. He took a quick shower, then began contemplating what method of punishment he should bestow upon his victim. After all, this was such a long awaited moment, he'd have to make it good. He needed to send a message to Shark, just in case everything he said was a ploy to lure Chino in for the kill.

Chino was going to yell for Knees to call him a cab, but then remembered you couldn't call cabs in that area. Yellow, only yellow cabs in Manhattan. He was going to have to get him some more wheels as soon as time allowed. This cab shit wasn't making it.

                    *   *   *   *

The security guard must have been on break or maybe making his rounds around the building. How convenient for Chino that he wasn't there. As he rode the elevator to his destination, he finalized his plans for Lil' James. He was let in by Free.

"My lil' nigga." Chino embraced Free as he entered.

Buck was next in line for his show of appreciation.

"Yo, where this motherfucker at? We've wasted much too much time already."

"He's over there in the other room." Buck led the way.

Lil' James sat straight up, waiting. He was fearless. He always knew that he would be when facing the end. He'd killed enough people to know his soul was marked for eternal damnation, but somewhere in the back of his sick and twisted mind, he prayed for that "exoneration" from the Lord that his mother always claimed he'd receive.

215

"Well, well, well," Chino teased. "Look what we have here. I think we have a scared bitch. A proud, scared bitch, but a scared bitch all the same," he continued, "See my lil' niggas, this is what I teach y'all not to fall into, and that's a fucked up situation where you have no wins," Chino lectured.

"Y'all pay attention now. See this nigga here. He threatened me. He told me he was gon' kill me. Now what's the rule when a nigga brave enough to tell you he gon' do you?" Chino asked.

"Do his ass first!" Buck replied.

"Good, good. I see my students have been paying attention. That's what's up."

Chino removed the duct tape from Lil' James' mouth. "What you got to say now motherfucker?"

Lil' James hurled a wad of saliva at Chino's face, catching the corner of his chin. Remnants of the foul liquid embellished the hairs of Chino's light beard. Nothing disgusted him more.

He took out his blade and grabbed Lil' James by his neck. He summoned his boys to come in closer and watch as well as help him hold Lil' James still.

"Hold that motherfuckers' mouth wide open! I don't care if both of you have to hold him. Open his motherfucking mouth!" Chino yelled furiously. "You want to spit motherfucker?"

Chino grabbed Lil' James' tongue and sliced it in half, just as a butcher would skillfully carve a freshly skinned animal. He left his tongue dangling in two pieces, in his mouth. Blood dripped, and spurted everywhere. Lil' James squealed like a baby.

"I wish I had a Polaroid camera motherfucker. I'd love to show you your face right now. You wanna' threaten people, huh? You wanna' spit on me? You should be begging for your fucking life bitch! What, you think you too good to beg?"

Chino fucked with him. "I should make you beg, but I'm afraid that probably wouldn't be possible right about now, huh?"

Buck and Free couldn't stop laughing.

Buck taunted him, "Where all that shit you was poppin' yo'?

"The cat definitely got your tongue now!" He said. They all began to laugh.

Lil' James was helpless. Chino looked him in his eyes. "All you had to do was mind your fucking manners and I would never have even fucked with you. My beef ain't with you."

Lil' James still tried to speak despite the fact his mouth was a pool of blood and his tongue was literally hanging out of both sides of his mouth.

"You a motherfuckin' trip Shorty. You just don't quit! You're like that little motherfucking energizer bunny an' shit, but I got somethin' for you."

Chino pulled out a flask. "I made a little stop before I got here. You know, I wanted to make this a religious ceremony, being that we sending you to meet your maker an' all. I figured I'd take my time. You ain't in no rush to die are you?"

Chino began to pour the gasoline that was in the flask into Lil' James' eyes, ears and mouth. "This is a going away party for James Murphy. James Murphy was a little man, probably with a little dick. Hmm, Is your dick little man? Let's see. Na I'm just fucking wit' you. I damn sure don't want to see it! I would like to set that shit ablaze before I set your fucking face on fire, but again, I ain't touching your funky ass. So I'll have to pass on that pleasure and settle for your face slowly burning, dripping your flesh, until you fry bitch!"

Lil' James gagged from the gasoline poured down his throat. His pupils were whitened by the liquid. It blinded him.

Chino took a lighter and placed it by his left ear. "You scared now ain't you motherfucker?"

The sound of the burning flame was amplified in his ears.

"Well don't sit there, say something. Oh, I forgot. You can't!"

He and the boys burst out in laughter again.

"Ok, ok let's get on with this. I've got more important shit to do and I'm just wasting time on this bullshit."

"Lil' man you do the honors." Chino handed the lighter to Free.

Lil' James squirmed in pain from his tongue being slit. His eyeballs were already on fire without being set ablaze, but he was more petrified of what was to happen next. Being shot he could take, but being burned alive, that was one of the most horrible deaths to suffer. He was no longer feeling fearless.

Chino took the lighter back from Free. "My bad. I gotta' do this one myself man. It's only right."

Chino lit the inside of Lil' James' mouth. He didn't get a chance to ignite the rest of his face. Lil' James squirmed around so much, every direction he turned his head, he would turn right into the direction of the flames, igniting the remainder of his face. All you could hear were bellowing shrieks from Lil' James. Until, he was ... No more.

"That's for Mari motherfucker!" Chino yelled.

Buck couldn't take the smell. "Lets get the fuck out of here!"

They all headed for the door. As they approached the door

leading to the stairwell, a neighbor opened their apartment door and began yelling, "Fire, fire!"

All of the residents began to emerge from their apartments as well. How sweet could it have been? Chino, Buck and Free walked calmly down the stairs as residents began to push by them to evacuate the building.

Chino told the security guard as he was leaving the lobby, "Yo man you might want to check the eleventh floor that's where you really smell the fire."

The security guard shouted as he continued to talk to the fire department over his walkie-talkie, "Good looking out my man."

FRIENDS TO THE END

"I know somebody better tell me something!" Ms. Rogers yelled.

"Ain't no damn way my baby laying up here like this and don't nobody know what happened. Somebody know what happened!"

"Chill Ma. I got this." Lamont decided he'd better take over. His mother was getting nowhere.

"Lisa, I know you're shook, but you here, so that means you got to know something."

"We haven't heard from Mari in two days. Mommy had been calling around looking for her. I've been calling you, Mommy's been calling you. You've been M.I.A., now we in the fucking hospital?"

Ms. Rogers couldn't help crying, "She was supposed to come to the house yesterday to do my hair. She never called. That's not like Mari. Lisa if you know who did this, please if I ever meant anything to you, if Mari ever meant anything to you, you have to help her."

Lisa was burdened with guilt and she was fading fast. Then she thought, 'What would it hurt to tell?' She then remembered Shark and replayed the events that had led to this very moment and changed her mind.

"Honestly, I really don't know what happened," Lisa stated.

That was not an outright lie. Lisa felt as if she really didn't know what was happening.

"I called to see if Mari wanted to go out to get something to

220

eat and the police answered."

"They wouldn't tell me much over the phone. They just told me where they were taking her, so I immediately came here."

"Well why wouldn't you call me and tell me that my one and only daughter was being rushed to the hospital Lisa?"

"I'm sorry Ms. Rogers," Lisa squealed. "Yes you should have been the first person I called, but I really didn't know what was going on and I didn't want you worrying unnecessarily. I know now, I realize that I was very wrong."

Lisa was as honest as she possibly could be. There were still so many unanswered questions, she just couldn't open up the floodgates right now, she'd surely drown.

Lamont wasn't buying it. "I know one thing! Mari doesn't attract violence and when she comes around and tells me who's responsible for this, they're going to wish they were never born."

There was a low moan. Camaria was attempting to come to. They scurried to her bedside.

"Mari ... " Ms. Rogers cried.

"I'd better get Dr. Raymond back in here." Lisa rushed out to find him.

"What happened baby? Who did this to you?" Ms. Rogers asked.

There was no answer. Just a few more moans that exuded agonizing pain.

Lamont stood to the side, watching his sister suffer. He was fuming with anger. He wanted to get Lisa alone. Something was very wrong with this picture. Lisa seemed too calm not to know what was really going on. Oh, she knew something ...

Lisa came back in the room with Dr. Raymond on her heels. The doctor rushed to Camaria's bedside. He checked her vitals. He noticed her eyes fluttering, which was a good sign.

"I think she's trying to come out of it and back to us." Dr. Raymond said.

"She's making very slight eye movements, however, that's a great start. Also if she was moaning, she apparently has some feeling as to her level of pain. Let's hope not too much feeling. We couldn't properly sedate her because of her condition, so she will definitely be in excruciating pain as she comes further and further out of the woods."

"I would like to say that it's amazing seeing what I've seen thus far. If she continues on this path, she should regain conscienceness anytime now." Dr.Raymond's face really held an abundance of hope.

Lisa introduced Camaria's mother and her brother, to Dr. Raymond. He explained to Ms. Rogers and Lamont, the extreme importance of the next twenty-four hours. Dr. Raymond also described the condition in which Camaria came to the hospital. He also revealed that she had been raped.

"I'm gon' kill me a motherfucker!" Lamont exploded.

"Calm down Monti. This is not the time for your temper, we in a hospital!" Ms. Rogers pleaded.

"Mama I don't give a…"

Lisa interrupted, "Lamont! Please! That's why I didn't want to call you. Can you just calm down?"

"Bitch you calm down. I know you know more than what you're telling me and my Mama! My motherfucking sister is laying here sliced the fuck up, now they sayin' she was raped

222

too and you telling me to calm down! What the fuck is your angle? You ain't no best friend! What kind of best friend are you?"

"Stop it Monti!" Ms. Rogers shouted.

Dr. Raymond now understood why Lisa didn't want to involve Camaria's family. He could see the pain in this young lady's eyes. He saw life and death day in and day out in his profession, but he had a feeling that the story behind this woman laying there, nearly cut to pieces was surely an unforgettable one.

Lisa needed to call and check on Donell. Donell ...What exactly did she plan to do about him? Lisa decided there was too much going on to even try to contemplate such a question. She'd deal with that later, right now she just wanted to know how he was doing.

"I need to step out and make a call." Lisa said.

"Yeah, I bet you need to make a call," Lamont sneered. "I'm telling you Lisa I better not find out that you know anything about this or I'm ... "

"You what Lamont?!" Lisa snapped. "Look. I don't know who you think you are, you may be somebody to your people, but you ain't pushing no weight with me! You are my best friend's brother and I'm really trying to keep my composure, but you're taking this shit a bit too far, " Lisa said, neck swinging, hands on hips, "I am telling you everything I know and I'm being as honest as I can be. I was not there. But as soon as I found out-- I was here, and I am Camaria's best friend, no matter what you or anybody thinks." Lisa stormed out of the room.

Lisa dialed Donell's room. The phone rang endlessly. She panicked. She then retrieved Dr. Brennan's number and called.

"Hello," said the very masculine voice on the other end.

"Uh, Hello, Dr. Brennan?" Lisa asked.

"Yes," not recognizing the female voice, he added, "This is Dr. Brennan."

"Hi Dr. Brennan, this is Lisa Spencer."

He was both surprised and pleased.

"Hello Lisa Spencer. How are you?"

"I could be better. I was calling to check on Donell. I tried to call his room and I didn't get an answer. I wanted to make sure he was doing alright."

"Let's see, I left the hospital around 3 a.m. and I know we scheduled him for some additional tests. So in that case, I would say he's with one of my staff members having tests run."

"I'm sorry I called you so early in the morning," Lisa said.

Dr. Brennan replied, "That's ok, really, I don't get much sleep anyway."

"Has there been any sort of change in Donell's condition?" Lisa asked.

"No, not really." Dr. Brennan answered. "We're keeping a close watch. He is stabilized, and that is a good thing. This second series of tests should give us a clearer outlook on what we're dealing with. I'd be glad to let you know how the tests come out as soon as we have all the results in."

"Yeah, I mean yes. That would be great. You do still have my numbers right?"

"Actually yes, I do."

"Good, well, leave a message if you have to. I have to go. I'm at Metropolitan right now, but I'll be back over there."

Dr. Brennan felt a surge of nervousness in his gut. He didn't want the call to end.

"Metropolitan. What are you doing there?" He blurted out.

"Uh, it's a long story and frankly I just can't get into right now. I'm truly mentally exhausted," Lisa admitted.

"Have you eaten?" Dr. Brennan asked.

"No, I haven't." Lisa responded.

"Now that's not going to work. You're the one that's going to be admitted to a hospital if you keep that up."

"Honestly, with everything that's been going on, I couldn't keep anything down."

Dr. Brennan had to seize the opportunity. He was not going to let her get away this time.

"Well, how about when you do get over to the hospital, we have a bite to eat? "

"I don't know Dr. Brennan," Lisa had a lot on her plate. Food just wasn't one of them.

"We don't have to eat inside the hospital. God knows you need a change of scenery."

He decided to go for it, "Or we can try going out to eat. How about dinner?"

There was silence.

"You know, forget I said that."

"No, Dr. Brennan. It's ..."

Dr. Brennan interjected, "Please, call me Chris."

"Ok, Chris. Honestly, it's nothing personal. I just have a ton of problems right now and I would be lousy company," Lisa said.

"There is nothing like an open ear." The doctor didn't want to take no for an answer.

"You know, you may be right," Lisa agreed.

"I am right and I'm glad you're agreeing to join me."

"I will join you, Chris." Lisa had a hint of a smile in her response. She was surprised at herself. She didn't know from where in her being this silent smile had arisen.

REASONABLE DOUBT

"You believe her Ma?" Lamont questioned his mother.

"I don't know what to believe until my child wakes up and tells me what happened to her. Until then, I'm making no assumptions." Ms. Rogers delivered a stare to Lamont that clearly told her son to drop it.

Camaria began to moan again. This time it was louder. She was beginning to feel the wretchedness of her wounds.

Lamont began pressing the "call" button for a nurse. Camaria's moaning soon turned to screams of agonizing pain.

Lisa rushed back into the room. The nurse had called for Dr. Raymond to return. She asked for everyone to clear the area. They all huddled in the corner, resembling a team discussing their next play.

Dr. Raymond arrived and immediately began to inject Camaria with a sedative.

"Wait!" Ms. Rogers yelled. "What are you shooting her up with? I need to know everything that you give my daughter."

Dr. Raymond replied without so much as a glance in Camaria's mothers' direction, "I'm giving her morphine."

"Morphine, ain't that for junkies?" Lamont asked.

Lisa was embarrassed. "They use it as a pain killer, Lamont."

"Ain't no other pain killer you can give her besides that?," he asked.

"Lamont, PLEASE!" Ms. Rogers shouted.

Lamont had enough. He felt highly unappreciated. "You know what? Fuck it! I'm outta here. You telling me to be quiet.

227

This bitch is trying to make me look stupid. I don't need this shit. When my sister comes out of whatever she's in, call me!" Lamont left the room.

"I'm sorry doctor," Ms. Rogers apologized.

"No apology necessary," advised Dr. Raymond. "Camaria will be in a lot of pain for the next few weeks, but I believe she is going to make it just fine. I still want to keep her in ICU today and tonight."

Lisa asked, "When do you think she may be able to talk?"

"Unfortunately, that's something only Camaria knows." Dr. Raymond replied.

"Is it alright if I stay here?" Ms. Rogers asked.

"Of course it is, Ms. Rogers." Dr. Raymond answered.

"I have to go check on some of my other patients, but I will be checking in on you guys quite frequently throughout the day and evening."

"Thank you for everything doctor," Lisa said.

"Just doing my job. I really wish I could do a lot more."
He left the three women alone.

"Ms. Rogers," Lisa felt more at ease now that Lamont was gone. She never did get along with him. He had asked her out years ago and she declined. Since that day, he treated her like dirt. He felt she thought she was too good for him. Lisa was not attracted to Lamont in any way. It was as simple as that.

"Yes Lisa?"

"Ms. Rogers, I haven't been totally honest about all of this. It's just that I know Lamont's temper and I was worried that he would try to seek revenge on the man who did this. I wouldn't blame him, but it would just make things much worse than they already are. I just can't lie to you."

Ms. Rogers was all ears. "Lisa, what exactly is going on?"

Lisa told Camaria's mother everything she knew. She told her about her conversation with Karen and how Lil' James most likely was the culprit. Lisa explained how Donell had been sick and how Camaria had cared for him, while she was "doing other things". Lisa revealed that Chino was involved and that's who Lil' James had been looking for. She told Ms. Rogers how guilty she felt and how she wished it was her lying in that hospital bed instead of her daughter. Lisa broke down and pleaded with Ms. Rogers to forgive her.

"Lisa ... if all you're telling me is true. This isn't your fault."

"Oh I swear. It's true. I couldn't take not being up front with you Ms.Rogers. In fact, my conscience feels a whole lot better now that you know," Lisa sobbed.

"There, there now child." Ms. Rogers pulled Lisa to her and held her as if she were her own. She patted her head until Lisa calmed down.

"Ms. Rogers, please know that I love Camaria like my own sister. I would never do anything to hurt her," Lisa said.

"I know that child ... "

"I need to tell that to Mari. I haven't been totally honest with her lately either."

Ms. Rogers said, "Sounds to me like you need to check on your man. I'll be here with Mari and if she should wake up, I'll be sure to tell her everything you have told me. And I'll make sure she knows you've been here and you'll be back."

"Thank you Ms. Rogers!" Lisa happily exclaimed.

"Lisa, if you don't stop calling me Ms. Rogers, I'm gon' die! You've known me too long for that. Shit, you grown. Go on and start calling me Barbra."

"Ok, Ms. Rogers. I mean Ms. Barbra."
"Just Barbra, Lisa."
"I'll be back as soon as I can, Barbra."

THE DISCUSSION

Lisa arrived at Bronx Lebanon shortly after 9 a.m.. She proceeded to Donell's room. Lisa missed Donell. There was so much going on. She had put her feelings aside, but now that everything was straightening itself out, she was able to place certain things into their proper perspective.

"Hey you." Lisa said.

"Hey you yourself." Donell replied.

"You look and sound one hundred and ten percent better," Lisa happily exclaimed.

"That's good. I actually feel one hundred and ten percent better."

"How did the tests go?" Lisa drew the curtains back to allow the sunlight to flow into the room.

"I don't know, they haven't come back with the results," Donell said.

Lisa avoided eye contact. She could not look at him knowing he knew about Chino. Donell sensed her uneasiness. He wanted to ease her concern.

"I don't know if you've talked to Chino, but Camaria may be in trouble. I called Chino last night to let him know, but ... " Donell noticed the somber look on Lisa's face.

"What happened?" Donell asked.

"I guess there is no easy way to say it."

"No easy way to say what!"

Lisa spoke sullenly, "Lil' James raped and stabbed Mari."

"What?!" Donell was shook.

"Please, don't make me say it again." Lisa pleaded.

231

"What the fuck happened?" He asked.

"Apparently, Lil' James was looking for Chino and he went and spoke to Karen. Karen mentioned Camaria's name, but she swears she never told him where Mari lived, so she says, but I spoke to Karen and I'm not buying her bullshit. She's very much the cause of this."

Lisa went on and on about Karen. Telling Donell, how she may be working for the enemy.

"So, you really think Karen is the cause of what happened to Camaria?" Donell asked sarcastically.

"Well, he went straight to Mari's after he left her house. She practically sent him there!"

Lisa's wide eyed expression found Donell.

There she was protecting him again. He wasn't going to let her get away with it so easily this time.

"So you're sayin' that Chino had nothing to do with this, huh?" Donell questioned.

"I'm not saying that he had nothing to do with it. I know damn well this is all Chino's fault, but he's not directly tied to Camaria, Karen tied her to him." Lisa continued, "He wouldn't have touched Camaria had it not been for their conversation. She probably sang like a fucking canary."

Donell needed no other evidence that Lisa was in love with Chino. She defended his honor even when she didn't realize it.

"Is Camaria going to make it? Donell asked.

"Hopefully, she will, but it's still a very critical time for her. The doctor said the next twenty-four hours are crucial to her recovery and that was last night. I left her in good hands though. Her mother came, and so did Lamont, unfortunately."

"I tried to get to her, but they shot me up with that shit and

I was out!" Donell said.

"There was no way they would have let you out of this hospital. What the hell were you thinking?" Lisa asked.

"I was thinking that Camaria was in some shit of trouble, and she needed help. I was on the phone with her when she went to answer the door. I'm the one who told her to call the police," Donell said. "The next thing I know I was getting shot up with some more shit. I did have a chance to call Chino and tell him what happened. Then I got wheeled into some bright, cold ass room and they plugged a bunch of shit up to me, then I must have went out again."

"I'm a kill that motherfucker when I get my hands on him," Donell was heated.

He thought out loud, "She had nothing to do with this."

"You seem very concerned for someone who doesn't even like Mari. " Lisa mentioned.

"I am concerned. She looked out for a nigga when no one else would. I could have died." Donell kept it real.

"I hear you." Lisa replied. She still felt the guilt of not being there when she should have. "I know it should have been me there with you."

"What was she calling you for?" Lisa quizzed.

"She was looking for you. She had just gotten off the phone with Karen and she was trying to warn you about Lil' James maybe looking to hurt you."

Lisa felt a thousand times worse about Camaria's predicament.

"What made her open the door?" Donell asked.

"I don't know. I still don't get it," Lisa replied.

"I guess we really won't know what happened until Mari wakes up and tells us," Lisa said.

"So were you ever going to tell me about you and Chino?"

Donell asked.

"Donell, there is so much going on. Can we please not talk about that right now?" Lisa asked.

"No, I'm sorry. This is something that we are going to have to discuss if we ever plan to have any sort of relationship Lisa," Donell stated.

Lisa didn't know if she wanted to maintain a romantic relationship with Donell. Her main concern was to see to it that he made it through this illness with her help. She'd had enough of the lifestyle that came with him. Lisa wanted more. She was destined for more. The mere fact that Donell went straight back to negative elements upon his release from prison was all the writing on the wall she needed.

"Donell, what I want, is to be honest," Lisa said.

"That is exactly what I want too, nothing but honesty," Donell replied.

This was it, an open forum to be totally honest with herself and with Donell, to make something right out of this whole mess.

Lisa started, "I love you and I always will ... "

"Uh oh, oh no. I know what comes after that," Donell attempted to cut her off.

"Please, hear me out." Lisa found the strength and courage to look directly into Donell's eyes. "Like I was saying. I will always love you Donell and I always will have a special place in my heart for you and for what we've shared, but I am in a different place in my life. I'm finding that I want different things. Things that can't be attained in your world."

Donell retorted, "My world, huh? My world and Chino's world are identical. So what are you saying? You can be with him and he can do all the dumb shit in the world and you're going to keep fucking with him, but we're through after eight years?"

"No, what I'm saying is I've had enough, period! I don't plan to see Chino anymore either." Lisa shocked herself.
She knew then at that moment what her answer to Chino's question was.

Donell had a feeling of great satisfaction once that was said. He couldn't take losing Lisa, but he could never take losing Lisa to Chino.

"Lis, I think you're thinking too much. I think you should take some time before you make any rash decisions about us. We have eight years of history baby."

"We've had two years of physically being together Donell. The last six were me just not letting you down while you were locked up because of everything you'd done for me. "

"So now you're saying you felt sorry me?" Donell asked.

"What I'm saying is a lot of the last six years were feelings of what we had, not who we are as individuals. We're going in completely different directions with our lives Donell. I'm sorry, but I have dreams and I'd like to one day fulfill at least one of them."

"So your dreams can't come true if we're together?" Donell pressed.

"Donell the last thing I want to do is hurt you at a time like this. You are going through a lot and this is just the beginning of your journey. With this disease you are going to need to focus all of your attention on getting better."
Donell stared at Lisa so long he appeared to be looking through her.

"Donell?"

"I can't fucking believe this shit!" Donell shouted.

"Donell please, don't. I'm just tired of the lies. I'm tired of the games. I won't play them anymore." Lisa's statement was final.

Donell reached out for Lisa. He couldn't grasp the thought of losing her. He had never thought he would ever have to. Donell was even willing to work through the disturbing fact that she had been with his best friend behind his back. He loved her that much.

"What if none of this would have happened?" Donell asked.

"What if I never went with Chino and you and I had never had the fight we had?"

"Would you have kept fucking him and me at the same time?"

"Were you going to leave me before all of this?"

"Honestly Donell, I was trying to make "us" work," Lisa said.

"Chino knew and understood what it meant when you came home. No, I was not going to see you both at the same time."

"Oh so you were still fucking with him right up until the time I came home?" Donell asked.

Lisa would not look at him.

"Damn Lisa!"

"It wasn't like that. It wasn't up until you came home. We hadn't been together for a while," Lisa tried to defend herself.

"So how long before I came home did he touch you?"
Lisa gave him an odd glare. "What difference does it make?"

"I'm just curious. Don't I have the right to know? ...You love him?" Donell had to ask. He just wanted her to be a woman and say it.

"Donell, why are you asking me all of these questions now?"

"When else was I supposed to ask them? I've been drugged up for two days straight."

"This is the clearest my mind has been since y'all blessed me with the good news about you two. I thought since you've decided not to be with me anymore, I could at least get my fucking questions answered!"

"Donell!," Lisa yelled.

"Pardon me if I appear a bit hostile," Donell snidely replied. "What if I told you that I fucked Mari before? Would that hurt you?," Donell wouldn't give up.

Lisa's chest sank. When could he have done that? Her mind began to race.

"Before, when?" Lisa asked.

"Before!" Donell answered.

"You know what Donell? If you have, oh well. I'm tired of all of this bullshit. Who's fucking who ... fuck whomever you like!" Lisa continued, "That's all a relationship is about to you, isn't it?"

"I know for a fact that's what Chino's relationships are all about! You think you're different?"

"I don't THINK anything. I know I am!"

"He got you straight trippin'!" Donell quipped.

"Oh I'm far from trippin, but that's neither here nor there." Lisa refused to entertain Donell's taunting.

"Look Donell, I just came to check on you, you know, make sure you were alright and see if there was anything you needed, but you seem just fine, so I'm gonna take off," Lisa said.

"Don't go Lis, not like this, please. "

"That's fucked up, you know I'm sick, and you're just going to leave me like this. You don't have no real love for me," Donell said.

"I thought about staying with you until you were better Donell, but it wouldn't be fair to either of us. I do want to be there for you, but we don't have to be romantically together for me to be there for you. I do want to help you through this, but as a friend," Lisa said. "Right now, that's all I can offer."

Donell decided to accept what she was offering. He looked at it as a sign of hope. She wasn't cutting him out all together, so she must care. He wondered why he even wanted her back after what she had done. Donell then reflected on all he had done to Lisa. Most events, she knew nothing about. There had been countless infidelities. He spared her the drama, always had, but what goes around, comes around, and he sure was getting his.

"Ok, so we're friends now. This is going to take some getting used to. Are we good friends, great friends, homey, lover, friends, what?," asked a smiling Donell.

"You crazy! " Said a smiling Lisa.

HEADS OR TAILS

Chino, Buck, and Free made it back to the Marriott. Knees was still in the exact spot he was in when Chino left.

"Lisa hasn't come back at all?" Chino asked.

"Nope," Knees answered.

"She buggin' the fuck out. She won't answer none of my pages. This is not the time for this shit. I have to figure out what I want to do about this cake. Am I giving it back? Na, I just don't trust it," Chino said.

"Yo, who got some trees?" Knees asked. "I'm fienin' in this motherfucka'."

"I got you dawg," Free said.

"Good lookin' out!" Knees replied.

Free proceeded to roll up. Chino went out onto the balcony. He reminisced on the episode he and Lisa shared there. Chino finally had a moment to concentrate and plan his next move. Lil' James' demise couldn't have been sweeter. He was very pleased with Knees for initiating his soldiers to move in for the kill. Chino reveled in the fact that he had taught them well.

This next move, however, was crucial to his survival.

Knees rolled out onto the balcony. "This is some fly shit Boss. I dig this hotel."

"Yeah Baby Boy it's a'ight." Chino had seen much better. "For real, this ain't shit. I could show you some shit that'll make you skeet nigga. Shit that will make you wanna stay caked up. Make it your permanent parlayin' spot. You know what I'm sayin?"

"Have you decided what we should do about Shark?"

Knees asked.

"No, I haven't, but there ain't gon' be no "we" in this one," Chino said. "I don't want y'all tangling with this nigga'. He ain't no joke."

"He's human ain't he?" Knees asked.

"Of course, what's that supposed to mean?" Chino asked.

"It means he's just like any other motherfucka' to me. He bleeds, " Knees said.

"I don't see the big deal. Let Buck and Free do their thing. We can all go back to Brooklyn tonight and it's done." Knees' plan was simple at best.

"Baby Boy, I don't know what I gotta' do to get you to understand that this man is different. This whole situation is different," Chino said.

"He's been like an old man to me. Like I've been to you. Like I've been to all my little niggas."

"Would it be easy for you to put a bullet in my head?" Chino asked.

"Come on Boss, you know that shit ain't even a thought. I'd never think about doing anything to ever do you dirty," Knees said.

"That is exactly what my response is supposed to be if Shark asked me that same question," Chino said.

"Do you now fully understand the position I'm in?" He asked.

"The only reason I took him off was to get revenge for my pops' death, and to make a shit load of cake, of course ... but for real, he didn't kill my pops," Chino admitted.

"This shit with us killing Shelly, turned this whole shit upside down."

"If there was one thing in my life I could take back, that

240

would be it," Chino revealed.

"Remember what you taught us, Boss?" Knees asked. He then followed with his own answer, "No regrets ... "

"Yeah, well, there is always a first time for everything," Chino replied.

"So if we're not going to take him out and we're not going to give him his money back, what are we going to do?" Knees asked.

"Just leave it to me and I told you it ain't no "we", it's me!" Chino chimed.

"Where the hell is Lisa?"

Chino was becoming impatient with Lisa. He could have any woman he wanted in this world, but he had to fall in love with her. He began to second-guess his decision. Chino snapped himself back to reality. He was addicted to Lisa. There was no turning back.

"Look, I want y'all to head back to Brooklyn," Chino said. "I gotta' take care of this shit and I don't want y'all nowhere around."

Knees felt that feeling again. He wanted Chino to change his mind. Knees felt Chino at least needed Buck and Free with him. He agreed he should go on back home to make sure the boys were good. No one had paged or called to say otherwise, but still ...

Knees knew his wheel mobile wasn't cut out for the excursions his crew were regularly involved in. He briefly contemplated giving up the game. He now had enough money to move his peeps out of the Projects.

"Buck, call the main desk for a cab. Make sure they know you need a big enough vehicle to place a wheelchair in the trunk," Chino said.

241

Chino knew he was wasting far too much time. Shark would be calling him in a few hours.

"Boss, have I ever steered you wrong?"

"No, you never have." Chino answered.

"Then please, let Buck and Free stay with you," Knees pleaded.

"I've made my decision Baby Boy."

"I want all of you to go back to Brooklyn together." Chino continued, "There is still a contract out on my life as far as I know. I really can't trust the fact that Shark said it's called off."

Knees barked, "See, that's what the fuck I don't understand! This man doesn't have a fucking problem placing a bounty on your motherfuckin' head, but you insist on treading lightly with him. This just ain't like you Boss!"

"Don't fucking question me!" Chino yelled.

This was the first time Chino ever truly yelled at Knees in front of any of the crew. Buck and Free looked to one another, not really knowing how to react.

Knees' eyes began to water up. Chino knew the extent of Knees' feelings, but there was nothing he could do about it, or at least that's how he saw it. He had to do what he had to do, and he had to do it alone. Too many innocent people had been hurt already.

"Look, Baby Boy, you know you like my motherfuckin' son. I don't want to leave y'all, but I'm not going to say it again. Now man up and cut out all that other shit. "

Buck picked up the phone to call the main desk.

"So what if something does happen to you, how are we going to know?" Knees cried. "Don't nobody know about us."

"Lisa knows about you."

"Yeah, and where she at?" Knees asked.

"I don't know where she is right now, but I do know she would never cross me," Chino said.

"I'll make sure you know what's going on."

Knees was still hesitant. He had a horrible vibe. His heart was palpitating too hard. Danger was lurking.

"I still don't like it, but you're the Boss!" Knees agreed.

"Finally! " Chino stated.

"The cab'll be here in fifteen minutes. We gotta' be out. We gotta' be downstairs," Buck said.

"Y'all go on ahead. Let me holla at Knees," Chino said.

"We'll be downstairs, yo'." Free said.

"Yeah, yeah, I'll be right behind you. I'm coming," Knees replied.

Buck and Free gave Chino dap and a half hug as they left the room.

"Now you see how Buck and Free are taking all of this?" Chino asked.

"They don't care, like I care," Knees said.

"That may be, but they know what it is, and you the one I got leading them. I know you know what it is, so don't get all sentimental on me man. This game ain't got no room for that shit."

"My gut is telling me you need back up," Knees said.

"My instincts are as sharp as a knife. You know it, and I know it." Knees felt he had to give it one last shot.

"I'm not doubting your instincts, Baby Boy. No matter what happens, you my mufucka. I got much love for you. Never forget that! "

"Stop talking like that! " Knees snapped.

"You know Baby Boy. I've been doing a lot of thinking. I

243

want a better life for my little niggas."

"I don't want y'all caught up in this shit no more. After all of this shit gets squashed, we're going to do something positive with this cake, like try to open up an after school center or something."

Knees said, "Or we could buy all the shorties in the neighborhood some throwbacks. They would love that shit."

"You wild nigga, I'm talking about doing something big!"

"Fa' shizzle," Knees replied.

"Now that's the Baby Boy I'm used to," Chino said.

Chino gave Knees a hug. They gave each other dap and Chino rode with Knees downstairs to an awaiting taxicab.

They had been riding for about five minutes when Knees ordered the cab driver to come to a halt.

"Yo, stop the cab man!" Knees yelled.

The driver became nervous. He had three black teenagers in the back of his taxicab demanding that he stop clearly before reaching their destination. This was never a good sign.

"I don't understand. " The driver responded.

"What the fuck? You don't understand the word "stop"?" Buck asked.

"Yes, yes, please I don't want any trouble," the driver pleaded.

"Ain't no trouble man, be easy." Knees said.

The driver pulled over to the nearest curb, almost causing an accident and nearly hitting a pedestrian.

"Look, I don't give a fuck what Chino says, he needs y'all watching his back."

"Knees, he told us to go back. Chino been making moves way before us. If he say he good, he good," Buck said.

Buck asked Free, "What you think?"

Free responded, "I'm with Knees, yo'. Look at how we had to hit off little man." He continued, "Maybe he just got too much on him to think right, right now. Ain't that what we for?"

Knees couldn't have put it better himself. "My point exactly!"

"Now y'all gone have to find a way to watch him without him knowing. I know he gon' flip on me, but I don't give a fuck."

"Don't even worry about that. You know we the niggas for the job!" Buck said.

"No doubt. We got him. We'll hit you up to let you know what's up a little later, " Free added.

Knees was pleased, "That's what's up. That's the business. I feel a whole lot better now."

Buck and Free exited the taxicab. Buck threw a one hundred dollar bill at the driver.

Knees, laughing, yelled out of the car window, "Come on man, y'all done shook Money up enough, y'all got him all nervous n' shit."

Knees tapped on the back of the partition, "Sorry about that man, but I had to straighten some things. Ain't nobody trying to beat you man. We ain't all alike, like y'all think."

The driver stayed silent and kept his face to the streets. Knees sensed the driver was still a bit shaken. He realized there was nothing he could do or say to make him feel otherwise. This bothered Knees, the misconceptions of black youth. Yes, he took part in criminal activity, but never had he deliberately hurt anyone. He took solace in the thought that one day things would be different. That people wouldn't be so eager to pass

245

judgment. Right now he chose to go with the flow.

"Yo, put some sounds on in this motherfucka', turn on HOT97."

MEDICINE MAN

He really didn't know why he was so jittery. He had gone on countless dates with some of the prettiest women, yet he had butterflies in the pit of his stomach. He felt like a teenager going out for the very first time.

Were they still on for the evening? He hadn't heard from her all day. He realized he said he would call, but when he saw her leaving his patients' room, he was sure he was about to receive a page from her.

"Oh hell, what am I doing?"

"I'm not new at this."

He picked up the telephone and dialed.

"Hello. " Lisa answered.

"Uh, hello."

"Dr. Brennan?" She asked.

"Chris."

"I'm sorry. Chris."

He thought maybe he should cancel dinner. She just didn't really seem interested.

"I thought you were going to call me?" Lisa asked.

She caught him off guard.

"Uh, yes, I was supposed to, wasn't I ?"

Lisa replied, "Yes you were."

"It's just that ... I uh, saw you leaving Donell's room and I ... well I thought maybe you changed your mind." Chris said.

"Why would I change my mind about you giving me Donell's test results?" Lisa was puzzled.

"Oh no, I meant that you may have changed your mind

about tonight, meeting me." Chris said.

"No, I haven't changed my mind. On the contrary, I'm actually looking forward to meeting with you," Lisa said.

"It would be a nice little get-away from all the drama in my life. Where did you want to meet?" Lisa asked.

Chris felt warm inside. He couldn't quite tell why he felt this way, but he was usually sure of his feelings. Chris always knew what he wanted since the day he was born. That would explain him becoming a physician at the tender age of twenty-two. Two years later a full- fledged surgeon. He aspired to be different, out of the ordinary, and most definitely not anyone's statistic.

"What type of foods do you like?"

"Oh I like everything, pretty much." Lisa said.

"Are you in the mood for anything in particular?" Chris asked.

"Hmm, well, yeah, I'd actually like some good ole' home cookin'."

Chris was surprised. He didn't see Lisa as the "good ole' home cooking" type. Again, he was impressed.

"We could go to Sylvia's! " Lisa exclaimed.

"That we could. " Chris responded.

"What time is good for you?" Chris asked.

"Let's see, how about seven o'clock?," Lisa asked.

"Seven o'clock it is."

"Ok, see you then," Lisa said.

"Yes, I'll see you then Lisa."

Lisa had gone back home. She figured Donell was in the hospital, so there was no question of her having a quiet home with the peace she needed. Surely Chino was still at the hotel waiting for her to return, or maybe he was out looking for her.

Her pager had broken when she'd thrown it earlier at the hospital. She wasn't ready to deal with him just yet. Lisa decided instead to have an enjoyable evening. She felt she deserved it.

Lisa wanted to check on Camaria to see if there had been any new developments. She retrieved the card given to her by Dr. Raymond and called. Unfortunately, there had been no change in Camaria's condition.

Lisa drew herself a nice hot bath. She selected her favorite jazz disc, and let it blare. Lisa remembered a box of scented candles she had purchased. She placed them around the outskirts of her Jacuzzi tub and transformed her bathroom into a sensual aromatic haven.

She thought about Christopher Brennan. Dr. Christopher Brennan...

There was a time when Lisa would have never contemplated going anywhere with a straight-laced gentleman. The type absolutely bored her, but there was something different about this straight laced gentleman. She couldn't quite put her finger on what made him so different.

Lisa had finished up her bath. She wondered what she was going to wear. She really didn't know how to describe the evening. It wasn't a quote, unquote "date". Lisa decided she would look her best as she always did. She'd go with a classic look. Lisa chose a black pair of slacks, a white button up silk blouse, with black open-toe, sling back pumps. She decided she'd go with a ponytail because she had been running for the past few days and it was just easier. As simple as the outfit was, she still managed to look as good as all hell.

Lisa took a few moments to savor the surroundings of her

home. She loved her house. It was one of the things she would regret losing due to the break-up with Donell. She had chosen this domain for the two of them when things were great between them. Money was flowing and everything was "all good". She even enjoyed it after he got locked up. She never disrespected her and Donell's home. Lisa never slept with Chino in her house. Not that it made it better, but in her own little world, she felt she was showing respect for Donell.

Lisa's mind flipped back to Dr. Brennan. She thought that he couldn't be too much older than she was and he was already a doctor. She thought very highly of him for that fact alone. He was very nice to her, even after she was not the nicest person to him in the hospital. Not to mention, he was fine. Lisa wondered why he was single, or was he?

Lisa was just about ready to walk out the door when the telephone rang. She couldn't imagine who it could be. She hadn't been there for a few days. No one knew she was there. Lisa was curious. She answered, "Hello."

"Where the fuck you been, Baby Girl!?" Chino yelled.

'Damn!', Lisa thought.

"Hey ... ," she sullenly responded.

"Hey?"

"What the fuck you mean "hey"?"

"What the fuck is up with you Baby Girl?" Chino asked.

"Ain't nothin' up with me," Lisa said.

"That's it? That's all you have to say to me?" Chino asked.

"What do you want me to say?" Lisa asked.

"I wanna' know why you left without telling me shit? I wanna' know why I haven't heard from you since?" Chino asked.

"You already know the answer to the first question," Lisa

said.

"As for the second, I still need some time to get my head together from all of this Chino. "

"Look Baby Girl, time is something that's coming up real short right now. And I ain't got a lot of it."

"Well I'm sorry to hear that, but that doesn't change my feelings." Lisa said.

"You're sorry to hear that?" Chino snidely asked.

"Where the fuck is this attitude coming from all of a sudden?" Chino asked.

"You just don't get it, do you?" Lisa asked in return.

"I get it, but there ain't shit I can do about the way things went down Lisa. What's done is done."

"Yeah, I know that!" Lisa said.

"Look, I'm supposed to get up with Shark tonight and settle everything, but I need to see you first."

Lisa didn't respond.

"What made you go back to your crib?" Chino asked.

"I live here don't I?" Lisa said.

"Yo', what is up with you? What, you flippin' on me too?"

"Chino I have a real bad taste in my mouth about this shit. My best friend is lying in the fucking hospital, cut the fuck up behind you and your bullshit. I don't even know if she's going to pull through!"

"Now you telling me you have to get with Shark? You robbed this man and killed his girl, and you're going to get up with him? How stupid does that sound?"

"What!" Chino snapped.

"You heard me Chino. You heard exactly what I said, so I'm not going to waste my time repeating myself!"

"I'm not feeling this attitude shit Baby Girl, stay put. I'm on my way over there."

"Uhh, um, I'm about to be out." Lisa said.

"Out where?"

"You know what Chino? You don't listen to me. Donell never listened to me either. When I say I need to get away from this shit, I mean just that. I'll call you." Lisa hung up. The phone immediately began to ring. Lisa grabbed her bag and darted out the door.

She had had enough of the men in her life steering her choices. Things were a lot clearer to her after witnessing the effects of her best friend being brutally wounded. She wanted out of being with men in " the game" and all the drama that came along with them.

*   *   *   *

Chris had arrived a little earlier than seven o'clock. He wanted to make sure he was there waiting when she arrived. He couldn't wait to see her again.

A tall, slim, very attractive waitress sashayed over to Chris' table to take his order. She had an expression on her face as if she had just hit lotto. She merrily greeted him and introduced herself as Simone. He politely informed Simone that he was expecting a guest, but he would like a shot of cognac. The waitress' face did a one eighty. Chris laughed inside. 'Women sure do wear there emotions on their sleeve', he thought.

He noticed his palms were moist. This never happened before. He thought about going to the men's room, but he didn't want to miss Lisa's entrance.

Simone returned with his drink. Her smile was back and stronger than ever. Chris was a little amused by her behavior.

"Will your guest be much longer?" Simone asked.

"Uh," Chris uttered.

"No. His guest has arrived," Lisa replied.

Simone stepped to the side, revealing a delightful sample of the best eye candy Chris had seen all day.

"Well hello there." Chris said.

"Hello yourself." Lisa said.

"Sorry I'm running a little late. Have you been waiting long?" Lisa asked.

"Not at all." Chris answered.

Simone gave Lisa a head to toe review. She guessed she would do.

"This is our waitress, Simone."

"I see. Hello Simone," Lisa said.

Lisa was a woman. She knew the deal. Honey was wishing he was dining alone. She was also wishing that her tip would be his phone number. Not tonight.

"Can I have a peach martini please?" Lisa asked.

"Peach?" Simone questioned.

"Yes, peach. Your bartender should be familiar with it. If not, tell him to add peach schnapps to a dry martini, and garnish it with a slice of orange." Lisa said.

A woman who knew exactly what she wanted and how. That was a definite turn on for Chris.

"That sounds delicious," Chris said.

"It is. It's very delicious," Lisa replied.

A chill flowed through Chris. She was so sensual, yet, she didn't seem to realize it. Another plus in his book.

"You look very nice tonight," Chris said.

"Thanks, you don't look so bad yourself." Lisa smiled.

"You have beautiful teeth," Chris said.

"Thank you."

Chris found himself staring. She was very interesting to say the least.

"So, how was your visit with Donell this afternoon?" Chris asked.

"He was much, much better. Whatever you guys gave him seems to have worked wonders." Lisa said.

"Yeah, well, he still has a serious struggle ahead of him," Chris added.

"What exactly did the tests show?" Lisa asked.

"The tests were conclusive. Donell has what we call "Myeloid Leukemia"."

"Is it curable?"

"Myeloid Leukemia is a cancer that attacks the immune system. It affects about 4,400 people a year in the U.S. and will kill 2,000." Chris explained.

Simone was back. She sat Lisa's drink in front of her. Lisa sipped lightly, nodding an approval.

"Are you ready to order?" She asked, looking directly at Chris.

Lisa told her, "Honestly, I haven't had a chance to view your menu. Can you give us a few more minutes?"

"Of course." Simone spoke, still looking at Chris.

Lisa also found her quite amusing.

"She obviously would like to take more than your order," Lisa said, as she looked over the tantalizing treats on the menu. Chris had no interest whatsoever in the waitress. He decided not to give the comment any merit.

"What looks good to you?" Lisa asked.

"You mean on the menu?" Chris lightly flirted.

Lisa was flattered, "Yes, on the menu."

"I was just about to ask you the same thing," Chris said.

"I'm going to have the smothered chicken with candied yams and greens." Lisa spoke with anticipation and delight. She hadn't had a decent meal in a few days with all that had been going on.

"Mmm, that sounds delicious too." Chris concurred. "I'd love to be your palate, you have very good taste. "

"Thank you."

Simone returned.

"Ah, you're just in time," Lisa teased.

"I take great pride in my work as a service technician. And my perfect timing is definitely an asset." Simone again directed her statement at Chris.

Lisa couldn't resist, "A service technician huh, that's a very clever synonym for a waitress. I like it."

Chris tried not to, but he snickered. Simone was noticeably embarrassed. She rapidly took their orders and disappeared.

"I'm sorry. I didn't mean to be cruel, but I didn't appreciate her attitude and I'd rather have a little fun than to make a scene. Cause a sister can get a lil' ignant."

"Oh it's cool. I'm flattered. I could do without the extra attention." Chris's cognac was long gone. He didn't want their table graced with Simone's presence so he suggested he go to the bar and get them some more drinks.

Lisa told him she didn't want to have too many drinks because she was driving. She told Chris two was her limit. He agreed and excused himself from the table.

Lisa's phone vibrated. The peach martini gave her the extra "umph" she needed to shed her inhibitions on her feelings. She wasn't hiding anymore. She answered.

"Hello."

"Don't hang up Baby Girl!" Chino demanded.

Lisa said, "I'm not hanging up. You have approximately three minutes. Then I'm hanging up."

"I need to see you in an hour at the room."

"Ok Chino."

"I don't know what you up to Baby Girl, but get it out of your system. You hear me?" Chino asked.

"Yes, I hear you."

"One hour." Chino hung up.

Chris returned as Lisa was closing her flip phone.

"Everything alright?" Chris asked.

"Absolutely." Lisa answered.

"Now back to Donell. That's just a little under a fifty percent fatality rate." Lisa stated. "That's not too promising."

"Look at it as the glass being half full, rather than half empty," Chris suggested.

"Yes, that would be best. I'm sorry. I should be more positive. I have been called a pessimist at times," Lisa explained.

"No problem," Chris said. "Some of the best attorneys I know are pessimists."

"As for a cure, well, what I can say is, there is treatment, very expensive treatment."

Lisa asked, "What's expensive?"

"It could be as high as $25,000 to $30,000 annually." Chris stated.

"Shit!" Lisa exclaimed.

"Yes, I know. There is a recommended drug called Gleevec, which is covered by a few insurance companies. I can obtain a list for you."

Their food had arrived. They had a different person serve their meal. They were thankful. They'd both had their fill of Simone for the time being.

"Donell doesn't have insurance." Lisa admitted.

"He may be able to obtain insurance through one of the special programs I know about. I have a few friends. We'll see what we can do," Chris offered.

"Wow, thank you. I know Donell would thank you too for your kindness, especially since I know you really don't have to do that."

"Oh but I do. It's all a part of being the best doctor I can be."

"Do you mind if I ask how old you are? " Lisa probed.

"No, I don't mind. I'm twenty-five. I'll be twenty-six in August."

"Isn't that sort of young, I mean, for you to be a physician already? " Lisa was intrigued.

"Yes, it is. I pretty much got skipped throughout school. Did the college thing really young. Med school at twenty and the rest is history." Chris looked to be enjoying his meal and his company.

"Lisa, even with the drug Gleevec, Donell would still need a bone marrow transplant. This treatment is most effective if done in the first year of discovery, which is why I still need to see Donell's medical records while he was incarcerated."

"You're going to have to ask Donell to help you there. And I'm sure his mother can help you with everything else you'll need." Lisa savored every bit of her meal. She too, was enjoying herself.

"I don't understand." Chris looked concerned.

"Well, Chris, that chapter of my life is closed," Lisa said.

"Sorry, I had no idea."

"No need to apologize. You really had no way of knowing."

Suddenly it seemed very quiet. Chris was still absorbing the great news he had just received. Lisa was fully absorbed in the remains of her dish. She was not the type to front as if she wasn't hungry. She had no problem consuming an appetizer, an entree, and yes, she would be taking a peek at the dessert menu.

"What are your plans for the future?" Chris asked.

Just then Lisa realized, no one had really asked her that, besides her professors of course.

"I'd actually like to break into television broadcasting," Lisa said.

Until that moment, Lisa never really knew what she wanted, but now it was all coming to her so clearly.

"You'd be perfect for that field." Chris said.

"How do you know?" She asked, smiling in comfort as if she'd known him for years.

"I just know." Chris confirmed.

Lisa cocked her head to the side and just looked at him for a few minutes. She felt peaceful. She was totally at ease. He contained an odd sense of familiarity to her.

"So, what do you do Lisa?"

"Nothing right now. I'm sort of taking a break. I just finished school last spring. Donell just came home about a month or so ago. I was taking some time off to spend with him."

"He doesn't seem like your type," Chris said. He instantly

regretted that statement. "Uh, I didn't mean ... "

"You mean because he was locked up?" Lisa asked.

Normally she would have been offended by what Chris was insinuating, but for some reason she took his words at face value.

"What do you think my type is?"

"Hmm, a tall, dark, handsome, hmmm ...   physician maybe," Chris prodded.

Lisa laughed as she smiled, and smiled as she laughed.

"Hmm ... Maybe," she agreed.

DOWN TO THE WIRE

Shark was ready to call in his men and let them know what the plan was. He would give Chino a chance to return everything he took by midnight. If he did not, he would be killed. Shantel would be upset at first, but she would come around. Shark had made up his mind. He could not let him live if he continued to play games. He was taking him for a fool and Shark was nobody's fool.

He called Lil' James first. He didn't get an answer. Shark thought Lil' James might still be resting, but it had been more than enough time. Hustlers rarely slept long, if at all. He then called Goo and Butch and told them the plan. Shark asked them to go check on Lil' James. His vibes were active and they signaled trouble. Shark paged Hench and told him to get over to the penthouse.

Hench arrived in record time. He too was ready for this ordeal to come to an end.

"Hey, what's up?" Hench asked.

"My motherfuckin' blood pressure is what's up!" Shark coldly responded.

"Any news?" Hench questioned.

"Not a word." Shark poured him and Hench their drink of choice, snifters filled with Hennessey.

"You spoke to Chino though, right?" He asked.

"Yeah, me a' talk to im'."

"What's his story?"

"He thinks that I'm responsible for the killing of his father," Shark explained.

"Wasn't that about thirteen years ago?" Hench asked in disbelief.

"Yeah. Something like that." Shark had nothing but love for Chino's father. He was torn about the probable outcome of the situation, but Chino was leaving him no choice.

"That's a long ass vendetta." Hench said. "You got some food in here?"

"Yeah, I always have food."

The phone rang.

"Yeah," Shark answered.

"Yo Boss." It was Goo.

"Yeah."

"He got to him Boss. The people in the building are saying he was burned alive. The area was swarming with police, so we didn't stick around. A couple of my connects said they saw some young kids running out of the building. They didn't recognize them from around the way. One dude said he thinks Chino was with them by the description I gave him."

"A' what in the bumba a gwon'!" Shark was furious. "The bwoy' done gon' mad you know! A' him a' tell me what him fa' do to Lil' James, but I thought after our talk that was squashed! That's it! I want him - Alive! " Shark yelled.

"Nobody knows where Chino is," Goo said.

"Bullshit! I'll find him my blood clad self. A' wha'? A' pure pussies me have working for me? You can't find one mon? One blood clad mon!"

Goo didn't react. This shit was getting way out of control. Chino had them running around like chickens with their heads cut off. Goo had to admit it, they did appear to be useless, but he knew that was not the case. Chino had just been very lucky thus far.

"I'm a' find him Shark, give me an hour."

"Wait! Why am I looking for somebody who is going to come to me tonight?"

Shark regained his composure. Chino had him playing way out of character. Goo didn't tell him, but word was out on the street. The syndicate was already calling Shark soft for the way the situation was being handled. Word had it that he was washed up. Ready to be plucked. An easy mark. Those phrases never entered the same sentence as Shark's name and here it was, his own protégé did him dirty and seemed to have gotten away with it.

"How do you know he's really gonna show?" Goo asked.

"Either he shows or everybody he loves dies. This blood clad game ends tonight!" Sharks' statement was final.

*   *   *   *

It was coming up on eight o'clock in the evening. Shark couldn't help but wonder what Chino was thinking, or better yet, what he was planning. He was not mentally up to this. The death of Shelly was too fresh in his mind and in his heart. He still hadn't planned her memorial service. Shark literally ached all over. Still, there was business to be handled. The more he thought about it, killing Chino was the only solution, even if he did return the money. Chino needed to understand what it meant to betray a true hustler.

Shark took a moment to reflect on his right-hand man. There was nothing he wouldn't have done for Lil' James, and there was nothing Lil' James wouldn't have done for him. Shark thought back on how Shelly and Lil' James would go at each other. He found the two of them to be quite comical during their disputes. Deep down he didn't believe they really hated each other, but you would never know it, listening to the two of them. They were both just standing in front of him arguing like cats and dogs. Now they were eternally gone. Both of them so brutally killed. Lil' James was no saint, but to be burned alive? Shark always thought that was one of the worst ways to go. There would be no open caskets for neither one of them.

As far as Shark knew, Lil' James had no family. Shark was his family. Shark made up his mind. He was definitely finished. He had to get out of the game. Yes the past few days of events were all a part of the program, but the shit was getting real old, real quick. Shantel meant too much to Shark. He had to protect her. He wanted to be there for her, to watch her evolve into the woman Shelly and he always knew she would be.

Shark decided to call Chino to set up the meeting. There was no sense in prolonging the inevitable. He dialed his cell phone.

"Talk to me." Chino answered.

"I see you're still having your likl' temper tantrum," Shark scowled.

"I told you he was as good as dead. He threatened my life. What was I supposed to do?"

"Do you have my money?" Shark asked.

"Na, not all of it. I need more time. Like, another day."

"Chino, you take me for a blood clad fool eh', a me' no pussyhole ya' know! A' me tired of bumba clad playing sien!" Chino knew when Shark resorted to mixing his English with his native tongue, he was hot.

263

"Come on man, you know I don't understand that shit, talk to me in English."

Chino knew exactly what Shark was saying. He was just riling him up even more.

"I swear on my blood clad Moma, Chino," Shark was unable to finish his threat.

Chino chimed in, "Hold up, hold up, for real I got a great idea. I just don't know how you would feel about it. Right now may not be the right time to present it to you."

"A' what the bumba you a' talk bout', idea?" Shark asked, with disgust in his voice.

"Come on Shark, don't sound like that. I'm serious." Chino continued, "See, what I was thinking is this- I don't have all the loot right? So I'll give you what I do have, and since your homeboy wound up late, I can take his spot. You know, I could be your partner."

Shark couldn't believe what he'd just heard. Did this man honestly think he was going to get away with killing the love of his life, the most loyal partner he'd ever had AND become his new partner? He didn't think, he knew, Chino had lost his damn mind.

Chino kept going, taking Shark's silence to mean he was contemplating his idea. "You said you were done with the game right? Well I could be your eyes and ears and the final word will always be yours." Chino had it all figured out.

Shark said, "I get it now. You're crazy! There is no raas clad way I would even consider the thought of you becoming my partner after the shit you just pulled. You really take me for a pussy!" He yelled.

"I'm just trying to make the best out of a situation gone bad." Chino replied.

264

"Too late, you fucked up. I gave you a chance to make it right. You chose murder. You get no more chances." Shark was past the point of being fed up with Chino.

"Midnight, at the entrance of Central Park at 116th street. Be there or your boy Donell will be the first to die. Hmm, let's see where did Lil' James tell me he was, oh yeah, Bronx Lebanon Hospital."

Shark continued, "Now that I think of it, weren't you and Donell's girl getting pretty close? What was her name? Lisette, no Lisa. Yeah mon. Lisa that's it!"

He struck a cord. Chino snapped, "Don't fucking play Shark. Shelly was an accident. Lisa is off limits."

Shark laughed and told him, "No one is off limits!" — "Midnight Chino!" Shark ended the call.

Hench came back into the room. He had gone to the kitchen and made them both sandwiches. Shark was not in the mood to eat. He gave his sandwich back to Hench.

"Was that Chino I just heard you talking to?"

"Yeah."

"What the fuck is he talking about?" Hench anxiously asked.

"Talking a bunch of crazy bullshit!"

"Does he have your money?"

"He says some of it."

"How much is some of it?"

"I didn't ask. If it's not all of it. I don't care how much he has."

Shark told Hench the insane scenario Chino had proposed. He told him that he threatened Chino's people and the threats were to be made into facts if the meeting was not a success. Shark informed Hench of the location of the meeting. He also

265

instructed him to handle the artillery that would be necessary for the encounter.

Once Shark explained the conversation to Hench, he also was ready to kill Chino. He knew Chino was taking Shark for a fool. Who in their right mind would even think of considering an offer such as the one Chino attempted to present?

"I hope you know you're going to have to kill him regardless." Hench looked to Shark.

"Yeah, a' dat me know ... "

RUNNING OUT OF TIME

'Damn--four hours just wasn't enough time, even if he did plan to show up', Chino thought. He had to warn Donell, get his immediate family out of town for a while and last but not least, meet up with Lisa and force her to go to Virginia with him. Her life now depended on it.

Chino had gone back to the room at the Marriott to wait for Lisa. She'd damn well better have a good excuse for being late. Lisa knew time was of the essence at this stage. Where was she anyway? Chino thought Lisa had been acting a little strange. Was she trying to break it off?

Chino had to admit it, this was all becoming a bit much. The whole ordeal was a simple plan that had snowballed into an avalanche of disaster, but there was no turning back now. He wasn't giving Shark back his money. It couldn't be done, even if he wanted to. He already divvied it up and out. He sure as hell couldn't get it back now.

Lisa's hotel room was in walking distance of Shark's penthouse. Shark would've blown a gasket if he had known Chino had been so close the whole time.

Chino didn't waste any more time. He knew when he didn't show for that meeting all hell was going to break lose. He called Donell to warn him.

"Hello," Donell answered.

"Yo dawg, you sound much better." Chino was glad.

"Yeah man I feel much better. Hopefully I'll be out of here soon."

"That's exactly what I was calling you about. About how

267

soon you think they gon' let you out?" Chino asked.

"I don't know. Maybe two ... three days, tops."

Chino sighed, "Yo man, that's just not soon enough."

"What you mean, it's not soon enough? What the fuck is going on Chino?"

Chino paused. He didn't feel like hearing the "I told you so's."

"Shit went a little off track with the plan. Shark wants me to give him all his money and he said he was gon' squash shit."

"You believe that?" Donell asked.

"Hell no. He wants me to meet him at midnight at Central Park and 116th."

"You going?"

"Hell no. But somehow he knows where you are. I gotta' get you out of there before midnight."

Donell was feeling a lot better, but clearly he was in no condition to be swept into this whirlwind of mayhem.

"I ain't goin' nowhere Chino."

"Look man, this shit ain't no game no more. I had to take care of Lil' James. Shark got a mark on you and Lisa and I know that nigga gon' try to go after my moms."

"Goddamn man! I told you not to fuck with him man!" Donell yelled.

Chino knew it was coming, "Yo, I don't need to hear that shit. Straight up. Not now."

"Not now huh? Well when do you think it's gon' be a good time? When we all in the motherfucking morgue!"

"You finished?" Chino asked.

Donell knew Chino's plan was going to blow up in his face. He tried to tell him he was going about it all wrong, but once Chino had something in his head, there was no changing it.

"You just don't get it dawg! That man is after all of us now. You can't get the money back?" Donell was still going to try to sway Chino to do the right thing. Surely Chino wanted to lessen the turmoil that was soon to be upon them.

"You said he told you if you give him back the money, he'd squash it right?" Donell asked.

"And I also said I don't believe he would do it. I heard it in his voice. As soon as I give him his money, that nigga gon' try to smoke me, or have one of his boys try to smoke me. I ain't settin' myself up for my own death. Now that would be crazy! The only thing to do is to make sure everybody's safe until shit calms the fuck down."

"And just how long do you think EVERYBODY can stay away Chino? We got lives, nigga, here. You gonna have to figure something out. Lisa ain't gon' just up and leave. Her whole family is here, and I know damn well when you tell your moms this shit, she gon' look at you like you out your motherfuckin' skull." Donell continued, "She been working for the Board of Ed for damn near twenty years and you gon' tell her she gotta' leave town because you took some money from Shark."

Chino wasn't swayed. "Look man. I can't go to that meeting. You can say what you want. If you don't want me to try to come get you that's cool yo, but just know I tried to come get you dawg. I gotta' go man. One last time, man. You want me to come get you?"

"Be easy Chino."

"No doubt. One love, nigga. If shit get really real, see you on other side." Chino hung up.

Chino dialed his mother's house.

The recorded message played, "Good evening, you've

269

reached the Wells residence. There's no one here at the present time, but if you'd be so kind as to leave your name, number, date and time of your call someone will get back to you at our earliest convenience. Thank you. And have a blessed day ... " Be-----ep.

"Yo Ma, you gotta' erase that damn paragraph of a message. If I was on a pay phone, my damn money would've run out by now! That's just too damn long."

"Look serious business Ma, cause I know you, you could be right there screening your calls, if you are, pick up the phone cause' this is one of the most important messages." Be------ep.

'Damn' Chino hated his mothers' answering machine. His cell phone rang. He saw her number on the display.

"I knew you were there."

"What's so important Chino?"

Ms. Cynthia Wells was a no-nonsense type of woman. She didn't take any mess from anyone. She never remarried after her husband was gunned down. She simply had "friends". All of the old timers from her era knew Poppo and the story behind his demise. Ms. Wells was a highly respected woman in her career and social life as well. She never approved of her husbands' profession, but she was madly in love with the man whom she endearingly termed, "Dr. Love". As far as she was concerned, he was always the treatment for whatever was ailing her.

She didn't approve of the avenue her son had chosen either, but he was her son, her only son. Chino meant the world to her.

"You have some vacation time left don't you?" Chino suspiciously asked.

"Vacation time? What in the world are you asking me that

for boy?"

Ms. Wells could only imagine what was going to come out of her son's mouth next. She had been trying to steer Chino in the right direction since the day his father died. When Poppo was alive, forget it, Chino emulated his every gesture. She felt bad for Chino when Poppo was killed. His father was his whole world.

"I messed up Ma."

"What have you done Chino?"

"I took some money from Shark," Chino admitted.

"So give it back! What the hell is wrong with you Chino? I raised you better than that."

"I can't give it back Ma, this is a lot of money we're talking about."

"Well what the hell did you do with the money?"

"It's too long of a story Ma. I promise once you're tucked away safely, I'll explain the whole thing, but right now, I really need you to trust in what I'm telling you."

"Chino, you expect me to leave my home and take time off from my job because you're out here playing Cowboys and Indians. I don't have time for this silly shit Chino. Now I don't care what you have to do, you give Daverton his money back. That man has never done anything, but help your black ass and you go and steal from him?"

"I just don't know what to do with you. You're too damn old for this shit Chino. Get a damn job and get your life together!"

"Ma, I promise, I will look for a job if you go ahead and take a little leave of absence. Go on down and stay with Aunt Pearl an' them. You ain't been down there in a while."

Cynthia detected that her son was in fact very serious.

"How much money did you take from him Chino?"

"About a million."

"Dollars!" Cynthia yelled.

"Yeah Ma, dollars."

Despite her slight use of profanity, Chino's mother was a woman of God. Cynthia attended service faithfully. She immediately started praying.

"Ah come on Ma, don't start with that. We don't have a lot of time."

"Daverton would never hurt me."

"There's more to it than just the money, Ma."

Chino didn't know how he was going to break the news about Shelly to his mother. They were fond of one another. They were very much opposites, but maybe that's what made them so compatible as "girlfriends", despite the age difference.

"I knew there had to be. What else Chino?"

"I made a terrible mistake. I thought I was shooting at Lil' James, but ... "

"But what, Chino?"

Chino reluctantly told his mother, "I killed Shelly."

"You what?" Cynthia knew she didn't hear what she thought she heard.

"Tell me you didn't say what I thought you said Chino."

"I wish I could tell you that Ma, I really do. Look Ma, things are real crazy right now and Shark is going to probably try to kill me. So I just wanted you to know what was going down. I ain't want you to hear nothing crazy."

Cynthia's heart sank. This couldn't be happening. Not again. She had already lost her husband to the streets and now her only son was so calmly informing her he too would most likely be killed. Not to mention the fact that her son just confessed to killing her long time friend.

"Why would you do something like this? What would make you do something like this?" As level headed as Cynthia had always been, she just wasn't grasping the words that were being spoken.

"Pack some things, Ma. Go to Aunt Pearl's house. I'm going to VA too. I'm a' go chill down there for a while myself."

"Since when are you interested in going South?"

"Ma, you asking too many questions. Are you gon' break out for a while or am I going to have to risk coming over there and packing you up and putting you on a plane myself?"

Cynthia Wells knew her son. He was serious. She needed to lay low for a while, see where the chips would fall. She wasn't ready to lose her only son. Hell, she was tired of working at the school anyway. "Kids just ain't kids, like they used to be", she had found herself saying, on numerous occasions.

"Alright Chino. I'll go," Cynthia finally agreed.

"Thank you, woman. I love you. And I'm sorry. I'll call you in the morning. If you don't hear from me take this number, 555-1750. That's a kid named Knees. He'll know what to tell you. "

"Be careful Chino. You know damn well I don't approve of what you've done, but you're all I've got, so handle this so we can get back to our lives. You just like your damn daddy." Cynthia's words were spoken with true concern and nothing but love.

"I'm good Ma. Tell Aunt Pearl I said hey and I'll call you in the morning. Ma, you really think I'm just like Pop?"

"Hell Yeah." Cynthia said.

Chino said, "Funny, I've always seen a lot of you in me

273

Ma."

"Chino," his mother called into the receiver.

"Yeah Ma?"

" Be careful!"

Chino called Amtrak. It was his best option. The only way he could have gotten a rental car was to wait until the morning, and he had no intention of still being in New York when the morning rolled around. He ordered two tickets. One for him. One for Lisa. They would be waiting for them at the station when they arrived. Chino thought about going back to his crib to get a couple of things he knew he would have wanted to take with him, but that was too risky.

Surely Shark had his place staked out. Whatever he needed, he was sure the cash in the duffle bag he possessed, would handle it. He wondered what was taking Lisa so long. It had been over an hour. Hell, it was going on nine o'clock.

He knew he was going to have a hard time convincing Lisa to go, but she would either go willingly or he would have to do what he had to. Lisa was not to be left behind, at any cost. Chino was sure she'd put up a hell of a fight, but he was not backing away this time. She wouldn't like it, but she would be alive.

Chino had made a big mess of everything. Yes, he had all the money and the ability to take his business to another state and pump all over again, but he was drained. The last seventy-two hours had literally exhausted him. He lay back on the bed and waited for Lisa. Overcome by fatigue, he dozed off.

LIKE WHITE ON RICE

Buck and Free were lucky they had a pocket full of cash. There would have been no other way they would have been able to get the room right next to Chino at the Marriott. The associate at the front desk thought they were kids playing a practical joke when they requested a room, but when they pulled out pretty much what the associate had made in a whole month, he was more than happy to assist the young men.

Buck wanted to let Chino know they were there so he would feel more secure. Free didn't think it was a good idea. He reminded Buck of Chino's mood before they were getting in the taxi to go back to Brooklyn. Buck agreed. They would simply have to follow him as best they could. They too were on foot, so this was going to be interesting.

"Turn on the t.v. man," Buck requested.

"We don't need to turn on the t.v., we need to have pure silence so we can hear what's going on next door." Free was serious about his business.

"Man I can still hear what's going on. What? You can't do two things at once?" Buck asked.

"I can do more than two things at once. That's not the point. This is some real shit Buck." Free said.

"Since when shit ain't ever been real man. It's always real for me. You know that." Buck didn't take kindly to the fact that his partner was insinuating that he wasn't being serious enough.

"It ain't even like that." Free continued, "I just think we should be on our p's and q's. This shit is all going down so weird. I still don't know what's really going on. I know this, if Chino is in danger, we're there."

"Word, tha's wha's up!" Buck agreed.

"I think we should hit up Knees and let him know what our position is, see what he wants us to do," Buck said.

"Yeah, good idea," Free said.

"Wha's good nigga?" Buck asked Knees.

"I'm back in the hood. It's all good out here. I just got through double checking the clubhouse," Knees said.

"Chino said we ain't using the clubhouse no more." Buck reminded Knees.

"I know what he said, but I still wanted to make sure we got everything out of there and nothing can be traced back to any of us. I also got the scoop on Pork. He's going to be getting out of the hospital in a day or two, so that's good news."

Buck was relieved, "Yeah yeah! My nigga. I knew he was gon' be alright. "

"So what's up with y'all? Everything good?"

"As good as it can be, I guess. We were lucky enough to bribe our way into the room right next to Chino's."

"That's perfect!" Knees said.

"Yep, but so far ain't nothing goin' down. I wanted to let Chino know we was here, you know, so he'd know we got his back." Buck waited for Knees' response.

"I don't know about that Buck. What did Free think?" Knees asked.

"He didn't think it was a good idea, since Chino was flippin' earlier."

"Yeah, exactly. Just keep a close watch, but don't reveal yourselves just yet. As a matter of fact, I'll give the word when it's cool to let him know you're there," Knees said.

"How will you know?" Buck asked.

"Don't I always know?" Knees asked.

"Yeah man. You always do. Just hit us back yo'."

Knees assured him that he would.

"So what did he say?" Free asked, although judging from Buck's end of the conversation, he already knew the answer to his question.

"He said to just chill and lay low until he gives the word."

"Cool." Free was relieved Knees' calmed Buck down. Buck could get quite excited at times. He was a wild child since birth, that's actually how he got his nickname. His family and friends would always tell him he was "buck wild."

"I still say we can at least turn on the t.v. I can't just sit here and stare at your ugly ass," Buck joked.

"Fuck you nigga," Free spat back, "You so ugly, when you was born, yo' mama said she didn't care if she was pregnant for the rest of her life as long as they shoved yo' black ugly ass back up her black ugly ass."

"Don't talk about my mother man," Buck warned. "That shit wasn't even funny."

"Come on man, your moms is like my moms man. You know I'm just fuckin' wit' you dawg!" Free knew Buck didn't like anyone joking about his mother. He cut the comedy short and turned the television on, but at a very low volume.

Free needed some air. He went out onto the balcony and marveled at the breathtaking view. 'The people who stay here sure know how to live', he thought to himself. He then noticed the balcony door to Chino and Lisa's room was slightly ajar. He didn't want Chino to spot him, so he quickly ducked back into the room.

"What you doing yo'?" Buck asked, flipping channels.

"I'm making sure we don't blow our cover." Free drew the heavy drapes across the balcony doors.

"We need to stop being so quiet. What's so strange about somebody else being in the next room?" Buck was not the discreet type.

"We need to be quiet, because we need to hear what's going on next door. Now how are we going to be able to hear what's going on over there, if there is a bunch of noise an' shit over here?"

Buck sensed that Free was getting annoyed. He decided to lay off. They were there to protect Chino and if for some reason something happened to Chino because of their inadequacy, it would be on their heads. He couldn't take that.

"I'm hungry." Free picked up the room service brochure, scanning it to see what appealed to his appetite.

Buck wasn't hard to please. "Just order me a hamburger with everything!"

Free wasn't havin' it, "We in a high class hotel and all you can think to order is a burger?"

"Yo', just who the fuck do you think you are man? You been talking like you better than a nigga or somethin'. What's up with all that?" Buck wanted to check the situation before it got out of hand.

"What's up wit' you nigga? I'm just sayin', when we gon' get a chance to lamp like this again. Let's live nigga!" Free wasn't trying to be better than anyone. He knew what it was not to have.

"My bad man, you dead right, I'm trippin'." Buck realized his homeboy wasn't flexing on him. It was he, who in fact was

278

acting "new".

Free thought he heard activity in the hallway. "Sshh," he told Buck.

He got up and went over to look through the peephole in the door. He knew he had heard the ring of the elevator signaling that it had just stopped.

"Who is it?" Buck was anxious. He couldn't sit still for long periods of time.

"Sshh! I don't know yet." Free was trying his best to get a good look through the microscopic hole.

"They need to make these damn things bigger. I can't hardly see shit!"

"Let me try!" Buck pushed Free to the side. The movement caused a stumbling noise.

Bucks' eye was pressed up against the tiny hole. The commotion behind the door caused the female to look toward their door.

Buck saw her. "It's just some lady." He turned and went back to watching television.

"That must be the chick Lisa they was talking about." Free attempted to look out of the peep hole once again, but she had already disappeared into the next room. "Well something should be hoppin' off soon."

"You gon' order our food or what?" Buck squawked. He was sprawled out on one of the queen-sized beds.

"Yeah, I'ma' order me a steak man. You still want a burger?" Free thought he would give his partner one last chance to sample the good life.

"Yeah. I still want a burger. "

Free couldn't resist, "Well I guess what my mother said

279

was true. You can take the boy out the ghetto, but you can't take the ghetto out the boy."

"I don't see no fucking boys in here nigga. Do you? For your information I don't eat no steak."

"You ever had steak?" Free asked.

Buck looked ashamed, "Na man, my moms said she ain't have it like that. Even when I give her money, she go smoke it up and bring us oodles of noodles and shit like that."
Free had a feeling that was the deal, but he wasn't going to blow his boys' spot up like that.

"Yo man, just try it. I'll order a burger too, just in case you ain't wit' it. "

Buck gave in, "That's wha's up!"

Free picked up the phone and ordered both of them the surf and turf special and two deluxe hamburger platters. Hell, he ain't never have no steak either, except for a steak and cheese sub. He heard his mother brag about it so much when her men would take her out, he knew he had to try it. When asked how he wanted their steaks cooked, Free mimicked what he'd always heard his mother say. "Well done. I ain't no vampire. I don't eat nobody's blood."

Buck went over to the wall and placed a glass to it and his ear to the other end.

Free screamed on him, "Nigga, that shit don't really work. You been watching way too much t.v.."

"How you know? " Buck asked.

"Do you hear anything," Free asked in return.

Buck just looked at him with a silly grin and they both began to laugh out loud.

There was a knock at the door. Buck rushed over to see who it was.

"Room service."

"Damn that was quick," Free said.

Without checking Buck swung the door open.

A 9 millimeter was pointing at his face.

"See what happens when you sleep?" Chino pushed Buck back into the room.

"How did you know we were in here?" Free asked, putting his gun away.

"I didn't know who was in here, but I knew something wasn't right." Chino locked the door and joined his two junior hit men. Chino actually seemed happy to see the pair.

"Ah come on man, I know Knees called you." Buck was a little shaken from being caught off guard.

"Na, Knees ain't hit me off. He knows I would have screamed on him and y'all."

"He's just lookin' out for you Boss." Free went back over to the balcony and drew back the drapes. Now that Chino knew they were there, he could enjoy the room like he wanted to in the first place.

"I know, but he is hardheaded as shit. I didn't want y'all mixed up in this shit, but since y'all here we might as well make the best of it."

Free's cell phone rang. He looked at the display, "It's Knees."

Chino grabbed the phone.

"Yeah," Chino tried to disguise his voice.

"Who's this?" Knees asked.

"Who you think it is?"

Knees had a smile in his voice, "Chino! Damn man. How'd they blow their cover?"

"They didn't. You could say, I blew mine. I told you I ain't

281

need no shadow on this one. "

"And I told you, I didn't agree." Knees stood his ground.

"A'ight, you win, as if you didn't know that already. "

"Just lookin' out for my boss man."

"Yeah, yeah I know. Look, Lisa is in the shower. We should be leaving out of here for Penn Station in about an hour. Shark thinks we're meeting at midnight. As long as we get on the train safely, that's that. "

"Sounds easy enough." Knees thought it sounded way too easy.

"Things should go as smooth as a baby's ass. None of his boys was good enough to find me," Chino gloated.

"Don't toot your horn yet Boss." Knees had an eerie vibe.

"My moms says things like that. How old are you again? Chino asked.

"I'm not feeling this shit." Knees let it be known.

"What shit? Me, getting on a train and breakin' out? I told you I would send for y'all later."

"I'm not talking about that. So Lisa's down with the trip?" Knees asked.

"Well, she don't know we're leaving so soon, but I'm sure when I tell her what's really going down, she'll go along with the plan."

"You sure about that?" Knees questioned.

"Baby Boy, if you got something to say, say it!"

"It's just that when I was there, I got the impression that she wasn't really down for you like that." Knees put it out there intentionally. He knew Chino did not want to hear that, but as his right-hand man, he felt it was his place.

"What the fuck you talking about Baby Boy?"

"I'm saying I don't want you gettin' caught out there

282

behind no broad."

"Lisa ain't no broad to me, Baby Boy. I got tons of broads. I don't give a fuck about them. She's different."

"Yeah, well she may be different to you, but I don't think you're so different to her. You get what I'm saying? That's just what I picked up from being with you two earlier."

Chino knew Knees was right ninety nine percent of the time, but he was in complete denial where Lisa was concerned.

"Na man, she'll see it for what it is. She's far from stupid."

"I hope you're right, Boss," Knees really wanted to believe Chino, but he knew better.

Chino didn't even notice the bus boy bringing in two large trays of food.

"I gotta' go Baby Boy. Lisa's waiting for me. I gave my moms' your number. I told her if something happened to me, you'd let her know."

"Be careful, Boss."

"Always, Baby Boy. Yo', thanks for the shadow."

"No doubt, Boss. No doubt!"

Chino ended the call. He then saw that they had company. For a moment, he thought he recognized the bus boy as an old schoolmate, but quickly dismissed the thought.

He served the meals and waited for his tip. When he realized the two of them were not even entertaining the thought of gratuity, he looked at Chino. Chino, knowing the boys had no clue of what a tip was, extended a ten-dollar bill in his direction. He took his tip and left without so much as a "thank you".

"Your welcome motherfucker!" Chino shouted as the bus boy left the room, "That's why y'all don't get no fucking tips. Ill-mannered motherfucker!"

Buck and Free found it amusing, they laughed.

"A'ight you two, I'ma' go chill for about an hour, maybe an hour and a half. I'll knock when I need y'all."

The boys were both devouring their steaks. They nodded to let Chino know they'd heard him.

Chino looked at the way they were going at their meals, "Damn, y'all act like y'all ain't never eat a steak before."

The two looked at one another, snickered, and continued to feverishly annihilate their dishes.

Chino realized they were serious, "I see, well, do you. I'll holla." Chino left.

IT'S NOW OR NEVER

Lisa was still in the shower. Chino decided to take advantage of the moment. He stripped off his clothing and entered the bathroom. The combination of steam and the aroma of vanilla cream stimulated his senses. He watched the silhouette of Lisa's body move with the grace of a seasoned ballerina. Chino adored her.

He slowly opened the glass door that was separating him from his goddess of gorgeousness. Chino embraced Lisa from behind, placing scintillating kisses on her neck leading down her shoulders. Feeling the tenseness of her muscles, he slowly massaged her skin, luscious kisses following every spot he kneaded.

Lisa moaned, releasing the tension the past seventy-two hours had caused. He left no part of her body untouched. Chino knew exactly what would hit the spot. He began to massage Lisa's scalp with one hand and her neck with the other, and oh what magical fingers and hands he had. She was putty in his hands.

"I want you," he whispered as his tongue tantalized her right earlobe. "Can I have you Baby Girl?"

Lisa wanted to resist. She was furious with Chino. She didn't want to forget that this was the man who turned her life upside down. The man who was responsible for Camaria being robbed of her beautiful physical appearance and most likely her spirit. The man that left her man to damn near die to handle his business, when he needed him the most. She couldn't possibly give in to him ... could she?

285

Chino situated himself so that his body was the shower heads' center of attention. He closed his eyes and let the water run down his olive skin like a waterfall. This was her opportunity to leave. He was no longer holding her.

A part of Lisa wanted to curse Chino out, burst out of the shower retrieve her things and leave him standing there ... alone. Then there was the other part of her. The part that was craving his touch. She still wanted him. She was mad at herself. How could she still want him, after everything he'd done!?

Lisa just stood and stared. Chino's eyes suddenly opened, startling her. He looked deeply into her eyes and held out his arms. She stepped into them. Chino held Lisa tightly.

"I want you, "he whispered again. "Can I have you Baby Girl?"

"Yes Chino, you can have me."

Chino immediately dropped to his knees and began to lavishly lick Lisa's pussy. The heat of his mouth along with the heat from the shower drove her into a frenzy. Chino couldn't get enough. He licked and sucked her pussy like it was a tootsie roll pop and he was trying to see how many licks it would take to get to the creamy center.

Lisa was ready to return the gesture. He was successful in placing her in her "zone" as she called it.

"Let's get a little more comfortable. Shall we?"

Chino picked Lisa up and carried her to the bed, both of their bodies still dripping wet.

He lay her on the bed and picked up where he left off.

"Damn Baby Girl, your pussy tastes so sweet. You just taste so fucking good." Chino said between the dips in between her thighs.

"You don't taste bad yourself. Can I have a taste?" Lisa was fully ready to participate. Whatever issues she had with Chino, didn't seem to be an issue anymore.

"Shit, you know you don't even have to ask. Na, better yet, ask and you shall receive." Chino said as he glided his pulsating dick into his favorite oral tunnel.

Lisa was giving it back, just as it was given to her. Hot and wet. Lisa deep throated the dick like the thoroughbred she was. Chino loved every bit of it. He fingered her pussy to show his appreciation. Lisa was dripping wet from the mixture of Chino, the shower and her own cum.

She was ripe and ready to be picked. He pulled his dick out of her mouth and flipped Lisa onto her stomach.

She protested, "I wasn't finished."

"Oh yes you are. I'm gettin' in that wet pussy."

Chino loved doggie style with Lisa. He watched as her juicy ass shook with every thrust of his cock. He grabbed a hold of Lisa's hair and pulled her head back to meet his lips, kissing her deeply. He then pushed her head forward with the slight force she'd come to like. He moistened his fingers and began to tease her butt hole, while pounding his dick into his "Baby Girl".

"Fuck me Chino. Uhm fuck me baby." Lisa was in another world.

"I am fucking you, and I'm gonna' keep fucking you. You hear me. I'm gonna keep fucking you 'til death do us part!" Chino's adrenaline was at its boiling point. He thought Lisa's body was incredible. He loved how she moved to meet his every stroke. His body gave in. Chino released an explosion of creamy thick liquid into Lisa's being, then collapsed on top of her.

"Chino." Lisa whispered.

Chino was still out of breath and trying to regain his composure. He lifted himself off of Lisa. He knew he needed to tighten up. Time was of the essence, and it was running out.

"What the hell was up with you earlier? Where were you, and why were you trippin' the fuck out?"

Lisa looked at Chino as if he wasn't the same person she had just allowed to have his way with her. Lisa had told herself before she had gotten there that she was not going to sleep with Chino no matter what. The shower was just to relax her. Yeah right. Who was she kidding? She was whipped, plain and simple. Lisa slid out of the bed and began to collect her things.

"You can keep this room as long as you want. I actually booked it for the month." Lisa scurried to get her clothes on.

"Yo, what the fuck is your problem?" Chino asked.

"Look, Baby Girl, fuck where you were. What matters is that you're here now. You know this shit is supposed to be going down tonight. It's supposed to go down at midnight. I need for you not to fight me on this and just come on and break out with me. Shit, we should already be at Penn Station getting on the train."

Everything that happened in the past couple of days came rushing to her mind. Lisa felt stifled. She was not going to abandon Camaria. She was not leaving her family. She was not going, period.

Lisa was now fully dressed. She had gathered her toiletries out of the bathroom and packed them into her bag. Chino was still lying in the bed, staring at her in disbelief.

"I'm not going with you Chino. I can't go." Lisa didn't look at him when she spoke. She couldn't.

He snapped. "Na' see that's where you're wrong! You're going, whether you fuckin' want to or not!" Chino leaped out of the bed and grabbed her.

"Chino what the fuck are you doing?" Lisa was shocked. She had never seen this side of Chino. He never acted this way before. "Have you lost your motherfucking mind?"

Chino's mind reflected on Knees' words, 'Was he on point? Is this bitch trying to take me for a fool?'

Chino's hands were around Lisa's neck. "What the fuck yo'? You tryin' to play a nigga?"

Lisa's voice was strained from the pressure of Chino's hands. "I ain't trying to play you Chino, I swear!"

Chino let her go. He immediately regretted his actions. "I'm sorry Baby Girl ... I didn't mean to hurt you." She had his emotions riled up.

Lisa was definitely ready to go. She didn't know what he would do next. "Chino I can't just pick up and leave everything," she stated, crying lightly while rubbing her neck.

"Leave everything like what? You're not working right now, so you don't have no job to call. What is so important that's holding you here?"

Chris Brennan came into her mind. Lisa had a very nice time with him. She was looking forward to seeing him again. Tell Chino she wanted to stay put so she could explore a friendship with someone new. She didn't think so.

"Chino my whole family is here and I can't just up and leave. My mother would have a fit. I can't worry her like that, you know she has heart trouble. I'm not going to be the one

289

that drives her to a heart attack."

"You don't have to tell her why you're going." Chino was not giving up.

"What happened to you sending for me?" Lisa was not giving up either.

"The tables have turned Baby Girl. It's now or never."

Lisa hesitated, "I really don't know what to say Chino. I can't leave right now."

"Would it be better for your mother to see your ass lying in a morgue? I got a better one for you. What would it do to her if she wasn't able to identify you at all? These motherfuckers ain't playing Lisa, but if you want to keep playing, fuck it, do you."

"Knees was right! I should have known. That nigga ain't never wrong. "

"Right about what!?" Lisa asked.

"Right about your fake ass. You don't really give a fuck about a nigga. All that bullshit you putting out, you lucky I love you, or I'd break your fucking neck right now."

"I love you too, Chino."

"Don't ever tell me that again. Go tell that shit to your boy." Chino looked at Lisa in disgust.

"Chino, I didn't ask for you to create this fucking disaster. You did it on your own. I do love you, but I can't leave my family. Maybe one day you will understand my decision. As far as me being fake, I'm as real as you'll ever get. Just because I'm not doing what you want, when you want, doesn't make me fake. It makes me a human being who thinks for herself."

Chino took it down a notch. He realized this was all very sudden, but that's how the game was. Lisa knew this. He didn't understand why she was being so difficult. Chino wasn't buying the "mother" bit. Lisa had left town plenty of times without letting her mother know. After all, she was a grown woman who had been living on her own for quite a while.

"Baby Girl, you know I wouldn't tell you nothing wrong. I need for you to understand the severity of this situation. Look at what happened to Shelly and Camaria. You fuckin' actin' like you can't be fuckin' hurt or killed. I can't stay here to protect you because if I stay I won't be alive to protect you."

"What about your little boys? Can't they look after me?" Lisa asked with a smirk in her voice.

"Ok, I see you think this shit is a game. My little boys as you call them, could very well protect you, but I'm not going to ask them to do that, Why should I let them risk their lives to save yours? You ain't fuckin' willing to risk a motherfuckin' thing for me. You got me mixed up with some other nigga. I ain't no fuckin' Herb."

"I never said you were. Chino. I'm fully aware of who you are."

"You know what? You need to go back to Donell. Y'all deserve each other. His bitch ass would rather sit in a hospital like a sitting duck. I offered to go get him, but he's on the same shit you are. I thought you were thorough enough. I thought I had a down ass bitch by my side. I should have known better, you fucked Dee over, why not me too, right?"

Lisa didn't want to hear anymore. She felt she had heard enough. "What we've shared has been incredible Chino, but I guess this is where I get off."

Chino looked at Lisa as if he had never declared his love. "Don't get it fucked up–you were never really on!"

"Oh it's like that now," Lisa asked.

"What the fuck should it be like? I risked my fucking life to stay here and try to get you out of harm's way, but you claim you just can't leave. What? You found some new nigga that quick? Or maybe he was there all along!" Chino was hurting inside. He really thought Lisa was the one. He was slowly realizing this was not the case.

Lisa had to take a minute to realize exactly what she was doing to Chino. This man had been there for her. He gave her whatever she wanted, whenever she wanted it, and plus, the lovin' was off the chain. Did she really want to just send him on his way?

She tried to switch it up. Lisa went toward Chino to embrace him. He now looked at her as if she was out of her mind. He figured maybe she was confused. He decided to un-confuse her.

"You know what? I'm not playing with you no fuckin' more, and I ain't asking you no more! I'm telling you! You comin' with me!"

Lisa was tired of fighting. She figured she would just go and slowly but surely work her way back to New York.

"Fuck it Chino! I give up. Let me at least check on Mari before we go." Lisa pleaded.

"Do whatever you gotta' do! " Chino flatly stated.

IT'S A SMALL WORLD AFTER ALL

This was too good to be true. Could the man he saw in room 415 possibly be who he thought it was? Darrel had almost tripped over his own feet trying to leave the room after delivering the meals. He had to make contact with Goo. This was his chance. He could prove he was qualified to be down with Shark's boys. Best of all he would make a shit load of money in the interim.

Darrel hadn't seen Chino in a while, but he was sure it was him. He felt sure enough to make the call.

"Yeah Hello. Is this Goo?"

"Who phone you calling?"

"Goo."

"Well talk."

"I found Chino"

"Who is this? This better not be no fucking joke." Goo had a strong feeling this was far from a joke.

"This is Darrel man. I mean Deezo."

"Word! What's up nigga? So you saying you found Chino huh?"

"No doubt. He's right here in the hotel I work at."

"And what hotel is that?"

"The Marriott on 59th. He's in room 415."

"You gotta' be kidding? That fuckin' slick motherfucker." Goo couldn't believe they were looking in all the wrong places. All this time, he'd been just blocks away from Shark's crib.

"Na man. I'm dead serious. I took food to the room and he was there on the phone. He had two young kids with him. He even gave me a tip. I looked right at him. Yo is that offer still good?"

"I gotta' see what Shark wants to do. Things have kind of changed for the moment."

"Changed?" Darrel asked.

"Yeah, Shark is trying to give Chino a chance to rectify the problem. He's supposed to get up with him at midnight."

"Damn!" Darrel was disappointed. He kept it real, "I really could have used that paper man."

"I feel you dawg, but like I said, let me hit Shark up, see what he wants to do. There may still be something in it for you because we've definitely been looking for him. It's damn near midnight now. He should be planning to leave your hotel any minute. I need you call me as soon as he does."

"You think Shark might finally think about letting me get down with y'all?" He asked.

"Now is not the time for that Deezo, but I'll definitely mention it soon. Don't forget – call me if and when he leaves."

"What about the two kids that's with him?"

"We don't murder kids."

Goo was anxious. It was close to midnight. He had a feeling Chino had no intention of meeting Shark. Goo struggled with the idea of telling Shark that he knew where Chino was. Maybe he would just let midnight roll around and let Shark see for himself that he wasn't going to show. Then he would divulge Chino's whereabouts. By then Shark would be furious and more than ready for Chino to be executed. Goo wanted Chino out of the way. He'd always thought he was a snake. He had a thought to go to the hotel and just kill him and explain it to Shark later, but he changed his mind. Shark needed to settle this. This was very personal to him.

Goo felt there was already too much disloyalty and secret keeping going on. He decided to call Shark and let him know what Deezo had told him and let him decide what course of action he wanted to take. It was already eleven o'clock.

"Boss."

"Yeah."

"I got some news. You remember Deezo?"

"No ...a' who is dat'?"

"Deezo. I had brought him around maybe two months ago. You said you was going to think about puttin' him on, but we just never got back to him."

"Goo I don't have time for this shit right now. What the hell does he have to do with anything?"

"He located Chino."

Shark was very attentive at this point. "Where is he?"

"Yo, you ain't gonna believe this shit! He's at the Marriott on 59th."

"What?"

"That's what he's saying. He says he works there. And he said Chino had some kids with him. Those are probably the kids that were spotted leaving Lil' James', so I guess they are still with him. Deezo said he brought them some food. They're in room 415."

"A' wha' da blood clad boy pussy for real. Him a' use likl' picknies fa' a man business, ya' know, me swear say da buoy gone crazy for real."

"It's close to midnight, did you want to give him a chance to still show or do you want to cut him off at the crossroads." Goo was hoping he would choose the latter.

Shark thought about his next move. Chino had kids with him. They had a rule. No kids would fall victim to their violence or distribution of drugs. Chino was operating totally against the rules. He was apparently using these kids as his vigilantes. He now viewed Chino as a pure coward.

Shark was determined not to waste any more time. Chino thought he was the one with all the surprises. Well, he was about to receive one of the biggest surprises of his life.

Shark told Goo, "Call your buoy and tell him we're on our way. Tell him to do what he has to do to keep Chino in that hotel!"

"I'll call him right now." Goo ended the call.

Shark told Hench to gear up. Butch was called in. Shit was on.

Goo got right back to Shark. Deezo would do what it took to keep Chino there. Goo was already in route to the hotel. Shark told him to meet them in the loading area where deliveries were brought.

Goo assured him he would find them.

Shark and Hench were heading out of the door, all of a sudden, Shark paused.

"What's up man?" Hench asked.

"I have to call Shantel." Shark knew that he wanted to come out of this the victorious one, but there were no guarantees. He needed to hear his daughter's voice.

"Call her while we are on our way." Hench was looking at his watch as if to signal to Shark that they were running out of time.

"Go get the car ready. I'll meet you in front." Shark headed for the phone. He didn't want to call Shantel from his cell phone. He wanted her to see their home number on the caller ID for some strange reason.

He dialed his mothers' home. There was no answer. He

wondered where they could be at such a late hour. He dialed Shantel's cell phone. There was no answer. He dialed his mothers' cell phone. There was no answer. Shark wished he would have just left without attempting to call, now he wouldn't be able to fully focus on the matter at hand.

'Where the hell could they be?' He thought.

There was no more time to waste. It was already twenty past eleven. Shark took the elevator from his penthouse down to the lobby, and proceeded through the huge glass double doors. He entered the black Lincoln Town Car. Once inside, they drove off, on their way to face the initiator of this mayhem.

Hench looked to his right and noticed Shark was deep in thought. He didn't want to disturb him, but he wanted to know where Shark's head was at.

"What's going on man? You don't seem like yourself." Hench was truly concerned. His cousin had been through hell and back in the past couple of days.

"Me can't get in touch with Shantel and Moma. It's late. Where would they go, and not tell me?"

Hench didn't have any answers. He didn't want to think the worst. "Maybe they're just sleep. It is pretty late."

"Maybe," Shark agreed, wanting to believe his cousins' words.

"The sooner you handle this shit with Chino, the better. We need to get shit regulated on the street. Niggas is talkin'."

"Me na' care what nigga's a' talk 'bout sien."

Hench said, "I know you don't care Shark, but you're still the man. Niggas look to you for leadership. It's as simple as that."

Shark dismissed his comment, "Yeah, yeah, me know."

They pulled up in back of the hotel. In all honesty, they could have walked to the Marriott. It was just that close. Shark was cursing himself inside. All of this time, Chino had been right under their noses.

They spotted Goo's car and parked along side of it. There was another person in the car with him. They assumed this person was Deezo.

Goo and Deezo quickly transferred themselves into the Lincoln.

"Fellas, fellas what's the deal?" Goo asked, slamming the door behind him.

"I told you about slamming my fucking doors. This ain't no fucking hooptie," Hench barked.

"My bad, my bad, dawg." Goo apologized and handled the introductions, "Y'all seen this nigga before, but just in case y'all don't remember, this is Deezo. "

"Yeah, me remember im'," Shark confirmed.

Hench remained silent. He didn't take well to newcomers. Hench didn't trust anyone.

"Is he still in there?" Shark asked in a venomous tone.

"Yeah, he's still inside." Deezo answered.

"Shouldn't you be in there, just in case he tries to leave?" Hench asked him.

"I wanted to show y'all how to get to the freight elevator and up to the room without nobody seeing you."

"And what if he's leaving the fucking hotel right now, how would we know this, with you here in the motherfuckin' car with us?" Hench questioned Deezo again.

Goo spoke up, "Look man, what the fuck you givin' my man the third degree for? If it wasn't for him, we still wouldn't

298

know where the bastard was, so shut the fuck up with all that bullshit and let's deal with the real shit!"

"Goo's right." Shark said. "We are wasting time."
Butch pulled up in his SUV. He noticed all the heads in Hench's car, so he stayed put. Shark signaled to acknowledge his presence.

Deezo didn't want the opportunity to pass by without speaking for his for tipping them off as to Chino's whereabouts, "Mr. Shark, uh I was wondering if I could be uh, be uh ... compensated for this information."

Hench screamed on Deezo. He thought it was in poor taste to bring up money at a time like this.

"Nigga, what the fuck? You a small time ghetto snitch motherfucker? You beggin' for money up front, shit, we ain't even seen the motherfucker yet!"

Shark's mind was stuck. Deezo called him Mr. Shark, that was the first name Shelly had ever called him. "Leave im' Hench. Look buoy, if you get me Chino I will promise you it will be well worth your while."

Deezo took Shark at his word. He told them the best way to get up to the room without being seen. Butch was advised via cell phone. Shark ordered that the kids be spared. The sight of Chino's torture and murder would surely be enough to guarantee their silence and hopefully persuade them to rethink their future.   Shark thought to himself, 'It was eleven forty-five. If Chino was still in his room, he had no intention of meeting him. If he wasn't there, well then, Butch was on his way to meet Chino at Central Park at the entrance scheduled. But if he was there, it was time. It was time for Chino to meet his maker.

TOO LITTLE, TOO LATE

It was too late to call the hospital. Lisa called Camaria's mother's cell phone. It rang to voice mail. She again remembered cell phones weren't allowed to be turned on in hospitals due to the interference with the equipment. She wouldn't be able to check on Camaria.

"Chino, we can't leave yet. I can't check on Mari until the morning."

"You know Baby Girl for someone who is so smart, you can be ... never mind. We don't have time to wait until the morning. We'll check on Camari from the train."

"Can't we just stay here tonight and pull out in the morning? Nobody knows you're here."

Chino really wanted to leave as soon as possible, but what could it hurt? Lisa was right, no one knew where they were. They could just as easily leave in the morning. Chino called next door to let Buck and Free know the plan. They didn't like it, but who were they to argue. Lisa emerged from the bathroom wearing a chocolate brown sheer teddy with matching thongs underneath. "Well since we're going to make a night of it, we might as well pick up where we left off before things got ugly." She spread herself across the bed, legs wide open revealing her neatly shaved tasty treat.

Chino looked at her suspiciously. "What's going on wit' you? You ain't been acting like yourself all night. One minute you hatin' on me. The next minute you want me. What the fuck you been smokin'?"

"I ain't been smoking shit, but I need to smoke somethin'

300

with all this shit goin' on, you got some trees?"

"Yeah I got some trees, but I don't know if I should let you smoke, it's hydro. And you know how you get."

"How do I get?" Lisa asked.

"You get fuckin' crazy, wanting me to do all kinds of crazy shit to you."

"And ... What's wrong with that? I know niggas that would kill to have a bitch like me. What Luda said? 'Y'all want a lady in the street, but a freak in the bed. So what's the problem? You made me this way."

Chino couldn't deny that. He went into his jacket pocket and pulled out the weed and the blunts and poured Lisa and himself a drink. Now this was more like it. This was how it should be, how it used to be when things were normal.

Chino and Lisa got high as all hell. Lisa wanted something different. No sex this time, just touching, and kissing. Chino utilized his skilled fingers to gratify both of her chambers of flesh as they laye side-by-side, his tongue deeply implanted down her throat. Chino was more than happy to oblige. Lisa was on fire. The mixture of the alcohol and weed had her feeling extra horny. Her hands began to explore Chino's body. She used her saliva to lubricate her hands and began to jerk him off softly. Chino's body was totally relaxed. All the trouble he had been facing was erased, at least for that very moment. Lisa's finesse with her hands brought Chino to ecstasy. He felt she was the epitome of erotica.

The reaction of Chino climaxing was enough to send Lisa into delirium. She jumped up and situated her pussy on Chino's face and rode his tongue to climax.

The two of them were exhausted. Lisa was out of it. Chino was feeling mellow, to say the least. He looked at the clock.

The digital display read 12:17. Chino wondered what Shark was doing at that moment. Surely he was heated. He would work it out later. Right now he was with his girl and her pussy was the bomb and he loved her and they were getting out of there first thing in the morning.

Chino looked over to Lisa who had fallen asleep. He slightly opened the balcony doors to give the room some relief of the fumes. He covered Lisa and called Knees.

"I was waiting for your call," Knees said.

"Yeah, I bet you was. Look, me and Baby Girl gon' pull out in the morning. She gotta' check on a homegirl of ours an' shit, you know Camaria, the one in the hospital. I already told Buck and Free."

"You think that's wise man?" Knees heard the liquor in Chino's voice. He wondered what else Lisa had talked him into.

"Nobody knows we're here. It's cool. We out first thing in the morning. It's already after midnight so Shark already know I ain't show." Chino was still smoking. He blew smoke as he talked.

"You sound a little lit up Boss." Knees put him on the spot. Chino was slipping, maybe because he knew the walls were closing in on him, maybe because of the mistakes that had been made, but Knees was going to snap his ass back to reality.

"I had a couple of drinks and a blunt or two. I'm good though." Chino assured Knees.

"You don't sound so good to me. You need to tighten up. You missed a very important meeting. That means the contract is back on. You need to be getting the fuck out of there right now." Knees was wondering what the hell Lisa had over Chino. Unfortunately Knees had never had a sexual encounter.

He was paralyzed before the opposite sex could get their hands on him. He was sure it had to have something to do with sex.

"Be easy Baby Boy. I'm still the Boss." Chino pulled rank. He heard the concern in Knees' voice.

"You gotta' keep your feelings outta' this type of shit Baby Boy. You ain't gon' last feeling shit."

"Right now I'm just trying to make sure your life lasts. " Knees gave it right back to him. "Your time is up. Don't sleep on them niggas man."

"Yeah I know. I'm a' lay down and get some rest. The morning will be here in a minute.

Lisa's ride is in the hotel garage. Like I said, we'll be out first thing in the morning. Buck and Free will drive her car back to Brooklyn. I want you to take it to her moms' house and park it. I'll hit you with the address when the time comes."

"If you want my opinion, you need to slap some water on your face and get the fuck up out of there and get your ass to Penn Station. Alone."

Chino was tired of Knees being on this anti-Lisa shit. What did he really know about her? Nothing.

"The plan is already in place. What, you uptight because I planned this move without you?"

Knees sighed heavily, "You high, man ...and you shouldn't be. This ain't the time."

"That's it Baby Boy! You still actin' like a fuckin' little boy, so stay in a fucking child's place. I run this shit. Don't fucking forget that!" Chino hung up in Knees' ear.

Knees' nerves were bad. It wasn't from Chino's harsh words to him. He attributed his outburst to the liquor and weed. Knees sensed trouble. He called Bones and told him to round up everybody. Everyone was to be strapped. He told him to hurry he felt there wasn't much time left, at all.

Knees called Free on his cell phone.

"Yo, we on our way up there."

"Word, what's up?" Free asked.

"Something ain't right." Knees flatly stated.

"What you mean?" Free was under the impression that everything was fine. Everything seemed pretty calm so far.

There was a loud knock at the door. "Yo man, hold up somebody's at the door."

Buck had taken the liberty of going over to check to see who it was. He couldn't see clearly. He hated those little holes, "Who is it?"

"Room service."

"Who is that?" Knees asked.

"Sound like the nigga said, "room service"," Free answered.

"What the fuck, y'all still ordering shit," Knees yelled.

"Na," Free said, "We ain't order nothin' since the first time."

"Don't open the door. That's an order." Knees felt his chest palpitating. Trouble was imminent.

Free told Buck to get away from the door, he demanded to know, "What the fuck is going on?"

Knees had no answers this time. "I don't know for sure, all I can say is eliminate anybody in your way to protect our boss. We'll be there as soon as we can."

THE FINAL CONFLICT

Goo and Hench knocked on the door of room 415. Deezo and Shark stayed in the cut. Deezo had an emergency key card. If they weren't asked in, they would force themselves in. They heard someone ask who it was, but there was complete silence thereafter.

"Fuck it, come on, let's go in." Goo was tired of playing. He looked to Shark. Shark looked at Deezo. Deezo came forth and handed the key card to Goo. He then asked if he could be excused. His job was done. He didn't want to be around when it all came down. He needed to keep his job. So far, there were no tempting offers on his plate. They told him he could go. They'd be in touch.

Goo slipped the key card into the door. The green light signaled them to proceed. They slowly opened the door. The room was pitch black. Not even a light from the city shone. The drapes were completely drawn.

The three men entered with caution.

Goo spoke, "Alright Chino, game over. Now y'all need to cut the shit and come on out. Let's make this easy."

Hench felt around the walls for a light switch, but he couldn't seem to find one.

"We ain't tryin' to hurt nobody," Hench lied. "So just come on out. We here to collect and we'll be out."

Shark remained silent. He didn't want his presence known just yet.

Free decided to let the "old timers" as he called them, feel a

305

little bit of what the young boys was puttin' out.

Both Buck, and Free were under the bed. Their plan-- aim for the legs. Immobilize their opposition and run get Chino to do with them as he pleased.

Free sensed someone near the queen size bed. He fired two shots from his 9 millimeter.

"Oh shit!" Hench fell to the floor, "I'm fucking hit."

Goo yelled, "Find the motherfuckin' lights "

Shark tried to find any source of light. He went to the window and drew back the drapes. That gave him the ability to spot a table lamp.

"There, the lamp!" Shark yelled.

Goo dove over to the lamp. He turned it on. Now the room was fully lit. They could see Hench lying in a pool of blood. His shin had been shattered. He could not move, besides the shaking he'd been doing from the trauma and shock.

Goo looked at Shark and signaled his eyes to go down to the floor. They read each other's eyes. They knew their target was under the bed. Goo fired three shots.

They heard the cry of a boy.

"Wait!" Shark yelled. "That's a buoy me hear."

"Fuck that shit Shark. They old enough to shoot, they old enough to be shot." Goo wasn't going for that save the children shit right now. These children were straight murderers.

Shark took a huge chance. He kneeled down and looked under the bed. He saw two young boys, who looked to be their teens. One was bleeding profusely. He pulled him out from under the bed. The other came out, out of fear of seeing what just happened to his homeboy.

Free was hit. He was hit badly. There was blood coming from his chest. His eyes were weakening.

"Where is Chino?" Shark asked Buck, relieving him of his weapon.

"Who?" Buck answered.

"Me can't believe this shit! You see your buoy here. A' you think you a' tough buoy sien. Normally we don't botha' kids ya' know, but I might make an exception, sien! Me want Chino. You tell me where he is, or you'll watch as I let my partna' here finish off your blood clad friend, Straight up! "

Buck remained loyal. "I don't know nobody named Chino."

"Finish him!" Shark ordered.

Goo pointed the glock. He aimed directly at Free's head.

"Alright, alright!" Buck broke down. He couldn't take the sight of Free bleeding to death.

"I'll ask one more time. Where is Chino?" Shark began to tremble. He was losing his patience.

Buck couldn't speak the words. He pointed next door.

Goo stepped over Hench who had passed out from the loss of blood. He immediately went to room 417. He didn't waste any time. Goo retrieved the emergency key card and entered. Shark was on his heels.

Buck ran to the balcony and tried to yell for Chino. There was no answer. He immediately called Knees to tell him what happened. Knees told Buck to make sure Free was still breathing. He went to check on him, but it was too late.

"He ain't breathing man." Buck was shook. He always knew it could happen, but he just wasn't ready.

"Get to Chino. I still got another ten to fifteen minutes before I can get there."

Knees told Bones, "Put the pedal to the motherfuckin' metal, my niggas is in trouble!"

Chino and Lisa were sprawled out on the bed asleep, their

naked bodies entangled. Shark noticed two duffle bags in the sitting area of the room. He motioned for Goo to check the bags. Goo went to the black duffle first. He opened the bag. To his extreme pleasure, he fingered through mounds of cash. He tossed the bag to Shark. Shark placed it on his shoulder. Goo checked the Louis Vuitton duffle, but there was nothing but clothes inside.

Shark used the .45 he retrieved from Buck to politely tap Chino on the chin. Chino blindly waved his hand in the air. Shark then grabbed him by his throat and shocked him out of his sleep and definitely out of his high. He lifted Chino out of the bed with his neck engulfed in his hand. Lisa was awakened by the stirring of Chino's body. She gasped loudly at the sight of a gun pointing directly in her face.

"Get the fuck up!" Goo yelled.

Lisa screamed, "What the fuck is going on? How the hell did y'all get in my room?"

Goo grabbed Lisa out of the bed, slapping her so hard, his entire hand print covered the left side of her face. It swelled immediately. He threw her to the floor. Shark dropped Chino on the floor next to her.

"Now pussy, a' what do you have to tell me now?" Shark was standing over the two of them. Buck's .45 in one hand, his own .357 magnum in the other. Goo was still aiming at Lisa.

"Yo, chill Shark. You got your money, man. Why don't you just leave it at that." Chino was holding on to Lisa who was crying uncontrollably. She now could relate to how Camaria must have felt when she was attacked. She didn't have to imagine anymore.

"Shut your bitch up man." Goo had no sympathy for Lisa

whatsoever.

"Fuck you Goo." Chino spit at his feet.

"Oh, you want to play big timer in front of your bitch motherfucka?" Goo rammed the glock down Chino's throat. "Spit now motherfucka!"

"Wait Goo!" Shark yelled. He bent down and looked into Chino's eyes. "Me' a kill you b'cau you'se a pussy, sien. You use young buoys to do a man's job. Well one of ya' likl' buoys dem, they dead ya' know. What you gon' do about that? Huh Mr. Big Time Hustler ?"

Shark circled around them, as a shark would circle his prey before an attack. He walked and talked as if he was in a trance. "You killed my Shelly. You killed my buoy James, so now it's time for me to do some killing, sien!" Shark aimed the 9 mm at Lisa and pulled the trigger.

Her warm blood splattered all over Chino. Lisa fell back, her body convulsed over and over. Chino couldn't believe what had just happened.

"No!" He screamed in sheer horror. He lunged at Shark, but was caught by a bullet to the chest, fired from Goo's weapon. There was a loud blast. Goo dropped to the ground. Shark looked in the direction of the balcony to see the young kid he left behind wielding another 9 mm. He knew he had better make a run for it. He was surely the kids' next target, but before he did, he pumped three more bullets into Chino to seal his fate. Buck emptied his clip firing at Shark, but he wasn't able to hit him. He got away ...

Buck went over to Chino to check him. There was too much blood. There was no way he could have survived.

Knees arrived with the rest of the crew. "Yo. What the

fuck!?" He spotted Chino. "Oh hell no!" He screamed. "Get him ... Let's get him out of here!"

"He's dead Knees," Buck cried.

"I said let's get him the fuck up out of here. The cops is on they way. Security is on to this shit! "

"What about her?" Buck asked.

"Fuck her," Knees said. "If it wasn't for her, Chino would still be alive."

"She still breathing man!"

"I said fuck her! " Knees said between tears.

They got Chino and fled.

THE AFTERMATH

The guests in the hotel were in shock when they heard what had happened. There had been a massacre on the fourth floor, but because of the soundproof rooms, no one heard a thing. If it wasn't for a tip called into the police, the bodies would have probably remained unnoticed, until housekeeping arrived.

There was a young boy, most likely in his early teenage years, found dead along with a man who appeared to be in his thirties. It was said that the older man's wound wasn't life threatening at all, he simply bled to death.

Miraculously there was a young female found in the next room, who survived. She was reported to be in stable, but guarded condition. The man found in the same room with her was not as lucky. He was dead on arrival.

Rumor was, it had to be an inside job. No forced entry had been proven. The hotel would be questioning their entire staff.

Shark had finally gotten through to his mother. She had decided Shantel needed undisturbed rest. She had turned off all of the phones, including the cell phones. He had to break the news to her about Hench. She was saddened, but relieved her son was still alive. Shark chose not to tell Shantel anything about what had happened at the hotel. He just wanted to bury his lady, his cousin and his right hand man in peace. He was through with the drug circuit.

*   *   *   *

311

The young surgeon had been paged. He was requested to rush to the hospital. There was a gunshot victim in need of emergency surgery. He scrubbed up and entered the operating room. The assisting surgeon briefed him on the matter. He knew what had to be done. As he turned to familiarize himself with his new patient, his eyes bulged. He knew this victim. He'd just had dinner with her hours ago ...

Chris had to brace himself. He was the one. He had to save her. The surgery lasted seven long hours. Miraculously, she pulled through. He couldn't wait until she was able to talk. He was anxious for her to explain to him how after such a lovely evening together, she wound up nearly shot to death. Chris vowed he would never let her out of his sight again.

EPILOGUE

A year had passed. It had been pretty hard for Lisa to get back into the swing of things. She still wasn't all the way "back" as she called it, but recovering from a severe gunshot wound to the chest, only to discover you're pregnant by your deceased lover ... that would take a little getting used to. Luckily, she had her best friend who was still by her side to help her with becoming a new mother, as well as her own mother, of course.

Lisa gave birth to a beautiful eight pound baby boy. She named him Jordan Christopher Brennan. She felt compelled to give him her husband's name, after all, he had saved her life.

"Let's go out to eat tonight," Chris mentioned.

"You don't think it's too soon for the baby?" Lisa hadn't been out too much since the incident. She wanted to make sure everything had died down.

"I think it's definitely time for you to get out. And the baby needs air too. You can't stay inside forever." Chris kissed her lovingly on the forehead.

She loved him so much. Lisa never thought the life she had at that moment was ever possible. No illegal activity whatsoever and she had more in life than she ever had before.

"What you feel like eating?" Lisa asked.

"Hmm, let's see...   How about some good ole' home cookin'?" Chris smiled.

"Sylvia's?" Lisa smiled.

313

"Sylvia's!" Chris agreed.

"I'll get the baby ready." Lisa headed on her way upstairs to get herself and the baby together for their very first evening outing.

The phone rang.

"I'll get it baby," Lisa yelled.

"Hello."

"Talk to me, Baby Girl!"

STAY TUNED FOR PARTS 2 & 3 OF THIS TRILOGY:

a dead man's vengeance

THE VENDETTA

ALSO: SOUNDTRACK & AUDIOBOOK FOR BETRAYAL OF A HUSTLER -IN STORES SOON!

www.4blunt.com

FUTURE TITLES:

HALLOWHOOD

STREETOLOGY 101

www.4blunt.com

ORDER FORM

D & D PUBLISHING
P.O. BOX 15473
RICHMOND, VA 23227
(804) 306-3160
www.4blunt.com

Betrayal Of A Hustler	$16.95
S&H (Via U.S. Priority Mail)	$ 3.50
TOTAL	$20.45

PURCHASER INFORMATION

Name:_____Reg.#:_____
(Applies if incarcerated)
Address:_____

City:_____ State:_____ Zip_____

QUANTITY: ___

D&D extends a 30% discount for orders that are shipped
directly to prisons. Costs are as follows:

Betrayal Of A Hustler	$11.87
S&H	$ 3.50
Total:	$15.37